Boo

## *Contemporary Romance Series*

## MacLarens of Fire Mountain

## Peregrine Bay

# Burnt River

Shane's Burden, Book One by Peggy Henderson
Thorn's Journey, Book Two by Shirleen Davies
Aqua's Achilles, Book Three by Kate Cambridge
Ashley's Hope, Book Four by Amelia Adams
Harpur's Secret, Book Five by Kay P. Dawson
Mason's Rescue, Book Six by Peggy L. Henderson
Del's Choice, Book Seven by Shirleen Davies
Ivy's Search, Book Eight by Kate Cambridge
Phoebe's Fate, Book Nine by Amelia Adams
Brody's Shelter, Book Ten by Kay P. Dawson
Boone's Surrender, Book Eleven by Shirleen Davies
Watch for more books in the series!

**The best way to stay in touch is to subscribe to my newsletter.** Go to www.shirleendavies.com and subscribe in the box at the top of the right column that asks for your email. You'll be notified of new books before they are released, have chances to win great prizes, and receive other subscriber-only specials.

# Rogue Rapids

## Redemption Mountain Historical Western Romance Series

## SHIRLEEN DAVIES

**Book Eleven in the Redemption Mountain**

**Historical Western Romance Series**

Avalanche Ranch Press, LLC
PO Box 12618
Prescott, AZ 86304

Book design and conversions by Joseph Murray at 3rdplanetpublishing.com

Cover design by Kim Killion, The Killion Group

ISBN: 978-1-941786-79-6

I care about quality, so if you find something in error, please contact me via email at
shirleen@shirleendavies.com

# Description

A painful betrayal and a past he chooses to forget. The dream of love and a future she desperately desires.

**Rogue Rapids, Book Eleven, Redemption Mountain Historical Western Romance Series**

**Adam "Mack" Mackey** vowed to never return to the family who betrayed him. Needing to forget and start over, the ex-Union officer accepted a deputy job in the Montana Territory. The new start offered satisfaction, purpose, and much needed peace. His nights with the women in Splendor saloons provided companionship. He required nothing else—including love, a notion he firmly rejected. At least that was what he thought until his gaze landed on a newly arrived mail order bride.

**Sylvia Lucero** escaped an arranged marriage certain to add to her family's riches while committing her to a lifetime devoid of love. Stepping from the stage onto the muddy street of Splendor, Montana, her gaze swept the area, halting on a handsome, and she'd soon learn, arrogant lawman—the last person she'd consider marrying.

Supper. That's all Mack wants, but the obstinate woman refuses all his invitations—until one evening when he wouldn't take no for an answer. Their first supper together changes everything.

Unfortunately, their tentative steps at a relationship face challenges neither anticipate. Threats to local ranchers, the town, and Sylvia strain their fragile connection.

Will the danger prove too much for two people with different goals? Or will the perils bring them together, forcing a shared strength greater than either imagine?

Rogue Rapids, book eleven in the Redemption Mountain historical western romance series, is a full-length novel with an HEA and no cliffhanger.

**Visit my website for a list of characters for each series.**
http://www.shirleendavies.com/character-list.html

# Acknowledgements

Many thanks to the wonderful members of my Reader Groups. Your support, insights, and suggestions are greatly appreciated. And as always, a huge thank you to my husband who is my greatest fan.

As always, many thanks to my editor, Kim Young, proofreader, Alicia Carmical, Joseph Murray, who is superb at formatting my books for print and electronic versions, and my cover designer, Kim Killion.

# Prologue

*Whiplash, Texas*
*January 1868*

From her seat inside the stagecoach, Sylvia Lucero's gaze darted through each window, hands clutched in her lap. Her heart pounded in a violent rhythm, breath coming in ragged gasps. Closing her eyes, she swallowed her growing fear, trying to calm her breathing while sending up a prayer. If she missed this chance, another might never come.

Worrying her bottom lip, Sylvia thought of her father, mother, and two older brothers, Cruz and Dominic. Making the decision to leave them had come after considerable thought. She loved them all so much, but the life she wanted wasn't going to happen—not with a father who protected her to the point of suffocation.

As the youngest, and a girl, Sylvia had been pampered and spoiled, seldom being allowed to make any decisions on her own. Even riding the short distance from their ranch to Whiplash required an escort. As a young girl, she'd thought her family's concern for her endearing. The notion faded as she grew, her body transforming from a gangly girl who loved riding with her brothers to a beautiful young woman who turned heads every Sunday morning.

Not that she ever noticed. Sylvia spent her time after church speaking with friends, making plans for visits, unaware of the attention from most of the young men.

Christmas had come like any other. She and her mother shopped, the family attended the church social, and church on Christmas Eve. And, as always, her family opened their spacious home to anyone and everyone on Christmas Day.

Staring out of the stagecoach, impatient for the stage to leave, she allowed herself to continue reminiscing, hoping it would take her mind off what would happen if her father found her.

Sylvia closed her eyes, remembering how she'd helped her mother set lavish amounts of food on the simply decorated Christmas table. She'd been happier than she'd ever thought possible. Heading for the library, she stopped to listen, overhearing her father discussing her future with Cruz and Dominic.

They'd talked of her father's requirements, not hers, mentioning several names of appropriate suitors. Not a single one was a man she could love. They were scions of other wealthy ranchers, men her father admired and who'd be thrilled to make a union with the powerful Lucero family. Love would play no part in the marriage.

Her stomach had clenched as she listened. Backing away from the library door, Sylvia's mind reeled at the future she'd planned for herself being stolen from her.

Confronting her father would've accomplished nothing. She loved him and knew he felt the same. Still, he expected total obedience, an acknowledgment he knew what was best for her.

Her dreams might be simple, something her father wouldn't understand, but Sylvia refused to give them up. Later that night, after all the guests had left, she'd begun making plans.

The jostling of the stagecoach stopped her thoughts. Glancing outside, she let out a breath, allowing herself to relax for the first time in over a week. A mile passed, then another before she ignored the distance and settled back against the seat. Closing her eyes, she thought of her future, the one she'd dreamed about. A future only she could claim.

# Chapter One

*Splendor, Montana Territory*
*September 1869*

Adam "Mack" Mackey drew his gun from the holster, pointing it into the air and firing. "Stop!" Cursing when the young cowboy kept running, he chased after him, glad for the full moon. At least the fool hadn't fired at him.

Mack didn't know how the kid stayed on his feet with all the whiskey he'd gulped down at the Dixie Moon. Right now, racing after the miscreant, Mack didn't care.

He and his fellow deputy, Caleb Covington, had stopped by the saloon for a couple drinks before going to Suzanne Barnett's boardinghouse restaurant for supper. They'd ended up in the middle of a dispute between groups from two ranches. It had nothing to do with cards or a woman. The fight began over a young mare one rancher sold to another. A mare one of the cowboys swore had been stolen out from under him.

Mack and Caleb didn't care who owned the mare—unless the ranch hand grumbling about his claim made a formal complaint to Gabe Evans, the sheriff. This seemed to be just a group of drunken cowboys having one of many arguments boys got into on a Saturday night.

Gaining ground, Mack shot into the air once more, slowing his pace when the cowboy tripped on a loose board, sprawling on the ground. Stopping next to him, Mack bent over, placing his hands on his knees and sucking in a deep breath.

Reaching out, he grabbed the fool by his collar, jerking him up. "What the hell were you thinking, drawing your gun in the saloon and firing toward the bar? You almost hit Paul. Is that what you wanted?"

Blinking a couple times, the cowboy shook his head, his brows furrowing. "The bartender?"

Mack let out a disgusted curse. "That's right."

"Weren't my fault," the young man sputtered.

Mack snorted. "It never is." Spinning the cowboy around, he pushed him into the street. "You're in luck. We happen to have an empty cell tonight."

"Ah, Deputy. I ain't done nothing wrong." His words slurred, his body slumped as they moved closer to the jail.

As they approached the boardwalk on the other side of the street, the door to Petermann's store opened. Mack slowed his pace, his attention focused on the young woman walking out, locking the door behind her. When she turned, Sylvia Lucero froze, her golden brown eyes locking with his.

Jerking the cowboy to a stop, Mack slid his gun into its holster, then touched the brim of his hat. "Miss Lucero. You're working pretty late tonight."

She eyed him and the cowboy in his grasp, her chin tilting upward. "I'm keeping the books for Mr. Petermann." Her words were clipped, strained. "It's easier to do them after the store is closed."

"Guess you're headed to the boardinghouse then." Mack jerked the cowboy's collar.

"It's where I live, Deputy. Now, if you'll excuse me." Sylvia stepped off the boardwalk, brushing past him as if he were a rabid dog she wanted to avoid.

"I'll meet you over there. Buy you supper."

Without halting, she yelled back at him. "No, thank you, Deputy. I'd prefer to eat alone."

Mack snickered at the familiar response. He'd been trying to get the mail order bride to have supper with him for weeks. Each time, she had the same excuse. Any other man would've given up, taken her continued refusals personally. He wasn't that man.

Shaking his head, a grim smile crossing his lips, Mack dragged the young man into the jail. After a quick explanation to another deputy, Dutch McFarlin, and a nod at Caleb, he secured the cowboy in a cell next to one of his friends, who Caleb had already hauled over from the saloon.

Removing his hat, Mack wiped a hand across his forehead. "You ready for supper, Caleb?"

Standing, he grabbed his hat from the desk, settling it on his head. "More than ready. Do you want us to bring something back for you, Dutch?"

The large, broad-shouldered man ran a hand through his unruly red hair. "Thanks, but I've already eaten. Are we going to keep those two overnight then let them go, or are they staying for trial?"

Mack's lips twisted into a scowl. "I don't think we have to keep them around for trial. They need to pay for the damage at the Dixie before they leave town. I'll be back early tomorrow morning and make sure they do."

Stepping outside, Mack and Caleb walked across the street and into Suzanne's. When he spotted Sylvia, Mack headed straight to a table a couple feet away. Giving her a brief nod as he removed his hat, he chuckled to himself at the way she shifted away from where he sat.

"Miss Lucero." Caleb took off his hat, smiling at the young woman before sitting down on the other side of Mack.

"What can I get you gentlemen tonight?" Tabitha Beekman, another of the mail order brides who'd arrived in town with Sylvia, looked down at them. "We have elk steaks and meatloaf. Both with mashed potatoes and gravy."

"Steaks," both responded at the same time.

Tabitha smiled. "And coffee?" When they nodded, she moved away, stopping at Sylvia's table for a moment before walking to the kitchen. Reemerging a couple minutes later, she set the coffee in front of the men. "I'll be back in a few minutes with your meals."

"Are you going to the fall dance, Mack?" Caleb took a sip of his coffee.

Not answering right away, a flash of mischief passed through him. Shifting in his seat, he leaned toward Sylvia, hearing her soft intake of breath. His voice lowered to a whisper.

"Miss Lucero, will you be attending the fall dance?" Mack watched Sylvia catch her lower lip between her teeth, then lift her chin.

"Yes, I will, Deputy Mackey."

He leaned closer, his gaze slightly heated. "Are you going with someone special?"

"Not that it's your business, but I'm going with Miss Beekman and Miss Bacon." She named two of the other mail order brides.

A wide grin tilted up the corners of his mouth. "Good."

She shot a look at him. "What?"

"You'll be available to dance with me."

Glaring at him, she pursed her lips. "You take too much for granted, Deputy."

"Probably, Miss Lucero. I'll see you Saturday night." He turned back toward Caleb, chuckling when he heard Sylvia release a frustrated breath.

Sylvia gripped her napkin between her hands, irritation spearing through her, along with the familiar attraction always present when Mack was anywhere near. And lately, he seemed to be everywhere.

On the days she worked at the general store, he tried to be her first customer, then often stood outside when she left at the end of the day. His constant presence had become annoying, alarming, and thrilling. It galled Sylvia, thinking his attention bordered on endearing.

Thank goodness she'd heard all about his background from Deborah Chestro, the fourth of the mail order brides. Deborah made it her business to learn about everyone in town, including all eligible bachelors such as Mack. And he was eligible in all ways, except the one mattering the most to Sylvia.

According to Deborah, he'd found enjoyment at one time or another with every girl at the Wild Rose, the Dixie, and Ruby's Grand Palace. Every...single...girl. Older, younger, slim, curvy, Mack made no distinction as to what he preferred.

And these women didn't include the three widows in Big Pine he'd courted for brief periods before moving on. Granted, it was assumed he paid for his time with the saloon girls. But three widows and nothing permanent resulting from any of those relationships? What kind of man went through women faster than water being poured from a bucket?

All this came from one of the girls who'd worked at all three saloons—a girl Sylvia suspected had been with Mack on numerous occasions.

He'd asked her to accompany him to breakfast, dinner, or supper so many times she'd lost count. Sylvia's response had been the same each occurrence. Hearing her polite but firm refusal, he'd grinned, shrugged his shoulders, and tried again a few days later.

It would've been easy if he'd given up, moved on to someone else. To her consternation, she found the ex-Union officer enjoyed a challenge, and she'd become a big one.

The problem wasn't that Sylvia didn't like Mack. The problem was she liked him too much. Ever since their first dance at the social the town had held for the four mail order brides, she'd been smitten.

Sylvia remembered the night with complete clarity. She let her gaze wander around the crowded room, seeing no one of real interest until Mack walked inside with Caleb. The impact had been immediate.

Not the most handsome man she'd ever seen, his piercing gray eyes with flecks of green missed nothing as they searched the room. When they'd landed on her, she'd felt the floor shift beneath her, breath catching. Tall with broad shoulders, black hair, and strong, angular features, Mack hadn't hidden his interest. Within minutes, he'd walked straight toward her, stopped a few inches away, and held out his hand, asking for a dance.

Sylvia could still feel how her body responded when she'd placed her hand in his. It had felt, well...magical. They'd danced three times that evening, and everything inside her screamed he'd been the one she'd traveled all the way from Texas to meet.

The next morning, Sylvia felt better than she had in a very long time. Lighthearted and full of hope, she'd slid into her nicest Sunday dress, praying she'd see him at church. Leaving her room at the boardinghouse, she'd headed downstairs for breakfast, taking a seat next to Deborah. Twenty minutes later, appetite gone and her chest tight, she'd left the table.

In an almost gleeful voice, Deborah had shared what she'd learned about Mack, not sparing a detail. It had been a good lesson for Sylvia about not allowing her heart to control her head.

"Would you care to take a walk after supper, Miss Lucero?" Mack's deep, somewhat raspy voice jolted her to the present. As much as she wanted to accept, Sylvia knew the only sensible answer was no. She just wished it didn't hurt so much to continue turning him down.

She stared down at her still full plate. "No, thank you. I already have plans." Sensing movement next to her, she glanced over, startled to see Mack had switched chairs. He now sat at her table, his knee touching hers. A quick look to her right confirmed Caleb had left, leaving the two of them alone.

Reaching over, he placed his hand over hers, his deep voice lowering. "Go to supper with me sometime, Sylvia."

Chest tightening, her breath caught as she desperately tried to calm her pounding heart. "I don't believe it would be a good idea, Mack."

His face brightened, a smile sliding into place. "That's the first time you've called me by my name. I like it."

She couldn't help the slight chuckle from escaping her lips before her face sobered. Inhaling, she tried to calm the anxiety his presence caused. "Why do you keep asking me out? Most men would've given up by now."

His gray eyes darkened. "I'm not most men."

She snorted. "Yes. So I've heard."

A deep crease appeared between his brows. "What have you heard?"

Shifting in her chair, Sylvia straightened her dress, swallowing her uneasiness. "It's nothing, really."

As he leaned closer, she felt his breath wash across her face. "It must be something or you wouldn't have said it. Tell me what you've heard."

Sylvia didn't know why she hesitated. Never in her life had she been afraid to speak her mind. Although not as bold or as insensitive as Deborah, she'd always been able to voice her thoughts without worrying about anyone's reaction. Somehow, her self-assured attitude slipped when it came to Mack.

"Truly, it's nothing." She looked down at her lap.

Mack shook his head, lifting her chin with a finger. "Did anyone ever mention what a bad liar you are?"

She pulled her face away from his grip, but not before he saw the blush creep up her cheeks.

"Well, Sylvia?"

A slight grin quirked up one corner of her mouth before she bit her lower lip. "Yes."

A deep laugh burst from his throat, grabbing the attention of the other diners.

She tilted her head to the side. "What?"

"Oh, darlin'. You are sweet."

Her back straightening, she pushed away from the table, standing. "I am not your darlin', and trust me, no one has ever thought of me as sweet." Turning her back to him, she headed to the stairs, stopping when a strong hand gripped her arm.

"My apologies, Miss Lucero. I meant no disrespect."

She studied his face, seeing the sincerity in his features. It was hard to stay mad at him, and that was just what she needed to do. She'd come to Splendor to find a husband and a safe life far away from a family wanting to take control of her future. Well, maybe not a family. Not her mother or siblings, whom she loved more than anything. She also loved her father, but his idea of a husband and a future held no resemblance to her own dream.

"It's all right, Deputy Mackey." Her voice was soft as she swiped hair away from her forehead. "I'm just tired." Seeing him blow out a deep breath before he released her arm, she turned back toward the stairs, stopping once more at the sound of his low voice.

"Join me for supper tomorrow night."

Three steps up, she rested her hand on the stair rail, shifting slowly. "I'm sorry, but it wouldn't be wise for me to spend time with you."

A brow lifting, he took a slow step closer. "Do you remember the night at the social?"

She nodded.

14

"We danced three times, and they were the best dances of my life. Something happened between us and I want to figure out what it was." He leaned closer, resting his hand on the end of the stair rail. "Join me for supper, Sylvia. Help me figure it out."

Sylvia wanted nothing more than to say yes, but she had a dream, and it didn't include a man who saw women as nothing more than a way to spend a few hours. She wanted much more from Mack.

Crossing her arms, she lifted her chin. "I'm not spending supper with you. Or breakfast. Or dinner. I'd appreciate it if you'd stop asking."

A look of surprise crossed his face. "Why not?"

"Because I won't be another of the ladies you cross off your list before moving on to the next."

# Chapter Two

*What the hell?* Mack's jaw dropped, watching her turn and hurry up the stairs to the second floor. Her response stunned and confused him. *What list?*

Shaking his head, he scratched his jaw, her words continuing to roll around in his head. Sure, he'd been with his share of women in Splendor and Big Pine, and in towns when he'd traveled west. But a list?

Walking back to the table, he tossed some coins down, glancing up the stairs before pushing through the front door. Mack stopped on the boardwalk, a deep breath escaping as he looked up and down the street. He needed a drink. Maybe two or three.

Unless the sheriff needed him, he'd spend most nights in one of the saloons before selecting a girl and taking her upstairs. One night would be at the Rose, another the Dixie. Sometimes he'd watch a show at Ruby's Palace before picking one of the dancers to help take away the loneliness haunting him.

It was a rare night he actually looked forward to his nights with a saloon girl. The time he spent with them filled an emptiness in his life, a deep, dark hole created during the last few months of the war. Keeping himself busy did an admirable job of easing his pain. Work, whiskey, saloon girls—whatever it took to keep his mind off the images triggering a never-ending stream of nightmares.

Tonight though, the thought of being with someone other than Sylvia held no appeal. Her mention of a list crossed his mind, causing him to flinch. He pinched the bridge of his nose, wondering where those words had come from.

Mack had never made a secret of how he spent his time when not working. He'd never cared what anyone thought about his choices. It was nobody's business what he did. Besides, it wasn't as if he courted eligible women, then walked away.

He'd heard the rumors about him courting widows in Big Pine, chuckling at the lie. Mack didn't know who started such nonsense, suspecting one of the saloon girls. Those women were always talking, making up stories, maybe as a way to pass the time between rising in the early afternoon and going downstairs to work in the evenings. Until tonight, he'd thought nothing of the rumors. People would believe what they wanted.

He stilled as his thoughts drifted to Sylvia. Maybe she'd heard the rumors. Her knowing about his visits with saloon girls was one thing. Thinking he'd courted and discarded widow women was something else. He cringed, muttering an oath.

Of course, Sylvia would've heard about the time spent with the saloon girls. As friendly and accommodating as they always were, not one of them meant anything to him. Those women were a way to spend time, nothing more.

Scrubbing a hand down his face, he glanced back at the boardinghouse, raising his head to look at the lights on the second floor. He wondered which room was hers. Mack didn't understand the immense attraction he felt for the young woman with ink black hair and golden brown eyes, or why he continued to pursue her after being rejected so many times.

Sylvia Lucero was a prize he couldn't let go, and Mack had never been a quitter.

Drawing the brush through her long, dark hair, Sylvia stared out the window to the street below. She hadn't been able to calm the rapid beating of her heart since running up the stairs, leaving Mack behind to contemplate her last words.

She hadn't meant to blurt them out. They were meant to be private, something she'd never planned to speak aloud—at least not to Mack.

It bothered her that the first time she questioned Deborah's story was tonight, after the words were spoken. Somehow, saying them to Mack triggered her first spark of doubt. What if they were untrue?

Pulling the brush down the back of her head, she winced, not realizing her strokes had become so fierce. Hand stilling, Sylvia set the brush down, braiding her hair as she stared into the mirror. When had she started to rely on tales women shared while sipping tea? More importantly, when had she begun believing anything out of Deborah's mouth?

Deborah, May Bacon, Tabitha Beekman, and Sylvia had left Philadelphia together. Their association through Pettigrew's, a company matching mail order brides with requests from the west, had given them an instant, if tenuous, bond during the long trip. Of the four, Deborah proved to be the most judgmental, and by far the biggest teller of tales.

At first, Sylvia thought she told the yarns as a way to pass the time. The problem was they weren't exactly fiction. They were comprised of hearsay, gossip she'd heard during her excursions through the railroad cars and at stops along the way. Although entertaining, none of the girls relied on them for accuracy.

Sylvia wondered why she'd put so much confidence in the stories about Mack.

Standing, she slipped into a wrapper, leaving her room to walk down the hall to Deborah's. Knocking, she waited a few moments before the door opened.

"Sylvia. It's a little late for a call, isn't it?" Deborah didn't draw the door open enough for her to enter.

"Do you have a minute?"

Deborah scowled. "Can't it wait until tomorrow, Sylvia?"

She leveled her gaze. "Actually, no." Pushing the door open enough to enter, she brushed past Deborah. Turning, Sylvia crossed her arms. "Do you remember the stories you told about Deputy Mackey?"

Deborah pursed her lips, brows furrowing. "The ones about his social activities?"

"Exactly. You said you'd heard about them from a dancer at Ruby's Palace. I'd like to know her name."

Brow lifting, Deborah cocked her head. "For what reason?"

The corners of Sylvia's mouth slid into a grin. "Nothing important. I'm curious about someone and thought she might be the best person to ask. Do you recall her name?"

"Of course I do. It's Malvina. When do you want to speak with her? I'll go with you."

Sylvia almost choked on the idea. "I don't want to bother you. I'll go myself."

"It's no bother at all. I work tomorrow, but not the following day. Will that suit you?"

Letting out a breath, Sylvia moved toward the door. "Let's talk tomorrow when you get back from work. We can decide then. Sleep well, Deborah."

Closing the door behind her, Sylvia bit her lower lip, stifling a grin as she hurried back to her room. Slipping inside, she sat on the edge of the bed, picking up her diary. Jotting down Malvina's name, she set it aside and removed her wrapper, a smile playing at the edges of her mouth.

Tomorrow was her day off, the perfect time to stop by Ruby's and speak with Malvina. By the time she left, Sylvia would know if the stories Deborah told held any amount of truth or were just one more bit of gossip meant to entertain. More significantly, she'd have an inkling if Mack Mackey was an honorable man or just another rogue.

"And what may I do for you?" A broad, if tired, smile twisted the corners of Ruby Walsh's bright red lips. She didn't hide the way her gaze moved up Sylvia's body, assessing her with an appreciative nod. "Are you looking for work?"

Sylvia concealed her unease, shaking her head. "Uh, no. I'm looking for Malvina."

Placing a hand on her hip, Ruby snorted. "And what would you need to see her about?"

Straightening her back, she squared her shoulders. "That is between Malvina and me. Is she up?"

Ruby's eyes sparked an instant before she threw back her head and laughed. "You've got spunk, gal." She stepped aside, motioning for Sylvia to enter. "Come in and I'll see if she's decent. I'm Ruby Walsh."

"Miss Sylvia Lucero."

Ruby glanced over her shoulder as she started up the stairs. "I know. I remember when you four gals got off the stage. You gathered almost as much attention as when I came into town with my girls. Take a seat. I'll be right back."

It took several minutes before her eyes adjusted to the dark interior. A few lanterns were scattered around the room, though not enough to get a good look around. What she could see impressed Sylvia. It was much larger than it appeared from outside, with at least two dozen tables, a long bar on one wall, and a stage taking up the entire span of another wall.

Lowering herself into a chair, she glanced up the stairs to see Ruby and another woman coming down. Much younger than Ruby, she had curly brown hair, pale skin, and couldn't have weighed more than a hundred pounds. When she reached the bottom of the stairs, Sylvia realized she couldn't be older than seventeen.

"Here she is. Malvina, this is Miss Sylvia Lucero. She came here to talk with you." Ruby looked at Sylvia. "She doesn't have much time. The gents will start wandering in real soon."

"Thank you, Ruby. I won't keep her long."

Sylvia waited while Malvina sat down, placing a hand over her mouth to cover a yawn. When finished, Malvina shot a tired gaze at her.

"What is it you want to talk about?"

Shifting in the hard chair, Sylvia clasped her hands in her lap. "Do you remember talking to Deborah Chestro about one of your customers?"

She choked out a weary laugh. "Deborah sometimes brings in extra cake from the St. James. We eat and talk about a lot of people."

"Deputy Mackey?"

An odd look, wistful and full of longing, crossed Malvina's face. "Mack?" she whispered out his name, her voice thick.

Sylvia almost didn't answer, the need to get up and run out almost overwhelming. The look on Malvina's face, the sound of her voice said more than any words about how the young woman felt about Mack. Sylvia understood at least a little of what she must be feeling.

Twisting her hands together, she nodded. "Yes. You know him." It wasn't a question.

Nodding, Malvina leaned forward. "He knows *all* the girls here at Ruby's, and *all* those who work at the Rose and the Dixie."

Sylvia looked down at her hands. "I see."

Malvina continued, as if Sylvia hadn't spoken. "He's a true gentleman. Takes real good care of the girl he's with." She let out a shaky breath. "Too bad he's not interested in anything more than conversation and a little fun in bed."

Clearing her throat, Sylvia felt heat creep up her face. She hadn't expected quite this much information and wasn't prepared with a response. "I see."

"Oh, I don't think you do, Miss Lucero. Mack isn't like most of the other men who come in here. He doesn't just pay for our time and leave. Whoever he picks gets a meal sent up. We eat and talk for a while. We never even get near the bed half the time. We talk for an hour or two before he leaves. The other girls say the same." She met Sylvia's gaze. "When he does take any of us to bed, he's real gentle, as if he cares about us. Does that make sense?" She didn't wait for a response. "Always leaves a little extra on the dresser before he leaves." Glancing around, she lowered her voice. "I think Mack is lonely. He pays for us just so he has someone to talk to."

The lump in her throat continued to grow with each word out of Malvina's mouth. Sylvia bit her lip, realizing how little she knew about what happened between a man and woman, and how little she knew about Mack Mackey.

Ignoring her embarrassment, Sylvia lifted her chin. "What about the widows he's courted? Does he treat them the same?"

Malvina's brows drew together. "Widows?"

"Deborah said he'd courted several widows in Big Pine. She said you talked about them."

Touching a hand to her forehead, Malvina's lips drew into a thin line. "I don't recall anything about Mack courting anyone. And I wouldn't know anything about his trips to Big Pine. Deborah must be mistaken." Pushing unruly curls from her brow, she focused her gaze on Sylvia. "If Mack courted someone, he wouldn't be the kind to seek out extra comfort with one of the saloon girls or dancers. He may not be interested in more than talk and a quick roll, but he's an honest man." Standing, she rested her hands on the table. "I need to get ready for the men when they come in."

Pushing up, Sylvia held out her hand. "It was a pleasure meeting you, Malvina."

Staring down at the hand, it took a moment for her to take it in a frail grasp. Letting go, Malvina tilted her head at Sylvia. "Are you the woman Mack is interested in?"

Eyes widening, her face paled. "Has he mentioned someone?"

"Not really." She shrugged. "It's a feeling I've gotten the last couple times he's asked for me." Malvina glanced behind Sylvia to see Ruby approaching. "I do have a good imagination, though. It's probably nothing. Good day, Miss Lucero."

Sylvia didn't budge from her spot next to the table as she watched Malvina climb the stairs. A wave of embarrassment washed over her, realizing how much she'd learned about Mack and his private habits. Poking into his private affairs no longer seemed right. She'd spoken to a woman he'd been intimate with on more than one occasion, a woman who held him in great affection.

Wishing she'd never entered the Palace, Sylvia spun around to leave, almost running into Ruby.

A knowing smirk appeared on her face. "Did you get the information you wanted?"

"Perhaps a little more than I'd sought." Sylvia's gaze moved to the door to see a couple cowboys enter. "I'd better go. Thank you for letting me talk with Malvina."

Ruby followed her to the door. "Mack is a good man, Miss Lucero. A woman couldn't do much better."

Mack pinned the badge onto his shirt as he left the small house he shared with Caleb. It was the same house Cash Coulter and Beau Davis shared before the two deputies found the women they loved and married. Cash now lived with Allie above her dress shop, and Beau shared his ranch with Caro.

His gaze wandered up and down the road behind Splendor's main street, a frown appearing at the sight of a woman emerging from Ruby's Palace. Shaking his head to clear his vision, Mack stared a moment before picking up his pace.

He followed her between two buildings before she reached the front of the jail. Looking around, Sylvia Lucero dashed across the street toward the boardinghouse, hurrying inside.

Mack stayed in front of the jail, wondering what would possess a fine, well-bred young woman to visit Ruby's. He didn't have to consider it long before an unwelcome thought had him wincing. Muttering a curse, he stepped inside the jail.

"About time you showed up, Mack." Dutch McFarlin sat back in the chair, boots resting on the desk, lowering the Big Pine newspaper to his lap. "Thought you might've forgotten about working tonight."

Setting his hat on a hook, he pulled up a chair, turning it around to sit down, resting his arms on the back. "Any excitement today?"

"Not unless you count Beau and Caleb riding out to the Murton ranch. Gil rode in to report missing cattle. He and Ty rode the entire ranch and couldn't find them." Dutch lifted his booted feet off the desk and set them on the floor. "Gabe's out at the Pelletier place." Dax and Luke Pelletier owned the largest ranch in western Montana. Standing, he walked to the wall and grabbed his hat off a hook. "That leaves you to take care of the town until Cash gets back from seeing Doc Worthington."

Mack lifted a brow. "Is he sick?"

Dutch chuckled. "Poison ivy."

"How the hell did he get into that?"

"Chasing a couple boys out of Petermann's store. They ran behind the boardinghouse, crossed the creek, and took off into the woods. He caught them, but the area is thick with poison ivy."

Mack shook his head, a wide grin tilting his mouth. "What'd the boys take?"

"The usual. Grabbed some lemon sticks from a jar on the counter and took off."

A deep laugh burst from Mack's throat. "Quite a price to pay for a few lemon sticks. I can't remember the last time I got tangled up in poison ivy. All I know is I don't want to do it again."

"Yeah. I know what you mean." Dutch grabbed the doorknob. "I'm on my way to the boardinghouse for supper. Come get me if you need help with anything."

After Dutch left, Mack rested his forehead on his arms, thinking about Sylvia. He could think of only one reason she'd visit Ruby's, and the thought didn't please him.

What he did on his own time was private. He didn't want some nosy young woman poking around in his business. If she'd wanted to know about him and his visits to the saloons, all she had to do was ask. He might not have given her the entire truth, but at least he wouldn't feel his privacy had been violated.

Mack didn't have much—his memories of life before the war, friends he'd lost in battle, the woman he'd once loved. Most nights, he'd give anything to forget all of them and find even a small amount of peace. He'd managed to do that by spending time with women who expected nothing, asked no questions, and smiled when he walked out their door.

Mack might be attracted to Sylvia Lucero, want to spend time with her and learn all he could about her. Still, she had no right to go behind his back. If she wanted answers, Sylvia should've come to him.

Standing, he flipped the chair around and walked to the window. Shoving his hands into his pockets, he stared across the street at the boardinghouse, a dark expression crossing his face.

Tomorrow, he was going to start his own investigation into Miss Lucero. By the time he was finished, he'd make sure she understood how it felt to have someone poke into her private affairs.

# Chapter Three

Sylvia wrote down the order from Gladys Poe, confirming the amounts. She'd learned from experience the woman would let the entire town know if the items didn't arrive as ordered.

"Now, you won't forget to order a blue and yellow dress, right, young lady?"

"No, Mrs. Poe. I won't forget."

"And the yellow flower pattern for the china. It's important it match what I already have."

"Of course, Mrs. Poe." It was the same pattern Sylvia's mother used every day back home. Her hand stilled a moment, a wave of homesickness squeezing her chest. It had been nine months since she'd left her family behind in Texas. Nine months of living without them and the warm, loving home they'd provided for so many years. If only...

"And those dime novels." Gladys scanned the list of titles, speaking each out loud, tapping her fingers on the counter.

"Yes, ma'am. They're all on the order. You do realize the china may take a little longer than the other items."

If possible, Gladys's expression became more sour. "Of course I do. This isn't the first time I've ordered through Petermann's."

Sylvia bit her lip, shaking her head. "No, Mrs. Poe, it isn't." She heard the bell over the front door ring, not looking up. It wouldn't be wise to get distracted. The sooner she had the order down, the sooner the woman would leave.

"Here you are." She turned the paper around for Gladys to read, keeping her gaze down. "Please make sure all is correct and sign at the bottom."

Gladys used a finger to go down the list, stopping midway. "Is this a six or a zero?"

Tilting her head, Sylvia glanced down. "A six, Mrs. Poe."

"Then it should look like a six," she huffed out, taking the pencil from Sylvia's hand and fixing it. Finishing, she signed at the bottom and handed it back. "It's fine, now that I've corrected your mistake."

Gritting her teeth, Sylvia took the paper, still not looking toward the door. "I'll give this to Mr. Petermann as soon as he returns from lunch."

"Timmy never made mistakes on my orders."

"Well, he's off at college, Mrs. Poe. Perhaps he'll be available to take your orders when he returns." Sylvia bit the inside of her cheek, grimacing at her curt tone. Glancing up, she noticed the cold stare in the older woman's eyes an instant before her gaze lit on a man standing by the door. Mack. She swore under her breath when an involuntary shiver rolled through her.

Gladys raised a brow. "Excuse me?"

Wincing, Sylvia shook her head. "Nothing. Thank you for your order, Mrs. Poe. We'll let you know when it comes in."

Gladys stared at her a moment. Letting out an exasperated breath, she snatched her parasol from the counter and turned away.

"How are you today, Mrs. Poe?" Mack removed his hat, making a slight bow.

Stopping next to him, she offered a forced smile. "Fine, Deputy. Now, if you'll excuse me."

"Yes, ma'am." He opened the door, shutting it behind her with an exaggerated sigh, loud enough for Sylvia to hear. His mood brightened when he heard her chuckle. "How do you put up with that woman?"

She gripped the edge of the counter with both hands, hoping the effort would keep him from noticing the slight tremble at his approach. All night she'd lain awake, Malvina's words rolling over and over in her mind, creating a mental picture Sylvia couldn't forget.

*"When he does take any of us to bed, he's real gentle, as if he cares about us."*

"Miss Lucero. Are you all right?"

Face flushing, she let go of the counter, crossing her arms. "Yes. I'm fine, thank you."

"I asked how are you able to put up with Mrs. Poe."

"Well, I...I suppose I've gotten used to her." Even with the counter between them, she needed more space. Taking a step away, she stopped when her back hit the floor-to-ceiling shelving, rattling some of the merchandise. "Oh." She turned quickly, holding up her hands to stop tin boxes from toppling to the floor.

"Do you need some help?"

She heard the slight chuckle in his voice and stiffened. "No. Thank you." Sylvia bit out the words, immediately feeling guilty at making him the object of her annoyance. Except he *was* the reason she'd gotten so little sleep, tossing and turning until almost dawn. Darn him...

Turning to face him, she lifted her head to stare into his eyes—a mistake she realized too late.

"What can I get for you today, Deputy?"

Resting his hands on the counter, he leaned toward her, his piercing gray eyes boring into hers. "Supper. Tonight at the St. James. I'll come by at seven to escort you." He didn't wait for her answer before shoving away and turning toward the door.

"Wait!"

Stopping, he shifted toward her. "Do you prefer six thirty?"

Her jaw dropped. "No. I—"

"Fine. I'll come by the boardinghouse at seven." He touched the brim of his hat. "Until tonight, Miss Lucero." Stepping onto the boardwalk, he couldn't stop a cocky grin from forming. She hadn't said no and didn't yell at him. In his mind, both were good signs.

Entering the jail, he glanced at the two deputies seated at the desk. "Cash. Beau." He grabbed a third chair, lowering himself into it. "Either of you know where Dutch is?"

"He and Caleb rode south. One of the sheepherders reported a number of slaughtered sheep," Cash answered.

"Wolves?"

"Nope. Their throats were slit," Beau said. "Real nasty business."

Mack rubbed the back of his neck. "Cattle rustling at the Murton's, now slaughtered animals south of here. Could they be connected?"

Cash steepled his fingers under his chin. "Doubtful. There's been trouble brewing for months between the sheepherders and cattlemen. Sheep farmers want to make a living, and the ranchers don't want them anywhere near their cattle. Fencing would help, but no one's interested. They want to keep the open range."

Mack stroked his chin. "Could the rustling be a diversion to draw attention away from the killings?"

"I suppose," Cash said. "I don't know what they'd gain, though."

Beau nodded. "They wouldn't need a diversion. The Murton ranch is miles west of the sheepherders. I'm thinking they're unrelated."

Scrubbing a hand over his face, Mack considered the new threats, wondering why they'd started now. "It's been quiet for a while. Now all this."

Beau leaned forward, resting his arms on his legs. "Trouble to the south and west. Let's hope nothing happens north at Redemption's Edge. We don't have enough deputies to handle any more threats."

The door slammed open, Caleb and Dutch walking inside, both looking angry and trail weary.

Cash stood, walking to the stove to fill two cups with coffee. Handing them out, he leaned his hip against the desk. "What'd you find?"

Dutch blew across the top of the cup, taking a sip. "It's a mess. Almost a dozen sheep slaughtered. They're moving the entire herd closer to the house, but they don't have near enough people to watch them. Hell, they've got their ten-year-old daughter sitting out front with a rifle in her hands."

Draining the cup, Caleb moved to the stove, refilling it. "On our way back, Lee Weston intercepted us. He's got at least two dozen cattle missing. Said he rode by the Murton's and they were raided again last night."

Beau shook his head, not liking what he heard. "Gabe should be back from the Pelletier's any time. We'll figure out what we can do."

"We need more men. The six of us can't go after whoever's rustling cattle and killing sheep and still protect the town." Cash pushed away from the desk, pacing to the window. "Someone needs to ride to Fort Connall. Colonel McArthur might be able to send some men until Gabe can hire more deputies."

The room quieted, all considering what to do next. After a few minutes, Mack looked at Dutch.

"Do you have a minute?"

Dutch's brow lifted. "Sure. What is it?"

Mack nodded toward the door. "Outside."

No one commented as the two left the jail.

"So, what is it you want to talk about?" Dutch took another sip of coffee.

"I need to ask a favor."

"Is this about Miss Lucero?"

Mack's jaw tightened. "It is."

"I've been wondering when you'd ask me to find out her story. Do you want me to contact Pinkerton?"

Snorting, Mack nodded. "I want to know where she's from and why she came out here as a mail order bride. Does she have family, and if so, why isn't she still with them? And most important, who's she running away from?"

Scratching his chin, Dutch's eyes crinkled at the corners. "That's all?"

"I found her coming out of Ruby's yesterday. When I went into the Palace during my rounds last night, Ruby told me Sylvia had come in to speak with Malvina."

Chuckling, Dutch drank the last of the coffee, tossing the grounds onto the street. "The woman's doing some checking of her own."

"Yep."

"So you're going to do the same. You sure that's wise?" Crossing his arms, Dutch's hard gaze focused on Mack.

"Probably not, but she needs to know it isn't smart to go checking on me. All she needed to do was ask and I'd have told her myself."

Dutch tilted his head back and laughed. "You're a brave man, Mack, telling a woman you've a hankering to court about your nights in the saloons."

"Better than her sneaking behind my back. Besides, I'm free to do whatever I want with my nights. She's got no say in it."

Dutch's face sobered. "Are you thinking of courting her and still visiting your girls?"

"Hell no. I'm trying to teach Miss Lucero a lesson. If she finally allows me to court her, I won't need or want the girls."

"You think Sylvia is the one?"

Mack drew in a breath, letting it out in a slow stream. He'd been asking himself the same for months, ever since the four young women got off the stage. The minute he saw her, Mack knew he had to take a chance, something he hadn't done since the woman he loved betrayed him. Something about Sylvia made him want to try again.

"Yeah, Dutch. I do."

Clasping Mack on the shoulder, he nodded. "In that case, let me get to work." He started back inside, then stopped, grinning over his shoulder. "Just know that you're going to owe me."

Sylvia paced back and forth in her room, mumbling to herself. Stopping next to the bed, she stared at the three dresses she'd laid out, telling herself she should stay upstairs when he called. It would serve him right. Mack was arrogant, bigheaded, and conceited. Too bad he was also incredibly good-looking.

Why hadn't Malvina and Ruby told Sylvia he was a rogue...untrustworthy and self-centered? No, they'd said the opposite, making her want to know even more about him. She kept telling herself this would be the perfect opportunity to get answers to all the questions rolling through her mind. When the evening ended, she fully expected to dislike the man and never see him again.

A soft knock on the door pulled her from her mental ramblings. "Sylvia. Deputy Mackey asked me to tell you he's here."

*Already?* "Thank you, Suzanne. I'll be down in a few minutes."

Grabbing a dress, she slipped it on, closing the tiny buttons in front. She'd already fixed her hair and placed her reticule and shawl on a chair next to the door. Placing her feet into shoes she'd already cleaned, she grabbed the hook, making short work of tightening them around her feet.

Straightening, she sucked in an unsteady breath, feeling the slight bit of moisture on her face. A trembling smile curved the corners of her mouth. She wondered if Mack had any idea she'd never been out to supper with a man who wasn't part of her family.

A ball of panic started deep in her belly, moving up so it almost choked her. What if he tried to kiss her? The thought caused a wave of heat to course through her body. She'd kissed two boys, both behind the church after services. Both quick, wet, and unsatisfying. Would it be the same with Mack?

Clenching her hands into fists, Sylvia reminded herself they were having supper, nothing more. If he tried to take liberties, she'd stop him, let him know she wasn't like the women at Ruby's or the other saloons. From what she'd learned from Malvina, Mack wouldn't try to take advantage. The thought depressed her, which was ridiculous.

Unable to put it off any longer, Sylvia picked up her reticule and shawl, then left her room. Stopping at the top of the stairs, she gripped the rail, steadying herself. She refused to be cowered by a tall, gorgeous man with a smile that lit his face and caused her heart to jump.

She was Sylvia Maria Pietro Lucero, only daughter of Antonio Lucero, cattle baron and a man others respected. Lifting her chin, she straightened her back. This would be a night she'd always remember, and Sylvia meant to enjoy every minute of it.

# Chapter Four

*Whiplash, Texas*

Antonio Lucero slammed his fist on the desk, a stream of curses erupting through his lips. "It's been nine months. *Nine months*," he shouted. "How is it these men cannot find a trace of my daughter? Sylvia is out there somewhere."

His oldest son, Cruz, sat across from him while his other son, Dominic, lounged on the sofa. Neither flinched at their father's outburst. They'd grown used to his explosive rants and barely controlled rage since their sister left. Both believed he'd brought it on himself, perhaps Dominic a slight amount more than Cruz.

They likened constraining Sylvia to breaking a wild mustang. It had to be accomplished with a great deal of patience and a soft hand. If not, you'd not only break the animal, but also its spirit. Sylvia leaving may have been the only way for her to maintain her spirit.

"Not even one lead." Antonio walked around his desk. "We know she left by stage and got off in Abilene, but nothing more." His face twisted in pain, the same as every time he thought of how he'd lost his daughter. "It's as if Sylvia disappeared without any trace."

"She's a smart girl. I'm not surprised she found a way to vanish without leaving a trail." Dominic pushed up, walking to a table to pour a drink. Lifting the glass to his mouth, he took a small sip, deep lines showing on his forehead. "What of the Pinkerton Agency?"

"What of them?" Cruz asked.

"They do more than hunt bank and train robbers."

Antonio studied his youngest son, his gaze narrowing. "Do they locate missing people?"

"I've heard they do." Dominic emptied his glass, setting it down. "A telegram to their offices will give us the answer." He took a few steps, stopping next to his father. "Are you certain you want to force Sylvia to come home?"

"She's my daughter, your sister. Her place is with her family." Walking back around his desk, Antonio sat down. "Dominic, I want you to ride to town. Send a telegram to the Pinkerton Agency and wait for a response. If they do track people, hire them right away."

Dominic glanced at Cruz, who shook his head, shrugging. Arguing would do nothing to change their father's mind. They didn't need to get drawn into an argument when the outcome would be the same.

"Yes, sir. Anything else you want me to do while I'm in town?" Dominic walked toward the door.

43

Antonio sent a hard glare at his son. "What I *don't* want you to do is visit any of the saloons. You're to take care of hiring Pinkerton, then ride home. Am I clear on this?"

A sheepish smile crossed Dominic's face. "I've no idea what you're implying. Like many of the men, after my chores are done on Saturdays, I head into town. Have a few drinks, play cards..." His voice trailed off when he saw the amused expression on Cruz's face.

Antonio shuffled the papers on his desk. "It's the other days you ride into town after supper, Dom. Perhaps you could refrain from stopping anywhere else and return home today."

Making a slight bow, Dominic smiled. "Whatever you want, Father."

Shaking his head, Antonio waved a hand in the air. "Get out of here before I change my mind and send Cruz."

Dominic chuckled as he closed the door and headed outside. Picking up his pace, he saddled his horse, reining it toward town. He had plenty of time to send the telegram, but he wouldn't sit around waiting for a response. The clerk would bring a reply to the saloon where he'd already made plans to meet friends for cards.

Thinking of Sylvia, he felt of stab of loss pass through him. They'd been close, much closer than either had been with Cruz. After she'd left, he'd been angry she hadn't confided in him, hadn't trusted him to keep a confidence. They told each other everything. *Well, almost everything*, he thought as he drew closer to town. There were some things an older brother simply didn't tell a younger sister, his activities at the saloons in Whiplash being one of them.

Dominic and Sylvia had always been alike. Pushing the boundaries their father set, creating their own dreams, which had nothing to do with the ranch. Both knew they were expected to marry, stay on the ranch, and continue the dynasty their grandfather started after arriving from Spain. Their father had done what was expected and he demanded no less from his three children.

Which they would've been more inclined to do if he allowed them to choose who they'd marry. Cruz had no issue with who their father picked for him. He and the neighboring rancher's daughter had been in love since they were young, and neither wanted anyone else. Plus, their marriage would unite two prominent families.

The woman their father planned for Dominic to wed was pretty, painfully quiet, and quite boring. In addition, she hated ranch life, dreaming of going to school back east. He had no idea what she planned to study and didn't care. All he knew was they weren't well suited.

Approaching the telegraph office, Dominic thought of his own dream, the one he'd shared with just one person—Sylvia. She'd supported him, encouraged him to tell their father. He snorted as he reined to a stop and slid to the ground. Antonio Lucero would've supported his son's wishes as much as he'd have supported Sylvia's. Not at all.

*Splendor, Montana*

Mack worked to keep his mouth from dropping at the vision coming down the stairs. His throat tightened, forcing him to swallow before holding out his hand to her, feeling a surge of energy when she accepted it.

"Good evening, Deputy Mackey."

"Adam."

Her brows knit together as she stepped beside him. "What?"

"It's my first name."

"Adam…" She almost whispered it to herself. "It's a wonderful name. Why does everyone call you Mack?"

He opened the door, escorting her outside. "It started when I served in the Union Army, although I can't recall who said it first. My father had always been called Mack. I never imagined using it myself."

She glanced up at him. "So, you were in the war?"

He nodded. "Caleb and I served under Gabe. That's why each of us came west."

"You must think quite highly of him if you rode across the country for work. Surely there must have been other jobs closer to your homes."

"Yes, there were." He didn't want to talk about home, what he'd left behind, or the woman he'd lost. "Gabe is one of the best men I've ever known. It's a privilege to serve under him now, as it was during the war."

They strolled along the boardwalk to the St. James Hotel, Sylvia's heart racing, afraid he'd notice her excitement. Letting him know how much she'd wanted to accept his prior invitations would embarrass her too much.

A young man Sylvia didn't recognize smiled as they walked in. "Good evening, Deputy Mackey. Your table is ready."

"Thank you, Thomas." He looked at Sylvia, seeing the look of surprise on her face. "Have you eaten here?"

"No, but May says it's wonderful. She works in the kitchen." Her gaze wandered around the dining room as they followed Thomas to their table.

"Here you are."

Mack pulled out her chair, taking the one beside her. "A bottle of wine please, Thomas."

She shot a look at him, her eyes wide. "I haven't had wine since..." Her voice trailed off when Sylvia realized what she'd almost said. "In a long time."

He stared at her a moment, wondering what she'd been about to say.

"Will this be all right?" Thomas held out the bottle, getting a nod from Mack. They remained silent as he filled their glasses before picking up the handwritten menu from the center of the table. "This is what is being served tonight." He handed it to Sylvia.

Reading it, her face brightened. "Oh, they have venison. If it's all right with you, that's what I'd like."

"You can have whatever you want, Sylvia."

Her soft gaze met his. "Thank you, Adam."

He startled at the use of a name no one had spoken in years.

"Is it all right if I call you Adam?"

Lifting his glass of wine, he motioned for her to do the same. "It's more than all right." He held out his glass to hers, touching the rim. "Here's to a memorable evening."

She wanted to tell him it already was, but stopped herself, glad when Thomas approached.

"What would you like this evening?"

"The lady and I will have the venison."

"An excellent choice."

When he left, Mack leaned toward her. "Where are you from, Sylvia?"

Biting her lip, she tried to remember what she'd been telling everyone. For some reason, being with Mack unsettled her, making simple answers difficult.

"I came here from Philadelphia." *It's not a lie*, she told herself. Pettigrew's, the company who'd sent the four young women west, was located there. So, in a sense, it was true.

He took another sip of wine, studying her over the rim of his glass. "Before then. Where were you born?"

"Well, I..." Her voice wavered with relief when Thomas approached with their meals.

"Venison for the lady, and the same for you, Deputy Mackey." Grasping the bottle of wine, Thomas poured a little more into each glass. "Please let me know if you'd like anything else."

Inhaling the aroma of cooked meat, Sylvia let out a deep sigh. "It smells wonderful." Picking up her knife and fork, she cut a slice, putting it into her mouth. "Oh, this is wonderful, Adam."

Mack's chest tightened, throat thickening at the use of his given name and the way her face lit up as she enjoyed her meal. It had been a long time since he'd paid attention to the small pleasures, such as a good meal or a beautiful woman who looked at him

49

as if he'd given her the moon. The truth was she'd given it to him.

They spoke little as they ate, saying a few words about the food or the setting. Sylvia had only been able to glance inside the Eagle's Nest restaurant a couple times, never spending more than a minute looking around. Tonight, she noticed everything.

"Did you know Gabe and Lena Evans own the hotel and restaurant with Nick and Suzanne Barnett?"

Lifting her glass of wine, she took a sip, nodding. "May Bacon told me as much. She says they're all wonderful to her." Setting the glass down, she once again looked around the room. "She's been encouraging me to ask about a job here, but..."

"But?"

Biting her lip, she lowered her gaze. "Deborah Chestro cleans rooms in the hotel. That's the only work available right now."

A grin quirked up one corner of his mouth. "And you'd prefer not to work with Deborah?"

Her face reddened. "It's not that...exactly."

"Then tell me what it is...exactly."

Lifting her napkin, she dabbed the corners of her mouth, her hand shaking enough for Mack to notice. "It's just...well, Deborah can be a little much sometimes."

"Such as?"

The example which sprung into her mind had her looking away from Mack, embarrassment flashing through her. What would he think if he knew she'd gone to Ruby's and talked to Malvina, learning the most important part of Deborah's story was untrue? No, she couldn't risk him ever finding out about how she'd gone behind his back, poked into his personal life.

"It's her stories," she blurted out, then covered her mouth a moment before lowering her hand. "Deborah embellishes quite a bit. Well, more than quite a bit at times."

Mack watched her eyes sparkle with a combination of annoyance and humor. "She sounds entertaining."

"She can be, except she often passes off her stories as true."

He leaned back in his chair and leveled his gaze at her. "Any you'd like to share?" Mack saw the instant her expression changed from amusement to horror.

"Oh, no. It wouldn't be right, as they, well..."

"Involve people here in town?" Mack began to put the pieces together, giving him some understanding as to why Sylvia might have visited Ruby's. He noticed her throat work, her face color once more.

She lowered her gaze, not knowing how to respond. Her mother always said it was best to tell the truth, or at least a close version. Sylvia wasn't prepared to do either.

Shrugging, she lifted her eyes to meet his. "Sometimes she does tell stories about local townsfolk. Other stories are about people she's met while working here at the hotel. It's just hard to know how much of what she says is real and how much isn't."

Reaching over, Mack placed his hand on hers and squeezed. "If there's something you want to know, I suppose you could just ask the person."

Catching her lower lip between her teeth, her eyes grew wide. "What do you mean?"

"For instance, if you heard something about me you suspected might be false, you could just ask me. Right?"

Her chest felt as if it were weighted down with lead, causing her to sink under the load. Guilt sliced through her. All Mack had to do was speak with Malvina or Ruby and he'd learn of her visit to the Palace. A soft groan escaped her lips.

He leaned closer. "Pardon me?"

Pulling her hand free, she shrugged, shaking her head. "I was thinking about what you said. It's not always easy asking someone straight out about something, well...personal. In most cases, it wouldn't be proper." Her brow lifted. "Would it?"

Settling back against the chair, Mack crossed his arms. "Well, now, I suppose it would depend."

"On what?"

"The reason for the questions. Who the person had to speak with to get the answers. If they thought the person would mind them going behind their back and not asking directly."

Pursing her lips, Sylvia thought about his answer for a few moments. "What if they didn't know the person well and the questions would be too embarrassing to ask directly?"

Rubbing his jaw, he appeared to be thinking. "Now *that* would be a dilemma."

"Exactly," she whispered, almost to herself.

"We have berry or apple pie tonight. Can I get either of you a slice?" Thomas's cheerful voice pulled them out of what had become an almost too personal conversation—a discussion at least she would like to end.

"Which one would you like, Sylvia?"

She placed a hand on her stomach. "I don't believe I could eat another bite."

"Same here," Mack added.

Thomas clasped his hands in front of him. "Coffee or tea?"

Mack raised a brow at Sylvia. "I'd love some tea."

"Coffee for me, Thomas."

"I'll take these plates and be right back." Leaning over the table, he picked up the supper plates before hurrying to the kitchen.

"You never did tell me where you were born, Sylvia."

Putting it off any longer wouldn't help. Mack would just keep asking. "I was born in Texas, but we traveled all over." Again, she'd told the truth from her own point of view. "Where are you from, Adam?"

Again, his chest squeezed at the use of his first name. He found himself wondering why it sounded so right coming from her lips. "New York, the same as Gabe, Noah, and Caleb."

"You grew up together?"

He shook his head. "No. Gabe and Noah did. I met Caleb while in the Union Army serving under Gabe. Just a strange coincidence we'd all grown up within a couple miles of each other."

Thomas set down the coffee for Mack and tea for Sylvia. "Let me know if you want more."

When he left, Sylvia picked up the cup, staring into the amber liquid. The mention of the four men growing up so close together reminded her of all she'd left behind. Her family and friends. She hadn't missed the affluence as much as the people. If only her father would've allowed her to marry for love. The wealthy, arrogant young men her father considered suitable never appealed to her. Looking over the rim of the cup, her gaze landed on Mack, the desire she felt increasing with every minute they were together.

"Are you all right, Sylvia?"

Shaking her head slightly, she set the cup down. "I'm fine. Why?"

"You looked a little peaked." Mack hid a wry grin, already loving the way he could read every emotion passing across her face. What he'd seen a moment before stilled his heart while triggering excitement he hadn't experienced in a long time. Maybe his luck hadn't run out after all.

# Chapter Five

"I'm looking for the sheriff." Elija Smith stood in the doorway of the jail, his brother, Ebenezer, behind him. Both were tall, wiry, with short beards sprinkled with gray, and an easy manner which belied their tough nature and unrelenting determination.

Mack stood, walking around the desk to extend his hand to each man. "Good morning, Elija, Ebenezer. Gabe should be back in a few minutes. Can I help you?" He'd been in the office since six o'clock, had gotten little sleep, yet felt better than he had in months.

Resting his hands on the back of a chair, Elija bent his head, letting out a breath. "We found five more head this morning. Slaughtered, the same as the others."

Ebenezer stepped beside him. "My son was guarding them last night. Took a bullet in the shoulder."

Mack's features hardened. "Did you get Doc?"

"Eb's good at doctoring. He took care of his son, but—"

"We need help finding whoever is coming after us," Ebenezer interrupted, his patience gone.

Mack had never seen either so agitated. For men who rarely showed emotion, it didn't bode well.

Elija straightened, fisted hands at his sides. "Gabe was out a few days ago, told us he didn't have enough men to do a thorough search. We're here to convince him otherwise."

All three turned at the sound of the back door opening, seeing Gabe walk inside. He took one look at the sheepherders' faces, guessing what brought them all the way to town.

Elija walked to him. "We've gotta have your help, Sheriff. We lost more sheep last night and Eb's son was shot."

"Mack, go find Cash and Beau. I'm going to need their help. Then locate Dutch and send him here."

Nodding at Gabe, he grabbed his hat before heading out. Crossing the street, he shot a look through the windows of the boardinghouse restaurant, seeing Cash and Beau, wishing he could get a glimpse of Sylvia.

After supper, they'd made a slow walk through town, talking the entire time. He'd wanted to take another turn, knowing the smart thing to do would be to get her back to Suzanne's. To his surprise, she'd asked him if he'd take her to Ruby's for the show. It had taken some fast talking, but he'd managed to dissuade her, saying he'd consider escorting her to the Palace another time.

It was then Mack had seen the gleam in her eyes, knowing she'd been teasing him the entire time. Still, he swore he'd also seen something else flash across her face. A look he couldn't quite define.

After saying good night at the bottom of the boardinghouse stairs, he left with a crooked grin, securing her consent for a second supper engagement.

Taking a quick look around the restaurant, his gaze stopped when he spotted her eating breakfast with May. He was about to move toward her when Beau's voice stopped him.

"Hey, Mack. Come join us." His invitation could be heard throughout the restaurant, garnering Sylvia's attention.

Turning to him, she smiled, causing his heart to stutter. He couldn't recall if he'd ever seen anything more beautiful than Sylvia when her face lit with joy. He'd gone to sleep with the same image on his mind the night before, waking to it that morning. Someday, he hoped to wake with her in his bed, instead of just a memory of her gorgeous face.

His brain stumbled on the thought. Until that instant, he hadn't considered anything beyond a few suppers together. The idea of something permanent with the lovely Sylvia Lucero wasn't repugnant at all.

Giving her a quick smile and nod, he joined Cash and Beau, providing a brief summary of what happened at the Smith ranch. Within minutes, the three left the restaurant, Mack forcing himself not to take another glance at Sylvia before walking out the door.

Fifteen minutes later, every deputy, except Caleb, stood inside the jail, waiting for instructions from Gabe. At least one man kept watch on the town each night. Last night had been Caleb's turn, and they all knew Gabe would let him sleep as long as possible. Judging by the mood in the jail, it wouldn't be much longer before someone would be sent to roust him.

"How do you want to handle this, Gabe?" Cash crossed his arms over his chest, his features grim.

"You and Beau will ride out to the three ranches surrounding the Smith place and question them. I want to know where all their men were last night."

"If they're involved, you know no one's going to admit it." Beau had met all three ranchers over the last year. None were anything like Dax and Luke Pelletier, who made friends easily, offering help to anyone in need.

The Millers had been one of the first pioneers to ranch in Montana. The grandfather worked hard, adding acreage whenever he could. When he died, his son, Norman, took over. A few years ago, he'd split the land in thirds, keeping one parcel for himself while deeding the other two to his sons, Curtis and Morgan. They worked together. If the father made up his mind about something, his sons followed.

"You'll go to old man Miller's place first. If they're behind any of this, you'll be able to get a good sense of it. The man is hard, but doesn't hide his emotions well." Gabe leaned back in his chair, his gaze moving to Ebenezer and Elija. "Do you two have any reason to think it's the Millers?"

Rubbing his stubbled chin, Elija glanced at his brother before answering. "We can't think of anyone else it could be, Sheriff. They've been none too subtle about their hatred of sheep grazing near their cattle. We've had animals go missing in the past, but never slaughtered."

"How many men do you have?"

"It's just me and Ebenezer. Then we've got our boys. The oldest is fifteen."

Gabe rubbed the back of his neck. "Cash and Beau, I'm going to ask you to stay out at the Smith's for a couple nights."

"Caleb and I will go, Gabe. There's no sense sending them out, leaving their wives at home. Plus, if anything happens..." Mack shrugged, leaving the rest for the others to figure out.

Gabe studied his deputy's face a moment before nodding. "Thanks, Mack. Why don't you let Caleb know what's going on, then come back here. You two can follow Ebenezer and Elija to their place, take a look around where the sheep were slaughtered, then ride out to talk to the Millers."

"If there's anything to be found, Caleb and I will find it."

Gabe nodded, no one else speaking as Mack left through the jail's back door. He walked the short distance to the house he and Caleb shared, opened the door, and shouted his name. Pounding on the bedroom door, he shoved it open.

"Enough beauty sleep, Caleb. Gabe has a job for us." He chuckled when his friend shot up, looking around while rubbing his eyes.

"What the hell, Mack? I just got to bed."

"It's been five hours. Plenty of sleep for you." He picked up a shirt carelessly dropped on the floor, tossing it at Caleb. "Get dressed. We leave in ten minutes."

Sylvia watched out the window of the general store, hoping to see some sign of Mack, the same as she'd done the last two days. He hadn't come in for breakfast or supper at Suzanne's, nor had May spotted him at the St. James Hotel. It seemed the man had disappeared.

Adjusting items on a shelf, she took one more look through the dusty front window, seeing Dutch McFarlin take dogged steps across the street toward the Dixie. A few moments later, he came out with Nick Barnett, Suzanne's husband and the saloon's owner. They stopped on the boardwalk, locked in deep conversation. Several minutes passed before Dutch nodded, turning to cross the street back to the jail.

She had the strongest urge to slip outside and intercept the deputy. He'd know where Mack had gone. A wave of embarrassment whipped through her at the thought of showing her interest, or concern, about Mack. She wasn't quite ready to let anyone else know of the attachment she'd begun to form for the charming, if seemingly lonely, lawman. Taking a breath, she decided no harm would come from a casual inquiry.

Sylvia's movement toward the door stalled when it opened, a young couple with two children walking inside. The opportunity had slipped away. A forced smile appeared on her face, pushing away thoughts of Mack to focus on her job. Mr. Petermann trusted her to take care of the store while he worked in the back, and she meant to do her best.

"May I help you find anything?"

"Is Mr. Petermann not here today?" the woman asked.

"He's in the back. I'm Sylvia Lucero."

"It's nice to meet you. I'm Tilly Murton. This is my husband, Ty."

He touched the brim of his hat. "Ma'am."

Tilly held out a crumpled piece of paper. "This is what we need. It's a good bit of supplies."

Glancing over it, Sylvia nodded. "Yes, it is. It will take a little while to get all this together. I should have it ready in less than an hour."

"That'll be fine. I need to speak with the sheriff before taking my family to dinner." Ty shifted his youngest boy in his arms. "Will that give you enough time?"

The mention of the sheriff returned her thoughts to Mack. Since their supper together, everything seemed to turn her thoughts to him.

"Yes, that'll be fine. If your wagon is outside, I can load it while you're gone."

The sharp gaze he cast at Tilly snapped to hers. "No, ma'am. I'll be loading the wagon. If you get it all ready, I'll take care of the rest."

Watching them leave, Sylvia slumped against the counter. There wasn't a smidgeon of doubt about how much Tilly and Ty loved each other and their children. She wondered if they'd met in school when both were young with an entire future before them. Something flashed through her, a wistfulness, an almost melancholy feeling, which made no sense.

Except she knew it did. The young couple had what she'd always wanted, something her father never understood. Love, respect, and trust. She supposed a man and woman could build mutual

63

respect and trust over time. Love, the kind she sought, either existed or didn't.

The fact her father didn't understand this still angered her, the same as it had back home in Texas. For a man who'd married her mother for love, he seemed determinedly detached from allowing his children to form the same type of union.

Antonio Lucero ignored the fact his oldest son, Cruz, had loved the woman he meant to marry since they were children. Their father had welcomed the idea, excited at the prospect. Sylvia supposed it was because the young woman's family ranch bordered the Lucero's, which would eventually enlarge the dynasty her father envisioned.

"As if he needs more land or power," she mumbled to herself.

"Excuse me?"

She whipped around, hand to her chest, releasing a breath at the sight of Cash standing across the counter. "Deputy Coulter. I didn't hear you come in."

He looked over his shoulder at the door. "The bell chimed. I guess you didn't hear it."

"Well, what can I get you?"

"Allie needs yellow, blue, white, and black thread for the shop. We're also short on flour and sugar. And I'll need some ammunition."

Within minutes, she'd gathered what Cash wanted. "I'll put this on your account."

64

"Thanks, Miss Lucero. I'd best get going." He picked up the items and started to turn away.

"Um, Deputy Coulter?"

A brow lifted. "Yes?"

Her courage vanished. She'd meant to ask about Mack, needing to know he was safe, but pride stopped her.

"Oh, it's nothing."

He stood there a moment, watching her face before nodding and walking out.

*Smith Ranch*

"We've learned nothing about who might've done this." Mack raked a hand through his hair. "I suppose we could stay a few more nights."

Caleb shook his head. "After talking with the Millers, I have no doubt they're involved. They also know we're still at the Smith's. They won't do anything as long as we're here. It might be best to leave, let them relax their guard, and return in a couple days with more men."

Mack sat atop his horse, staring into the distance. "Gabe doesn't have enough men to send more than two out here at a time."

"We sure could use at least a couple more men. He's been thinking about hiring more deputies, but money's a little tight. Last week, he told me the town leaders were going to meet soon to come up with a solution."

"The trouble is the solution may not come before it's too late. The Millers know we don't have enough men to take care of the town and handle threats miles away. I wouldn't be surprised if they're the ones who rustled cattle from the Murtons and Westons. It keeps us thinner than normal. The first group of sheep were slaughtered at the same time."

Caleb scrubbed a hand down his face. "We were still trying to figure out the missing cattle when the second group of sheep were laughtered. As disgusting as it makes me, Ebenezer and Elija are right. The Millers are trying to run them off, and from what we've seen, they might very well succeed."

Swearing under his breath, Mack's grip tightened on the saddle horn. "Not if I have anything to say about it. I've seen too many people swindled out of their land, losing their homes to greed."

"This is more than greed. It's a desire to drive out anyone who doesn't agree with the Millers' way of life. They're cattlemen with all the prejudices of past generations. To them, sheepherders aren't worth the air they breathe." A haunted looked appeared in Caleb's eyes. He wasn't a man who spoke much about his past, but something about this angered him beyond the normal injustice he fought.

Mack noticed the change on his friend's face, saying nothing, not wanting to intrude on the man's private past. "Let's get back to town. We'll explain what we learned to Gabe. Maybe we can at least hire a few men long enough to help us figure out what's happening to the Smiths, possibly finding the cattle taken from the Murtons and Westons."

"You're right. Delaying the return won't help the Smiths. We have to come up with a plan. Running them out of the area isn't acceptable." Caleb's hard voice said more than his words. Something deep inside drove him to make certain the Smiths could continue making a living the only way they knew how. A look of determination hardened the deep lines on his face. Without another word, he reined his horse around, Mack following.

The ride to town seemed to take forever, longer than the trip out. Mack kept his mind occupied, switching between the problems at the Smith ranch and a more pleasurable topic—Sylvia. She hadn't been far from his thoughts the last two days. As odd and uncomfortable as it seemed, he missed her.

After his first experience with love ended in disaster, he had no desire to try it again. Not even with someone as lovely as Sylvia Lucero.

Memories of the woman he'd once loved raked over him as they continued along the trail. Unbeknownst to him, his fiancée hadn't spent much time alone after Mack left to serve the Union.

They'd known each other for years, fallen in love, and planned to marry when he returned after the war. The thought he wouldn't return never occurred to either of them. Now he understood why his leaving didn't seem to bother her. She already had other plans, which didn't include him.

At some point, her affections switched from Mack to his cousin, and he'd never suspected anything. She'd never broken their engagement, and his parents had not seen fit to forewarn him. Instead, he'd learned of her marriage to his cousin while preparing for another battle. It came as a brief mention in a letter from an aunt, as if the news meant nothing to him. The callous actions of his entire family stunned him. As far as Mack was concerned, he no longer had a family. He didn't need people in his life who betrayed him. It was also why he hadn't considered marriage again—until meeting Sylvia.

Mack had no objection to marriage or raising a family. He knew love didn't have to be a part of a union benefiting both people. Sylvia was a beautiful, vivacious young woman—someone he could forge a life with, even if it didn't include love. He already liked her, respected her—two important aspects of a marriage. Wooing her wouldn't be a hardship.

The toughest job would be convincing her of his way of thinking.

# Chapter Six

*Splendor*

"The town leaders approved two more deputies. I'm sure Dax's strong support made a big difference. Cash and Mack are riding to Big Pine tomorrow to talk with Sheriff Parker Sterling. Last I heard, the town is growing faster than the jobs. With any luck at all, the boys will come back with a couple more men." Gabe let out a deep breath, lines of frustration on his face.

Mack and Caleb had spent considerable time explaining what they hadn't been able to find during their stay at the Smith ranch. Dead animals and horse prints, but nothing else. Meeting with the Millers had been a waste of time.

"The territorial capital is your best chance of finding men quickly." Mack pinched the bridge of his nose. "Have you sent telegrams anywhere else?"

Gabe shook his head. "I thought I'd wait until the boys return. If they don't bring back anyone, I'll send word to all the big towns within a few days' ride."

Mack stood, walking to the window to glance outside. As soon as they were finished, he'd take a bath and hunt down Sylvia, hoping she hadn't already made plans for supper. It wasn't what he should do. As tired as he was, Mack knew he should stay home, get a good night's sleep, and look for her tomorrow.

*That's not going to happen*, he mused.

"Dutch and I are working tonight. You two get supper and sleep." Gabe chuckled. "You both look like you're about ready to fall over."

"See you at first light tomorrow." Mack headed out the back door, Caleb not far behind him.

"Where are you headed in such a hurry?"

Mack shot him a quick glance. "I'd think the same as you. I'm in need of a bath before getting a table at Suzanne's."

Caleb snorted, shaking his head. "If I didn't know you better, I'd think you were trying to impress someone."

"You'd be wrong. I just don't want to chase out any of Suzanne's customers because of the smell." Mack threw open the door of the house they shared, wasting no time building a fire in the stove and placing the pot of water they kept beside it on top. He wouldn't wait for it to get hot. All he wanted was for it to be warm enough to dip in a rag and drag it over his grimy body. Tomorrow, when he wasn't in such a rush, he'd take a real bath.

Tossing off his dirt-encrusted clothes, he grabbed two rags from the cupboard, throwing one to Caleb. He nodded at the water. "Help yourself."

Rushing through the process of cleaning and dressing, they were back outside twenty minutes later. Neither spoke as they made the short walk to the boardinghouse.

Mack stopped the instant they stepped inside, his gaze scanning the room, heart pounding when he saw her sharing a table with May. "Come on."

Caleb shrugged, following him to the back, a rush of air leaving his lungs when he realized Mack's destination. A few seconds later, the two men stood next to the table.

"Good evening, Miss Lucero." A jolt of satisfaction rushed through him when Sylvia looked up, surprise mixed with concern on her face.

"Deputy Mackey." Sylvia breathed out his name, relief flooding her. "I haven't seen you in a few days."

Taking off his hat, he motioned to the two empty chairs. "I'll tell you all about it. Do you mind if Caleb and I join you?"

Sylvia didn't consider checking with May. "Please. Tabitha just took our order." She started to push away from the table. "I'll go get her so you two can order."

Before Mack could stop her, she'd dashed off toward the kitchen, stopping Tabitha as she walked out. A moment later, both women were back at the table.

"Good evening, Deputy Mackey, Deputy Covington. We have roast, quail, and chicken tonight. What would you like?"

Both ordered the roast, Sylvia not missing the way Tabitha's gaze lingered on Mack a little longer than necessary. Nor did she miss the way he grinned back at the attractive young woman. Sylvia kept her features neutral, even though their silent interaction angered her. Tabitha had never mentioned Mack taking her to supper or showing any interest in her. Still...

"Were you both gone?" May asked, unaware of Sylvia's internal battle.

Caleb nodded. "Yes, ma'am. Gabe sent us to a ranch south of town for a couple days. We just got back a little bit ago."

"I hope it wasn't anything serious." May picked up her tea and took a sip.

Caleb's mouth twisted in disgust. "I'm afraid it was." He didn't say any more, not wanting to discuss the gruesome scene with the women.

Sylvia's gaze locked on Mack. "Will you need to go back?" She worked to keep her voice calm, fighting the dread she felt at the danger always stalking a lawman.

He shrugged. "There's a good chance we will." Seeing the worry on Sylvia's face, Mack knew he needed to change the subject. "Tell us what you two ladies have been doing."

May opened her mouth to speak, shutting it when Tabitha set plates in front of her and Sylvia. "I'll be right back with your food, gentlemen."

Again, she lingered, gracing Mack with a warm smile, which he returned. Sylvia's heart sank at his obvious attraction to her friend. And who could blame him. Tabitha's soft brown hair, caramel eyes, and ivory skin had attracted a good deal of attention on the way west. All she had to do was smile to gain someone's notice. It seemed to be working too well with Mack. Swallowing the ache in her throat, Sylvia conceded the supper they'd shared hadn't meant as much to him as it did to her.

Caleb waited until Tabitha had walked away before giving Mack a wry grin. "Seems Miss Beekman has an interest in you."

Before Mack could reply, Sylvia picked up her fork, stabbing a piece of chicken. "And it appears you share her interest, Deputy Mackey. Perhaps you'd like to take *her* to supper at the Eagle's Nest."

May bit her lip, doing her best to hide her amusement. Sylvia had shared her interest in Mack with the condition the information not be shared with either Tabitha or Deborah.

"Here you are." Tabitha set down Caleb's plate, then moved to Mack, brushing his shoulder as she set his down. "You be sure and let me know if you'd like anything else, Deputy Mackey." She brushed his shoulder again before returning to the kitchen.

A sick feeling built in Mack's gut. Until Sylvia's sarcastic comment, he hadn't realized the impact his innocent flirting with Tabitha had on her. Staring across the table, he noticed the tensing of her shoulders, features grim as she chewed her food. After swallowing, she set down her fork.

"If you all will excuse me, I'm a little tired."

May's eyes widened. "But, Sylvia, what about your supper?"

Glancing at the almost full plate, she shook her head. "I'll stop by the kitchen. Perhaps Tabitha would have a moment to join you." She looked at Caleb, avoiding moving her gaze to Mack. "Good night, Deputy Covington, Deputy Mackey."

Slipping between the tables, she headed toward the steps, her chest squeezing with every movement. As she reached the bottom of the stairs, a strong hand tightened on her arm, turning her around.

"Do you want to tell me what that was about, *Miss Lucero*?" Mack's jaw tensed, his gaze boring into hers.

She glanced behind him, seeing Caleb and May staring, but no one else. Keeping her voice low and even, she tugged at his grip. "Would you please let go of me?"

"Outside."

Her brows furrowed. "What?"

"We're going outside where we can have some privacy."

"I don't want to go outside with you." She tried and failed to pull her arm free. It wasn't a painful grip, angering her more than it hurt.

"You don't have a choice." Opening the door, he guided her past him into the cooling evening air. Walking down the boardwalk away from the restaurant, he stopped in front of the darkened clinic. Drawing her to face him, he leaned down. "Now, tell me what all that nonsense was about."

The hurt turned to anger, her chest heaving in outrage. "I don't owe you an explanation. Besides, I'd think someone of your intelligence would understand simple English."

He closed the gap between them to mere inches, his gaze locked on hers. "Simple English?"

"I only stated what everyone else at the table heard and saw. You are obviously attracted to Tabitha, and she seems to return your interest." Her voice dripped with sarcasm, her eyes sparking. "Perhaps she'd enjoy an evening out with you at the—"

He didn't let her finish, stopping the tirade as his mouth covered hers. What he'd intended to be a convenient way to stop the outburst quickly turned into something more, hearing her soft moan. Without breaking contact, he moved her into the darkness at the side of the clinic. Loosening his grip on her arm, his hands moved to her back, drawing her close. He smiled against her lips, feeling her arms wrap around his neck, pulling him down.

Letting his tongue graze across her lips, he groaned in satisfaction when she opened to him. He'd never tasted anything so sweet. Moving his hands down her back to rest on the soft swell of her hips, he pulled her tight, hearing her quick intake of breath at the feel of his hardened body. When one hand moved down her dress, caressing her thigh, a whimper escaped a moment before she stiffened. He felt her arms drop away from his neck, her hands moving to his chest.

"Mack." She broke the kiss, her body stilling as she pushed against him. "Mack, let go." Her voice was hard, unyielding.

It took him a moment to realize what she asked. Dropping his arms, he stepped back. "I'm sorry..." His voice trailed off at the frightened look on her face.

Glancing away, Sylvia sucked in several breaths to clear the desire still pulsing through her. "I'm not..."

He tilted his head, trying to get her to look at him. "You're not what, sweetheart?"

The endearment drew her attention back to him. Keeping her voice even and low, she stepped farther away. "I'm not your sweetheart, and I'm not one of your women at Ruby's."

His features turned to granite, body stilling as if he'd been slapped. "What did you say?"

Blinking, she took a deep breath. "I believe you heard me." Sylvia tried to sound indignant. Instead, her voice came out shaky and weak.

"You're right. I did," he growled. Placing fisted hands on his hips, he tilted his head up, drawing in a deep, ragged breath before returning his gaze to hers. "I apologize, Miss Lucero. My actions were inappropriate. I'll not let it happen again." His voice was stilted, unyielding. "I'll take you back to the boardinghouse."

Placing a hand on her elbow, he guided Sylvia to the front door of Suzanne's. Taking her chin between his fingers, he lifted her face to meet his. "Good night, Miss Lucero. And to clarify any misunderstanding, I've never once considered you to be anything like *my women* at Ruby's." Stepping back, he turned away, leaving her standing alone.

Sylvia continued to push her hand against her chest, hoping the unremitting pain would stop. She'd lain awake for hours, hurt coursing through her at how he'd walked away, not looking back as he shoved open the doors of the Wild Rose and slipped inside.

Forcing herself not to watch the saloon from her bedroom window, Sylvia dressed for bed. Sleep never came, at least not until an hour or two before dawn. Staring at the ceiling, she berated herself for her careless comment about his saloon women. It was uncalled for, and unlike her to say something so mean spirited. The look on Mack's face continued to stab through her hours later. He'd been stunned, confused, then enraged at the outburst. She didn't blame him. He'd done nothing wrong, even if they had gone a little far in the dark space outside the clinic.

The incredible desire she'd felt scared her. She'd never been kissed with such passion or need, having no idea how to handle the emotions exploding through her.

Sylvia stared at the ceiling for hours, trying to find a way to fix what she'd done. Apologizing was such a weak action, but she couldn't think of anything better. Mack seemed the type of man who would appreciate a simple, direct apology.

Dragging herself out of bed, she finished her morning ritual, slipping into the nicest day dress in her wardrobe. Sylvia took extra time with her hair, looking into the full-length mirror, pleased with what she saw.

Taking a deep breath, forcing herself to calm the thumping of her heart, she walked downstairs. Ignoring the smells of frying bacon and fresh coffee,

79

she pushed through the doors and stepped into another of Montana's beautiful mornings.

Her movements stalled as she stared across the street at the jail. Mack had told her about meeting with Gabe early. Reaching out, she placed a hand on the post of the handrail, steadying herself. From the moment she'd left her bed, Sylvia had been practicing what to say, how to phrase the apology in a way he'd accept.

Even if he never wanted to see her again, share any more time together, at least the apology would've been made. The thought didn't provide the comfort she'd hoped.

Pushing away from the post, she stepped into the street, moving between groups of riders and wagons laden with supplies. Before Sylvia knew it, she stood in front of the jail, the pounding in her chest incessant and painful.

Straightening her spine and squaring her shoulders, a shaky hand gripped the doorknob, turning it. Disappointment clogged her throat when she stepped inside. Mack was nowhere in sight, Gabe and Caleb the only two people in the jail.

"Good morning, Miss Lucero. What can we do for you?" Gabe walked around the desk, the corners of his mouth sliding upward.

Clearing her throat, she clasped her hands together. "I was wondering if you know where I might find Deputy Mackey."

"On his way to Big Pine. He and Cash rode out early this morning."

A sense of defeat wrapped around her. "Do you know when he'll return?"

Gabe leaned against the edge of his desk. "Could be more than a week. It depends on what they find."

"Oh." She heard the distress in her voice, determined to correct the slip. Lifting her chin, she forced a slight grin. "Thank you, Sheriff."

"If you want to get a message to him, I'm sending a telegram to the sheriff in Big Pine. I can send another one for Mack. He'll make sure he gets it."

She shook her head. "Thank you, but no. I'll let you gentlemen get back to your business." Stepping outside, she didn't notice Caleb following until he came up beside her. "Is there something you want, Deputy Covington?"

Crossing his arms, he stared into the street. "I haven't seen Mack as drunk as he was last night in a long time. I'm thinking it has something to do with you." He glanced down at her. "Am I right?"

Biting her lip, her mind reeled as she searched for an answer he might accept. "I'm sure I don't know."

He chuckled, shaking his head. "I surely doubt that, Miss Lucero."

Sylvia's gaze rose to lock on his. "You wouldn't be calling me a liar, would you, Deputy Covington?" Her voice held a hint of amusement.

His lips twitched. "I'd never call you a liar, ma'am. I do, however, believe you know exactly why Mack buried himself in two bottles of whiskey last night."

She gasped. "*Two* bottles?"

"Well, one full bottle and half of another. I honestly thought I'd find him dead this morning."

She couldn't hold his questioning gaze. "I said something to Mack last night that angered him." Letting out a shaky breath, she wrapped her arms around her waist. "I'd hoped to apologize this morning."

His jaw worked, but Caleb remained silent for several long moments. After a bit, he looked back down at her. "It's best Mack left this morning. Believe me, he wouldn't have been in any mood to speak with you."

The bravado she felt a few minutes before vanished. "He hates me, doesn't he?"

"Hate is a strong word."

A brow lifted. "Never wants to see me again?"

He snorted. "I doubt it. What Mack needs is to be away for a spell, give himself time to figure out what he wants." His gaze narrowed on her. "You may not know, and he sure doesn't show it, but it's hard for him to trust anyone. Most times, he doesn't even try. The fact he's been trying with you says a lot."

Her brows furrowed. "What happened to Mack to make him have such intense distrust?"

Caleb shook his head. "It's his story to tell, Miss Lucero."

Dread clogged her throat. "What if he won't speak with me?"

"Then you'll know what he's decided."

# Chapter Seven

*"You'll know what he's decided."*

Caleb's words stayed with Sylvia two days later. She couldn't shake them from her mind, not while working at the general store, eating supper with May, or taking short walks on the boardwalk as the sun set each night, as she was doing now.

She knew what Caleb meant and the thought caused her chest to squeeze. Sylvia didn't want to consider Mack wouldn't want to see her again, that she'd crossed a line he couldn't forgive.

Taking a seat on an empty bench outside the St. James, she stared up, her gaze concentrating on a sky filled with bright stars and an almost full moon. Sylvia found herself wondering if Mack might be looking at the same stars and moon from wherever he happened to be in Big Pine. She doubted it.

Thick sadness washed over her, imagining what he might be doing. Playing cards, drinking, possibly getting friendly with one of the girls in a saloon. It made no sense, but the thought sickened her. They'd shared a meal, conversation, and a kiss that still played across her mind, causing her body to react in ways she didn't understand. In truth, there'd been nothing more. Because she'd ruined it with her thoughtless comment.

"All alone out here, Miss Lucero?" A man she didn't recognize stood over her, his gaze sparking with interest. She may not be experienced, but that didn't mean she didn't know when a man showed an interest in her.

"I'm sorry. Have we met?"

"At the community dance when you and the other mail order brides came to town. I'm Morgan Miller. I own a ranch south of here." He took off his hat, nodding at the empty space on the bench next to her. "Do you mind if I join you?"

Sylvia did, but courtesy wouldn't allow her to say no. "Not at all." She scooted as far to one side as possible, allowing a good deal of room between them.

"Nice night."

She glanced toward him at the comment, noticing he looked at the sky the same as she'd done before he'd arrived. For a brief moment, Sylvia studied the hard, strong lines of his face. Morgan wasn't handsome in the normal sense. Still, she found him quite attractive in an unconventional way. Before he noticed her staring, she forced her gaze away.

"It's beautiful. I don't believe I've ever seen a sky so blue during the day or bright with stars at night. There are times I believe there must be at least a million stars up there. Can you even imagine?"

He chuckled, a deep, robust sound tickling her senses. "I read there are many more than a million. There are millions up there. I don't know how anyone would know, but the journal seemed legitimate."

She quirked a brow. "Journal?"

Clearing his throat, he looked at her. "A few years ago, I traveled back east to attend medical school. The journal was in the library."

"You're a doctor?"

A sad expression crossed his face. "No. My family needed me back here. I came home before I could finish my studies. I learned a lot, but not enough to practice." His eyes fixed on the bright sky once again.

She felt a rush of sadness at the longing in his voice. "That must have been hard, giving up your dream to be a doctor."

Morgan didn't stop staring at the sky. "At first. Over time, I got used to the idea of following my father and older brother in ranching." He snorted. "Although they do call me the black sheep of the family."

"Why's that?"

He shook his head. "Pa and my brother agree on everything. I rarely agree with them, which isn't easy for any of us. It's good I own my ranch. Most of the time, I can do what I want without too much interference. It's not easy being at odds with your father. You probably don't understand."

*How well I know,* Sylvia thought, then chuckled. "I understand better than you might think."

Morgan looked at her, a smile tugging at his mouth. "Where is your family, Miss Lucero?"

A nervous laugh bubbled up. "I came here from Philadelphia."

"Were you born there?"

She shook her head, deciding to tell a small part of the truth. "No." She breathed in the cooling night air and stood, noticing him stand with her. "I need to get back to the boardinghouse. It was good speaking with you, Mr. Miller."

"I'm walking that way myself. Let me escort you."

Sylvia thought about it a moment, seeing nothing wrong with Morgan walking beside her for the short distance. "That would be lovely."

They continued to talk as they passed stores and the clinic, finally stopping outside the boardinghouse. She turned toward him.

"Thank you, Mr. Miller."

"My pleasure, Miss Lucero. Perhaps you'd allow me to escort you to supper sometime."

She let out a tired breath. "Perhaps."

Morgan touched the brim of his hat. "I'll bid you good night then."

"Good night, Mr. Miller." She watched him walk away. That was when Sylvia noticed Caleb standing across the street, his gazed fixed on Morgan.

*Whiplash, Texas*

Dominic stared down at the telegraph in his hand, reading it through a second time. The Pinkerton Agency had tracked Sylvia to Philadelphia, where she'd signed an agreement with Pettigrew's. He pinched the bridge of his nose, unable to understand what would possess his smart, beautiful sister to become a mail order bride.

Looking up, he let out a disbelieving breath. Pinkerton's hadn't been able to find out where the company sent her. Pettigrew's policy was to contact the potential bride, obtaining her permission to provide more information.

"Thank God for that," he mumbled to himself. Knowing his sister, she'd never allow the company to reveal where she'd been sent.

As much as Dominic loved his father, he loved Sylvia more and respected her desire to create a life built on love, not on the wishes of a man blinded by the need for more land. He hated his father's obsession for more property and increased power, especially when the cost was the happiness of his own children.

Sliding the telegram into a pocket, Dominic stopped at his favorite saloon, played a few rounds of cards, consuming a couple glasses of whiskey. He needed to get his thoughts in order. Afterward, he'd ride home to give his father the news. Antonio wouldn't be happy. He expected no less than the exact location of his daughter.

Taking a seat at a table with two other men he knew, Dominic played three hands, finishing two glasses of whiskey. Instead of using the time to focus on the cards, he spent the time thinking through what his father's reaction would be to the Pinkerton telegram. The more he considered it, the more he became convinced his father would take matters into his own hands. Which meant he'd send Cruz or Dominic to Philadelphia to obtain the information unavailable to the agency.

Tossing down the last of his cards, he decided it was time to ride home and face his father's displeasure. He thought of the older man's reaction the entire ride to the ranch. It was how Dominic always dealt with his father, doing his best to keep one step ahead of him, ready for any response.

By the time he reined to a stop in front of the large hacienda, he felt confident whatever his father said, he'd be prepared with an answer. Dismounting, he noticed a buggy he hadn't seen as he rode up. Dominic's brow lifted as he tried to figure out who it belonged to, but could think of no one who owned a black buggy with a red and white crest painted on the side. This was no ordinary carriage. It belonged to someone with means. Someone new to Whiplash.

His interest piqued, Dominic walked inside, hearing his father's voice coming from the library. An instant before joining them, he stopped at the sound of a woman's laughter. It was throaty, not the tittering sound of stilted or forced amusement, nor the giggles of a young girl. Whoever she was, Dominic knew without doubt he'd never met her.

Walking through the doorway, he stopped at the sight of three people. An older man stood next to a woman of about the same age. A younger woman in a green dress and some odd concoction on her head stood near his father, her back to Dominic.

"Ah, there he is now." Antonio walked toward him, stopping a foot away. "This is my youngest son, Dominic. Dom, I'd like to introduce Mr. and Mrs. Givens and their daughter, Edith. They recently purchased a ranch several miles on the other side of Whiplash."

Removing his hat, Dominic greeted the couple before turning his attention to Edith. "Miss Givens. It's a pleasure to meet you."

Her face flushed a charming soft pink. He thought her pretty in an odd, unconventional way.

The green eyes staring up at him were set a little farther apart than normal, her lower lip fuller than one would expect, and her nose uncommonly broad. Still, when Dominic studied her features as a whole, she did have a certain appeal. Then she opened her mouth to speak.

"Hello, Mr. Lucero."

Dominic steeled his features so as not to outwardly cringe at the high-pitched squeak of her voice. This was followed by a trilling giggle, causing him to wince. With regret, he realized the woman he heard laughing earlier must have been Edith's mother.

"They will be staying for supper, Dom. I'd like you to give Miss Givens a tour of the ranch while the meal is being prepared."

His jaw tightened when he figured out what his father had planned. As with Sylvia, he had begun a mission to find him a wife. The same as his sister, Dominic wouldn't be pushed toward a woman because of the potential benefit to the Lucero family. Nor would he lead on someone such as Edith, pretending he held an interest in her.

"As much as I'd enjoy showing her around, I've business to attend to." He turned toward their guests. "If you don't mind, I need to speak with my father for a few minutes. I wouldn't ask, except it is quite important."

"Of course, young man." Mr. Givens took his wife's arm, guiding her and Edith from the room, closing the door behind them.

It didn't surprise Dominic to see the anger on his father's face when he shifted toward him.

Antonio glared at his son. "How dare you be rude to our guests, especially the young woman who'd expected to spend time with you."

Instead of answering, Dominic pulled the telegram from his pocket, handing it over. The change in his father was immediate, his anger now directed at the company behind the telegram. Murmuring several strong oaths, Antonio paced away, slapping the paper against his thigh.

"I cannot believe an agency such as Pinkerton isn't able to discover Sylvia's location."

"Pettigrew's policy wouldn't allow them to disclose where she is, Father."

"Damn their policy. She's a young, vulnerable woman with a family desperate to find her." He slammed his fist against the top of his desk, spewing a series of curses. "It could take months to get an answer, and by then, she might not be where they first sent her. There must be another way to get the information."

Dominic shoved aside the lump of indecision stuck in his throat. He knew the answer his father sought. When he'd first thought of it, he envisioned

Cruz making the long trip to Philadelphia, using his charm to gain the answers needed.

After meeting Miss Givens, understanding his father's intention of pushing them together, Dominic had a swift change of heart. He could think of no better way to assist his family and extricate himself from his father's schemes. A wry grin formed on his face. Of her two brothers, Sylvia would want him to be the one to discover where she'd fled—not Cruz, and definitely not their father.

"I believe there is a way to get the information we need, Father. I will go to Philadelphia and obtain what we need to find her."

Antonio blew out a frustrated breath, his irate stare narrowing on his youngest son. "If Pinkerton can't get the information, what makes you think that damnable mail order bride company will provide her location to you?"

Lowering himself onto the elegant, quite masculine leather sofa, he stretched out his long legs. Clasping his hands behind his head, a wry grin curled the corners of his mouth.

"For once, you're going to have to trust me, Father."

His jaw clenched, Antonio said nothing, recognizing the look on his son's face. Nostrils flaring, he nodded once, a curt movement of his head, giving his consent.

Pushing himself up, Dominic walked to stand in front of him. "I'll need money."

His father took four long strides to a safe concealed against a wall. Reaching inside, he grabbed stacks of money, handing them to Dominic.

"I'll be taking the stagecoach to Abilene, then the railroad to Philadelphia. I doubt it will take long to obtain what we need."

"When do you plan to leave?"

Dominic lifted a satchel from its usual spot on a shelf and stuffed the money into it before closing the latch. "I'll be on the stage tomorrow morning."

*Splendor*

Sylvia found it hard to keep a positive disposition after six days without any news about Mack. Even May had asked if something bothered her. She'd told her friend everything was fine—but it wasn't.

The days passed as they had before she'd started spending time with the complicated deputy. Mr. Petermann increased her hours at the general store, a welcome change providing additional funds, which she dutifully added to her small account at the bank.

Breakfast and supper with May, and sometimes Tabitha or Deborah, helped fill the hours, keeping her thoughts from Mack. The hardest time occurred at night, lying in bed while staring at the ceiling. She continued to think about her cruel outburst, the hurt look on his face, the way he'd walked away without looking back.

Sylvia thought Caleb might come to her if he heard any news about his friend, but he'd been as elusive as Mack. He'd even been brusque the couple times she'd stopped by his table at the boardinghouse restaurant to say hello. Polite, yes. Friendly, not at all.

Sylvia wondered if she'd done or said something to anger Caleb, but hadn't spoken with him since the morning she visited the jail, asking about Mack. He'd seemed fine when she walked away.

"What time will you finish work tomorrow?"

Sylvia looked up from the paper on the counter, smiling when she saw May walk inside the store. "The same as today. Five o'clock. Why?"

Her friend's face brightened. "Lena Evans invited us to supper at the Eagle's Nest. You, Deborah, Tabitha, and me. Please say you can join us."

Sylvia almost laughed. "Well, my social calendar is a little full..."

May's brows furrowed. "You're teasing me, aren't you?"

Setting a hand on her friend's arm, she nodded. "Yes, I am."

Smart and a quick learner, May held a deep thread of naïveté, making her a target of her friends' good-natured teasing. Sylvia hoped being so trusting didn't hurt her in more serious ways.

She squeezed May's arm, then let go. "I'd love to have supper at the Eagle's Nest tomorrow evening."

The chiming of the bell over the door drew her attention, her eyes widening at the sight of Caleb strolling inside. As he walked forward, his gaze seemed to lock on May, an action which surprised and delighted Sylvia.

"Good afternoon, Miss Bacon, Miss Lucero."

May's face flushed when he stopped next to her, his arm brushing hers.

"May I get anything for you, Deputy Covington?" Sylvia asked.

He reached into a pocket, pulling out a list hastily scribbled in bold strokes. Caleb handed it to Sylvia. "Not much there, but I thought I'd better stock up a little for when Mack gets back."

She stared at the list, her eyes widening. "Um...will Deputy Mackey be returning soon?"

Caleb shrugged. "It's been a week. Gabe expects him and Cash to ride back any day now. With luck, they'll have a couple new deputies with them."

The bell rang again. Morgan Miller smiled when he spotted Sylvia. Coming forward, he removed his hat, nodding at Caleb and May. "Good afternoon, Miss Lucero."

A slight grin curved the corners of her mouth. His appearance at the store surprised her, while at the same time creating a sense of disappointment. She'd hoped to see Mack when the bell sounded.

"Hello, Mr. Miller." Sylvia noticed Caleb run his gaze over Morgan, his mouth drawing into a thin, tense line. She found herself wondering at his reaction to the rancher. "I have a few items to get for Deputy Covington before I can help you."

Morgan grinned. "I can wait." He looked at Caleb and smirked.

May watched the reactions of the three people around her and cleared her throat. "I'll be at the boardinghouse if you want to have supper together, Sylvia."

Caleb wrenched his gaze away from Morgan. "I'll walk you across the street, Miss Bacon."

Blinking, May looked up at the tall lawman. "Um...that would be nice."

He glanced at Sylvia. "I'll be back in a few minutes for my order." Casting a hard look at Morgan, he cupped May's elbow, guiding her to the door.

Sylvia hurried to gather what Caleb needed, listing the prices on a piece of paper before totaling the order. Setting everything aside, she turned her attention to Morgan.

"What may I get you, Mr. Miller?"

He leaned against the counter, his eyes meeting hers. "Flour, sugar, molasses, and salt."

She grabbed the items as Morgan spoke. "Is that everything?"

The bell rang again, but she didn't look to see who had entered.

"Actually, I hoped you would consent to having supper with me tonight."

She stilled, not sure how to answer. "Well, I, um…" That was when her gaze moved past Morgan. Sylvia let out a soft gasp at the steely, cold look on Mack's face.

# Chapter Eight

Sylvia's breath caught, chest squeezing at the first sight of Mack in almost a week. For a tense moment, she worried he might turn around and leave. Instead, he stalked forward, his gaze never wavering from hers.

"Miss Lucero already has supper plans this evening."

Morgan straightened, glaring at Mack before looking at Sylvia. "Is that right, Miss Lucero?"

Glancing between the two, her mind whirling at Mack's resolute claim, she nodded. "Yes, it is, Mr. Miller."

Picking up the items she'd set aside for him, Morgan gave a brisk nod. "Perhaps another time, Miss Lucero."

Swallowing, she gave him a slight smile, her voice almost a whisper. "Perhaps, Mr. Miller." Sucking in a shaky breath, Sylvia waited until Morgan left before shifting her gaze to Mack. "That wasn't exactly accurate, Deputy Mackey. I don't recall you asking me to have supper with you tonight." Her lips curved upward as she finished.

"Never said I always tell the truth, Miss Lucero." He stepped up to the counter. "Besides, you and I need to talk."

The hard look on his face told Sylvia she might not like what he had to say. Still, Mack was right. They needed to discuss what happened the other night and decide if they had reasons to continue seeing each other. If not, it would be better to find out now.

She blew out a shaky breath, lifting her chin. "You're right. We do need to talk."

"I'll ask Suzanne for a quiet table at the back of her restaurant. Is six o'clock all right?"

"Yes, that would be fine."

He studied her face a moment before giving a curt nod. Without another word, Mack turned around and walked out, closing the door with a soft click.

Sylvia didn't realize she'd been holding her breath until he left. Shoulders slumping, her heart squeezed. Something about the set of his jaw and cold look in his eyes told her she wouldn't like whatever Mack wanted to say. A slight chill washed over her. She looked down at her hands clasped together in such a tight grip, her knuckles had already turned white.

She remembered all the times Mack had asked her to supper, all the rejections she'd given him. Even so, he'd never stopped asking, always hopeful she'd change her mind.

During those months, Sylvia felt in control, not allowing herself to get snared by the charming deputy. She snickered at the term her friends used to describe the formidable, dark-haired lawman with a broad smile and easy laugh.

Sylvia thought of the first few weeks she and her friends had spent in Splendor. The three single lawmen—Mack, Caleb, and Dutch—had been the subject of their conversations on many occasions.

May had made no secret of her attraction to Caleb, acknowledging the tall, gorgeous, sociable deputy would never have an interest in a woman such as herself. Quiet, shy, and rather fearful by nature, May held no hope he'd even noticed her since she and the others had arrived in Splendor.

Deborah had expressed an interest in Dutch. Although the broad-shouldered deputy with a deep red beard and personable manner had shown his own interest at first, his attention had lessened as time passed.

Tabitha hadn't voiced her attraction to any of the three until the night she'd flirted with Mack at the boardinghouse restaurant. The same night Sylvia thrust a knife into the tenuous relationship she and Mack had started.

*Mack*, she thought, swallowing the ball of dread building in her stomach. If only she'd kept her mouth shut and not mentioned anything about not being one of his women at Ruby's. She groaned at the memory, feeling a flush of heat spread up her cheeks.

Her mother would've been appalled if she knew her daughter spoke of such a sensitive topic as soiled doves. Ladies simply didn't speak of such things. Mack obviously felt the same. If she could take the words back, she would.

She shuddered, thinking of the stunned look on his face before he'd left her at the front door of the boardinghouse. A wave of resignation washed over her, already knowing what Mack wanted to say. Dampness pooled in her eyes as she succumbed to the inevitable.

On a deep, shuddering breath, Sylvia accepted by the time she climbed under the covers tonight, her brief relationship with Adam Mackey would be over, as would her ridiculous dream of love with the taciturn, yet quite charming lawman.

Dominic stared out the train window, looking without seeing the miles of open land racing past. His thoughts had been on Sylvia the entire trip, wondering where she'd been sent and if she'd already married. He hoped his sister hadn't jumped into some ill-advised relationship with a man not at all worthy of her.

Sighing, he pinched the bridge of his nose before shifting in his seat. Dominic missed Sylvia—her bright smile, vibrant personality, ability to put everyone at ease. She built friendships without regard for social status or money. He couldn't think of a single person who didn't like her or wished her well, except perhaps their father.

It wasn't because he didn't love his daughter. The elder Lucero loved each of his three children more than many fathers. He wanted them to find happiness, as long as their definition of the word matched his.

Antonio Lucero expected his children to bow to his wishes and do whatever they could to build the ranch and grow the dynasty. Anything less would be unacceptable. Sylvia leaving dealt a tremendous blow to their father's dreams.

His body jostled as the train went through a narrow pass, jolting him out of his thoughts. He pulled out his pocket watch, checking the time. They'd reach Philadelphia the following day. Lifting his hand, he patted the pocket holding the slip of paper where he'd scrawled Pettigrew's address.

Dominic didn't worry about obtaining Sylvia's destination from the mail order bride company. Once he explained their relationship and all her family wanted was reassurance of Sylvia's safety, he hoped they'd provide what he asked. If not, he'd smoothly switch to his alternate plan. Charm went a long way, but money went further. Dominic had both.

"We'll be arriving at our next stop in a few minutes. You'll have an hour for supper before the train leaves." The conductor swayed a little as he walked along the aisle, looking at the passengers as he passed by each row. "One hour only, ladies and gentlemen."

Dominic watched a young boy across the aisle jump up and down, excitement coursing through him. He suspected the long train ride had grown dull after a few hours for a boy of five or six. Chuckling, he admitted it had also become dull for him.

He'd never been a person who could sit still for long. Dominic would've preferred to ride his horse, stopping at small towns, playing cards over a few glasses of whiskey in the evenings. The thought had him pulling out the thin flask from an inside pocket. Opening it, he turned away from the other passengers to take a small sip.

Within forty-eight hours, he'd know Sylvia's location, then he'd face a hard decision, one he didn't welcome. Taking one more sip from the flask, he slipped it back into his pocket, glancing out the window as the next stop came into view. A surge of unease passed through him. Whatever decision he made, it would change the course of Sylvia's life, and perhaps Dominic's as well.

Sylvia took one more look in the mirror, sliding both hands down the fabric of her favorite green dress. She didn't know why her appearance mattered so much tonight. Within the hour, Mack would tell her all the reasons he wouldn't be calling on her again.

She should be spending her time preparing her reaction instead of doing her best to make a good impression. Nothing she could do at this point would change his mind.

No matter what happened, the reasons he gave, she wouldn't allow him to see the hurt his rejection caused, how much she'd miss his company. Instead, she'd hold her head high, keep her expression neutral, and accept his decision. After all, they hardly knew each other. Certainly not enough to feel much of a loss. Sylvia would keep telling herself the lie until she believed it.

Unable to stall any longer, she stepped into the hall, taking the stairs to the first floor. Her throat thickened when her gaze landed on Mack. He leaned a shoulder against the wall, arms crossed, expression unreadable. His gorgeous face gave away nothing as he regarded her.

"I hope you haven't been waiting long."

Pushing away from the wall, he didn't respond before sweeping his hand toward the dining room. "Suzanne has a table ready for us."

Biting her lip, Sylvia lifted her chin, moving past him toward the table at the back where Suzanne stood. She forced a smile. "Good evening, Suzanne."

"You look beautiful, Sylvia. Is that a new dress?"

"It's one Allie Coulter designed. She had it hidden in a wardrobe and brought it out for me to see." She glanced down, unaware Mack watched her every move. "I'm afraid it was an extravagance I should've ignored."

"Honey, we all need to be extravagant every once in a while." Suzanne turned her attention to Mack. "Good evening, Deputy."

"Suzanne." He pulled out the chair for Sylvia, then sat down beside her. "Thank you for keeping this table for us."

She lifted a hand. "My pleasure. We have venison stew, roast beef, or chicken tonight. Oh, and I made both apple pie and berry pie."

Mack looked at Sylvia, a brow raising, an indication for her to make a selection. She looked at Suzanne.

"I'll have the chicken, please."

"I'll have the stew, Suzanne. And save me a piece of berry pie." Mack grinned, although the gesture didn't quite reach his eyes. "Coffee for both of us, please."

Sylvia kept her gaze averted when Suzanne walked away. She had no appetite, didn't know why Mack wasted his money on supper when he could've given her his decision without spending a cent.

Neither of them spoke, the tension increasing with each breath. She could feel Mack watching her, but he kept silent. Sylvia's heart pounded so painfully, she felt certain he could hear it. Pushing aside the ache in her chest, her gaze locked on Suzanne as she approached their table holding two plates laden with food.

"Here you are. I'll get your coffee."

Mack still said nothing after Suzanne filled two cups and left. He stabbed a piece of venison, chewing slowly, washing it down with coffee. All the while, he never took his gaze off Sylvia, studying her as if she were some kind of foreign creature. Unable to take the close scrutiny any longer, she squirmed in the seat, setting down her fork.

"You're staring at me."

He didn't flinch or change his staid expression. "Yes, I am."

Annoyed, she glared at him. "Why?" Sylvia hissed.

Unperturbed, he finished the last of his stew, then settled back in his chair. "You're a confusing woman, Sylvia Lucero."

One corner of her mouth scrunched as her gaze narrowed on him. "I'm certainly no more confusing than you, Adam Mackey."

A brow quirked upward, his mouth sliding into a grin. Crossing his arms, he let his gaze wander from the top of her head to her waist, then back up, resting on her confused expression.

She clenched her hands in her lap, teeth grinding together at his open perusal. "If you have something to say, please, just say it." She wanted to scream when a flash of amusement crossed his face.

"All right. You obviously know I've spent time at Ruby's, the Dixie, and Wild Rose. I've never made a secret of my activities or tried to hide what I do with my nights."

Sylvia swallowed, not sure she wanted to hear any more.

"I also don't discuss it outside the doors of the saloons. My actions are private and nobody's business but mine."

She wanted to cover her ears, shrink away, and run upstairs. "I—"

He held up a hand, stopping whatever she'd planned to say. "I've been with many of the women who work at the saloons in Splendor. I'll not apologize for it or say anything more about those meetings."

Sylvia felt her face heat, her stomach clench. She couldn't handle hearing any more. Pushing the chair back, she started to stand, stopping when his hand clamped onto her arm.

"You don't need to say any more. I'm sorry about the other night. If I could take back the words, I would." The misery in her voice almost stopped him from continuing. Almost...

"Sit back down, Sylvia."

Ignoring the pain in her chest, she did as he asked, staring at the clenched fists in her lap.

"I don't want your apology." He kept his hand wrapped around her arm.

Raising her gaze, she tilted her head to one side. "Then why are you telling me all this?"

Mack took a deep breath, exhaling it slowly, keeping his voice low. "While I'm courting you, I won't be visiting any of *my women*, as you call them."

"I—"

He held up a hand, moving a finger back and forth for her to stop. "As I was saying, while I'm courting you, Sylvia, you'll be the only woman I'll spend time with. Just you, no one else."

Her eyes widened, breath catching. "You, um...you still want to see me?"

Mack leaned closer, his face softening. "See, this is why I find you so confusing. Didn't I just say I wanted to continue courting you?"

Sylvia couldn't clear her head enough to know for certain what he'd told her. "Well, I think that's what you said."

Closing his eyes for an instant, he shook his head. "Let me be real clear. If you agree, I would like the honor of courting you, Sylvia Lucero. While I'm courting you, there will be no other women or long nights in the saloons. Is that agreeable to you?"

Sylvia felt tears well in her eyes and worked to control them so Mack wouldn't notice. The tightness in her chest began to ease. Lifting her chin, she nodded.

"Yes. I would be agreeable to that, Adam."

Letting go of her arm, he sat back, taking a sip of coffee. Looking around, he spotted Suzanne, lifting a hand to get her attention.

"Yes, Mack?"

"We'll have our pie now, please."

# Chapter Nine

Sylvia stared at the remaining pie, unable to take another bite. Her appetite hadn't returned, not even after Mack admitted he still intended to court her. She'd prepared herself for him to give excuses about not seeing her again. Instead, he'd stunned her, saying the opposite.

Mack's easy acceptance of her answer and nonchalant way he'd gotten Suzanne's attention and ordered pie left her speechless. The tension between them lessened, even if the confusion she felt remained. He had said she confused him. Sylvia would argue she felt the same about him.

"Are you finished?" Mack's question brought her back to their surroundings.

"Yes." A tentative smile crossed her face. "I can't eat anything more."

"Good." Standing, he pulled out her chair, cupping Sylvia's elbow as he led her toward the stairs. "Are you ready to go to your room, or would you like to take a stroll with me?"

"Being outside for a while would be wonderful."

Stepping into the cool air, he offered his arm. Mack guided her toward the schoolhouse. Before stepping off the boardwalk, he glanced down at her shoes.

"Do you mind walking on the street?"

She shook her head, and Sylvia realized she'd forge a river if it meant being with Mack. It was the strangest and most frightening acknowledgment she'd ever made.

"Good, because if we stay on the boardwalk, our time together will be much too short."

They took a footpath toward the school, then veered behind it to the creek running at the back of the buildings on the east side of town. He stopped at a spot where the creek widened, creating eddies on both sides.

Mack stared at the whirling water. "Someday, I'm going to pay Noah to build a bench and place it right here."

Sylvia saw the wistful look on Mack's face, wondering what he saw in the depths of the rolling creek. Following his gaze, she understood his desire to have a place to retreat from anything weighing on his mind.

"Mr. Brandt would do an excellent job creating a bench. Will you place it right here at this spot?"

A grin curled his lips. "This exact place." He looked up. "See how the moon shines through the branches?"

Once again, she followed his gaze, following the path of the moon's light to see it sparkle on the water. "It's quite beautiful."

Mack's attention shifted to her face. "Yes, it is."

They stood there several more minutes in silence before he tugged on her arm to continue along the creek.

"Do you fish?"

Her question surprised him. Most times, when he came to this spot to clear his head and find some peace, he'd thought about bringing a pole. He had yet to do it.

"I do, but haven't since moving to Splendor. Caleb and I talk about it, but there never seems to be time. The town is growing. Along with the law-abiding people, there's a certain percentage who have few morals about stealing or killing."

"Isn't that why the sheriff sent you to Big Pine?"

Mack stopped, turning to face her. "How did you know?"

Her chin tilted upward. "After our, well...our disagreement, I sought you out. He told me where you had gone and the reason. Nothing nefarious, I assure you."

He chuckled. Thinking of Sylvia and nefarious together made him smile. He didn't know anyone less wicked or disreputable than the beautiful woman standing next to him. She might be opinionated and frustrating at times, but she was also guileless, her emotions obvious for all to see.

"You were checking on me?"

She let out a breath, glancing away. "*Looking* for you. I wanted to apologize—"

He placed a finger against her mouth, silencing her. "We'll not speak of that night again." When she nodded, he dropped his hand, continuing their walk. "We rode to Big Pine to see if we could find a couple decent men to follow us here. Splendor needs more than five deputies."

"Was your trip successful?"

His mouth twisted. "Time will tell. We brought back three men. I doubt one of them will last a week before riding away. The other two..." He shrugged. "They have potential."

"Do they have experience as lawmen?"

"No. The two brothers fought together in the Confederate Army during the war. Afterward, they had nothing keeping them from leaving the South. The same as Cash, the two worked as bounty hunters for a few months before deciding to ride farther west. They happened to be passing through Big Pine with plans to ride south into Wyoming." He guided her past the schoolhouse, across a broad patch of open area, then behind the lumber mill.

She looked up at him, her eyes bright. "You persuaded them otherwise."

"Cash having fought for the South helped. They're more skeptical of me."

"As they should be, Deputy Mackey." Her lips twisted into a smirk.

Halting, he pulled her in front of him, moving his hands to rest on her waist. "Are you skeptical of me, Miss Lucero?"

She licked her lips, lifting her gaze to meet his. "If you're asking if I trust you, yes, I do. If you want to know if I understand you, I'm afraid not. You're a puzzle."

His mouth twitched. "One you mean to solve?"

Shrugging, Sylvia continued to study his face and gray eyes, which had darkened to almost black. "I haven't decided yet."

He threw his head back and laughed. It was a deep, rich sound she'd missed while he'd been gone. Before she knew his intentions, Mack lowered his head, his mouth meeting hers. At first, she stiffened, surprised at the quick move. As his soft, warm lips brushed across hers, she raised her hands to clutch his shoulders, unaware she tugged him closer when he deepened the kiss.

Long moments passed, both lost in the feel of each other before Mack raised his head. "I've not decided about you either, Sylvia. All I know is I can't stay away from you."

Her glassy, languid eyes locked with his, a hint of amusement in her features. "Isn't that what courting is about? To learn about each other and make determinations about a future?"

"Or lack of one," he murmured, sorry he'd said the words the moment they left his lips.

The soft amusement on her face vanished, replaced with a resigned expression. With a jolt, Mack realized Sylvia expected him to find fault, any excuse to walk away when he became bored. He wondered what caused her to doubt herself or her ability to hold a man's attention. She certainly held his.

Placing a kiss on her forehead, he slipped her arm through his, continuing on the footpath to emerge in front of the saddlery.

"Tell me about your family, Sylvia." He noticed her jaw clench and the way she caught her lower lip between her teeth. Mack wondered if she meant to lie or would trust him with the truth.

"There isn't much to tell. My parents and two brothers live on our small ranch, raising horses and cattle."

"Your brothers aren't married?"

She shook her head. "Not that I've heard."

A door closed near them, a large, broad figure stepping into the street. "Is that you, Mack?"

Mack recognized the deep voice. "Working late again, Noah?"

"I need to find someone to help at the saddlery before Abby throws me out of the house."

Sylvia chuckled at the image his words created. "I believe that would be physically impossible, Mr. Brandt."

A smile curved the corners of the big man's lips. "Don't underestimate my wife's abilities, Miss Lucero. She can be quite formidable."

"And scary," Mack added.

Noah laughed. "That's true. I'd better get home before she tosses out my supper. Have a good evening."

"You, too, Noah." Mack pulled Sylvia closer as they watched him swing into the saddle, taking the trail home.

"I don't believe I've ever seen two people more in love than Mr. and Mrs. Brandt."

He couldn't miss the longing in her voice. "I've never been in a town with so many devoted couples. Dax and Rachel, Luke and Ginny, Gabe and Lena. The number grows almost weekly." Mack shuddered. "It's a little unnerving."

A shot of laughter broke through her lips. He looked at Sylvia, his brows drawing together. "What?"

"You, Mack. Are you so adverse to marriage?"

His features stilled. "I've no issue with marriage. It's just I've never been in a place where there are so many couples who are completely in love and devoted to each other. Each town has a few, of course, but Splendor seems to have more than its share."

"I think it's quite nice. There are still so many places where marriages are made for convenience, not love. It's quite sad." She thought of her family and her friends who'd already succumbed to arranged marriages to strengthen alliances and increase power. Sylvia wanted no part of such an arrangement.

"Love is important to you?"

Her brows drew together. "How could it not be? I mean, why else would you commit to a lifetime with someone if you didn't love them?"

"I've known couples who've made a good union when love wasn't involved. They care for and respect each other, even if the passion is lacking."

"You don't believe in love?"

Mack's jaw clenched, thinking of the woman and the cousin who'd betrayed him. "No."

Letting out a breath, she shook her head. "I'll not marry unless it's for love. It's the reason I came here."

Mack tightened his hold on her arm. "To escape an arranged marriage?"

Sylvia winced, knowing she'd already said too much. "The prospect of an arranged marriage. My father didn't have a specific man selected for me." She shuddered. "Can we speak of something else?"

Mack let it go for now. Sometime soon, he'd learn about her family and what she was hiding. "Of course."

They stepped onto the boardwalk, passing the telegraph and post office as the tinny music of the

Wild Rose's piano spilled onto the street. Loud laughter came from inside. Mack couldn't help noticing the way Sylvia looked across him, trying to get a glimpse inside.

"Have you ever been inside a saloon?"

Her gaze shot to his, eyes wide. "It wouldn't have been proper."

Mack grinned. "That isn't what I asked."

Sylvia groaned. "No. I've never been inside a saloon."

Before they left the Wild Rose behind, he moved closer to the last window, stopping. Mack guided her in front of him so she could look through the grimy glass, resting his hands on her hips.

"Take a good look. Downstairs, the men drink, play cards, and listen to music. Upstairs..." He considered his next words. "I'm pretty certain you know what goes on up there." Mack looked over her shoulder, seeing her mouth slightly open, gaze moving across the large room before traveling up the stairs.

"How long do they stay?"

"Stay where?" Mack asked.

Turning her head, she gave him an exasperated glare. "In the bedrooms, of course."

He thought about it a moment, picking his words carefully. "Some men spend a few minutes. Others an hour or two. Although not often, a few pay for an entire night."

119

She lifted a brow. "A few minutes? Is that all it takes to, well...finish?"

Mack started to think stopping at the Wild Rose was one of his worst ideas. "For some."

Nodding, she bit her lower lip. "Is that how long you stay?"

Gritting his teeth, Mack turned her to face him. "No. Now it's time we move along."

"But..." Her voice trailed off as he whisked her away, his arm around her waist, keeping her close to his side.

Neither spoke as they passed the jail, general store, and bank. Allie Coulter's shop stood at the far end of the street. Each one had closed long ago, light from the oil lamps extinguished.

Crossing the street, Mack continued to hold Sylvia close as they stepped onto the boardwalk in front of the St. James. There were so many questions he wanted to ask, so much mystery surrounding her background and where she'd lived before coming to Splendor. She'd deftly deflected each of his questions, giving as little information as possible, leaving him more curious than before.

"Have you ever been married, Mack?"

Her question surprised him, as did much of what came out of her mouth. "No."

"Engaged?" she pressed.

"Yes."

Stunned, she stopped, pulling her arm from his. "What happened?"

Mack let out a breath, his jaw clenching. He had no desire to talk about his fiancée, or the way she and his cousin betrayed him. The way his entire family betrayed him. It had been years since he'd been home or heard anything from them, and the pain at what happened still burned hot within him.

"It didn't work out as planned." He took her arm again, slipping it through his, glad Sylvia didn't push further.

Reaching the front of the boardinghouse, he stopped, an almost imperceptible grin on his face. He had a good time, enjoyed her company and curious mind.

"Do you have plans tomorrow night?"

"Lena Evans has invited me and the others to supper."

His brows scrunched together. "The others?"

"May, Tabitha, and Deborah. Lena's the one who worked with Pettigrew's to bring us to Splendor. Well, along with Abby Brandt, Suzanne Barnett, and a few others."

"What about Sunday? May I escort you to church?"

Sylvia worried her bottom lip, wondering if he knew what he asked. "Are you sure you want most of the town to know you're courting me?"

"We've had supper at the Eagle's Nest and Suzanne's. Spent time walking the town. Do you believe me courting you is a secret?"

She shook her head. "Well, no."

"Would it bother you if everyone knew?"

"Not at all, Mack. It's just, well...I wasn't sure if you wanted everyone to know."

Moving his hands to rest on her shoulders, his voice softened. "Look at me, Sylvia."

Hesitating a moment, she met his gaze.

"You need to know three things about me, sweetheart. First, I want to spend time with you, get to know you, see where this may take us. Second, I do want to marry and have a family with the right woman. Someone who understands the limits of what I can give."

Her nose scrunched. "Limits?"

He nodded. "The third thing. I'm not interested in a union built on love. I don't believe in it and don't expect it in return." He saw her eyes widen, felt her shoulders slump. Ignoring both, he continued, knowing he had to be honest. "Companionship, respect, and trust are all I ask. In return, I'll take care of her and our children. I won't cheat and would never leave them to take care of themselves. I'd be willing to give everything a successful marriage needs."

She blinked a few times, looking away. "Except love."

He took her chin between his fingers, forcing her to look at him. His gaze hardened on hers. "Except love." Mack dropped his hand, taking a step away. "I don't want you to have any illusions about what I'm after, Sylvia. You deserve honesty."

Forcing herself to swallow the bile his *honesty* caused, she nodded. "I see."

He sighed, seeing the light in her eyes dim. "Think about it, Sylvia. If you're still interested, meet me in front of the church ten minutes before services. If not, I'll understand, and hope we can still be friends."

Sylvia felt numb, unsettled in a way she hadn't expected, especially after he'd declared his intention to continue courting her. Holding her arms straight at her sides, she straightened her spine and lifted her chin.

"Thank you, Mack, for being honest with me. I will need to consider what you've said."

Something akin to loss swept through him at the resignation in her voice, the closed look on her face. All traces of joy were gone, swept away as his words settled in.

"Good night then, Sylvia." He turned away, stepping from the boardwalk onto the street.

"Good night, Mack." She breathed the words out, knowing he couldn't hear her or the way her voice cracked.

# Chapter Ten

*Philadelphia*

Dominic stood outside Pettigrew's, ready to get his business finished and be on his way to finding Sylvia. Turning the knob, he stepped aside to let a young woman pass by. He let his gaze wander over her, wondering if she'd put in her name as a mail order bride.

He couldn't deny his curiosity about the women who found themselves walking inside. What drove them to travel across the country to meet and marry a man they knew little about, accepting an uncertain future? What made Sylvia do it?

Shaking his head to clear the questions always circling in his mind, he walked inside. Standing in the foyer, he read the sign next to each of three doors, the center one being for Pettigrew's Mail Order Bride Company. Taking a breath, he walked inside. Sitting at a desk was a prim and proper looking woman, a pair of glasses perched at the end of her nose, her attention focused on the papers in front of her.

When she didn't look up, he cleared his throat. "Excuse me."

Huffing out a frustrated breath, she looked up, her face pulling into a false smile. "May I help you?"

"I need information on a missing woman. We have reason to believe she applied at your agency and may have been sent west."

Her face twisted into a scowl. "I'm sorry, but we don't—"

The badge he dropped on her desk stopped whatever else she meant to say. "I'll start again. I was sent here to locate a woman believed to have been kidnapped. There are those who believe Pettigrew's is involved." The woman gasped, her face flushing. Dominic leaned forward. "You can give me the information now, or I can close you down while we do a complete investigation of your records." He picked up the badge, slipping it into a pocket.

She picked up her pen with trembling hands. "What is her name?"

"Sylvia Maria Pietro Lucero. She's been missing for about nine months."

The woman's brows knit together. "The name doesn't sound familiar. I'll need to access the files. If you come back tomorrow, I should have the information."

"I'm not leaving without answers." Walking to a chair, he sat down, stretching out his long legs and crossing his arms.

"It may take some time."

Dominic shrugged. "Take whatever time you need. If anyone comes in, I'll let them know you're busy and to come back tomorrow."

Anger flashed across her face before she turned and hurried into another office. Dominic relaxed, expecting to wait a long time, surprised when she emerged less than five minutes later holding a slip of paper.

"I believe this is what you'll need to find her. We've had no word she's left this location."

Standing, Dominic took the paper from her hand, glancing down. "Thank you. I'll let you know if we need anything further."

"There isn't anything else in the file. You're looking at all we have."

He gave her a hard look before leaving. Stepping outside, he walked down the steps to the walkway, holding the paper up to read it once more.

"Splendor, Montana Territory. The contact is Magdelena Evans, St. James Hotel. Four mail order brides."

*Splendor*

Sylvia dusted the shelves in the general store for the third time since arriving Saturday morning. Mr. Petermann had been there all day, handling most of the orders while she cleaned and stocked shelves until boredom threatened to overwhelm her.

Supper with her friends and Lena last night had been wonderful, even if her appetite hadn't returned since being with Mack Thursday evening. She hadn't seen him on Friday, nor had he stopped by the general store today, as he sometimes did when he knew she'd be working.

"Sylvia?"

Straightening, she walked toward her boss. "Yes, Mr. Petermann?"

"I need to work in the back for a while. Would you mind watching the front?"

"Of course not."

One hour passed, then another without any sign of Mack through the large front windows. It gave her time to think about what he'd told her on Thursday. He wanted to marry, have a family. He just didn't want it with a woman he loved.

She left her family, traveled across the country to get away from a marriage of convenience, only to fall for a man who didn't believe in love. Sylvia didn't doubt her feelings for him, which made his decision about marriage much more difficult to accept.

If she continued to see Mack, Sylvia believed they would eventually marry and have children. The fact he didn't believe in love couldn't kill what she felt for him, no matter how much she wished it would.

She couldn't help wondering what kind of marriage it would be without love. If she'd grow to resent him over time, becoming bitter and withdrawn. Oddly, her instincts told her Mack would love their children. He just wouldn't love her.

Sylvia thought of the home and family she'd left in Texas. Her parents loved each other, which made her father's demand his children marry to enlarge their holdings so hard. Now she found herself loving a man who believed the same as her father, even if Mack's reasons were different.

The thought made her pause. Mack hadn't shared why he had no use for a marriage based on love. Although she suspected it had something to do with his broken engagement, Sylvia hadn't asked. She'd been too stunned to ask anything at all when he'd confessed the type of union he expected.

She hadn't made a decision about whether to meet Mack outside before church or go inside with May. Without words, not meeting him would send the message she wasn't interested in being courted by a man who had such disdain for love.

There was another option, one exposing her to more pain if it didn't end in her favor. She could consent to a courtship for a period of time, making a decision when it suited her, and not before.

Along the way, Mack just might fall in love with her as she had with him.

Sitting outside the jail, Mack whittled on a piece of wood, paying no attention to the shape he created with his short strokes. The action passed the time while he thought of what he'd told Sylvia, wondering what she'd decide. He hadn't realized how much he wanted her to be standing outside the church in the morning.

After leaving her at the door of the boardinghouse on Thursday night, he'd walked behind the jail to the house he shared with Caleb. A light shown, letting him know his friend was inside. Stomping up the steps, he'd opened the front door, seeing Caleb slipping into his boots.

"Where are you off to?"

"Ruby's for a couple drinks. Why don't you join me?" He had stood, tucking in his shirt and buckling the belt.

Mack remembered thinking about what he'd told Sylvia not fifteen minutes before about no more saloons. In his mind, that meant not seeing other women. It didn't mean no whiskey with friends.

An hour later, he'd returned home, leaving Caleb to watch the show, and do whatever his friend did when Mack wasn't around. Taking off his boots, he'd fallen back onto the bed, staring up at the ceiling until almost dawn, unable to forget Sylvia's dismayed look when he'd mentioned his thoughts on marriage.

Tonight, whittling the piece of wood while glancing up at the light in her bedroom across the street, he still couldn't keep his thoughts off her. He'd known she wanted love, and a part of him wished he could be the man to provide it. Unfortunately for both of them, that man died long ago, and he had no intention of ever bringing him back to life.

He'd made the decision to be honest with her. Mack liked and respected Sylvia too much to let her think he shared her beliefs on love. He didn't see love as a requirement for a successful marriage.

Seeing her bedroom light flicker and go out, he stopped whittling, staring at the darkened window for several minutes. It had been a long time since he'd met a woman who held his interest and stirred his desire. Sylvia did both, so it wouldn't be easy to let her go. Mack could only hope the terms of his proposal weren't too steep. He'd convinced himself they could build a strong union, enjoy a long and fruitful marriage. All she had to do was agree to a marriage without love.

Dominic rested his head against the seat, scanning the horizon as the train made its way to Denver. Pulling the badge from his pocket, he held it in his hand, chuckling. If the woman at Pettigrew's had taken a good look, she'd have seen the Texas Ranger engraving and realized he had no real jurisdiction in Philadelphia.

He'd been accepted into the elite group of lawmen a week before leaving Whiplash. With the turmoil surrounding Sylvia, Dominic hadn't risked his father's wrath by giving him the news right away. The arrival of the Pinkerton telegram increased the urgency for the Luceros to do something on their own.

Suggesting he be the one to travel to Philadelphia gave Dominic more time to prepare an explanation as to why he applied to the Rangers. He hadn't thought the acceptance would come so soon or be accompanied by a badge. Before leaving Whiplash, he'd sent a telegram to the Ranger's headquarters, letting them know he might be gone for several weeks.

He'd received a quick response, his captain asking him to pass along information to several lawmen about a new string of bank robberies. Dominic agreed, feeling pride at being given the request.

Crossing his arms, he closed his eyes, thinking about the decision he'd made after leaving

Pettigrew's. Not hesitating to reconsider the action, he had gone straight to the telegraph office, sending a quick message to his father. The elder Lucero would explode when he received the news. Dominic didn't provide Sylvia's location. Instead, he let his family know he was going after her and would send word once he learned more.

The way he saw it, his mother would be distressed, his father enraged, and Cruz accepting of his brother's decision. Because he looked forward to a marriage with the woman he'd loved for years, their brother understood Sylvia and Dominic wanted the same. Unfortunately, the only answer for the two youngest Luceros seemed to be leaving the family ranch, getting themselves out from under their father's rule.

Scrubbing a hand down his face, he took a deep breath, knowing there'd be hell to pay upon his return to Texas. Dominic didn't know when that would be, but he knew his relationship with his parents would never be the same.

*Splendor*

Sylvia couldn't stop chewing on her lower lip as she paced around her small bedroom. Thirty minutes before church and she still hadn't made a decision about whether to agree to Mack's conditions or protect her heart and let him go. She knew the safest choice would be to walk away, allow him to find a woman happy with a marriage absent of love. It would certainly be the best for Sylvia.

Something inside her wouldn't give up. The attraction to Mack started the moment she'd met him after arriving in Splendor. He'd done nothing except welcome her. But his gray eyes had latched onto hers, making an impression she'd never forgotten.

Settling a bonnet on her head, she tied it, giving the strings a sturdy tug. The winds had picked up over the last several days, sending hats flying, forcing dirt into every slivered opening. Windows, doorways, saddlebags—nothing was safe from the dusty gusts.

Taking a last look in the mirror, Sylvia met May in the hall, taking slow steps downstairs. Her stomach churned as they made their way along the boardwalk, holding their bonnets down during the short walk to the church.

Stopping at the end of the walkway, Sylvia stared toward the church, scanning the open area in front for Mack. Her breath caught, chest squeezing when she spotted him talking to two men she'd never seen.

When one turned, Sylvia's gaze lit on a star pinned to his shirt. "One of the new deputies," she murmured.

"What?" May's brows furrowed.

"I believe Mack is talking to two of the new deputies who rode back with him and Cash from Big Pine a few days ago."

Sweeping a lock of hair from her forehead, Sylvia did her best to calm the incessant pounding of her heart before allowing herself to join Mack. Still unsure of her response, she let out a breath, taking the steps to the street and walking across the short expanse to within a few yards of him and the two men.

Mack finished what he was saying, his gaze locking on hers, a slight smile curving his lips. Her heart pounded harder, seeing his gray eyes darken as he took several confident steps to stand in front of her.

He lifted his hat. "Good morning, Miss Lucero, Miss Bacon."

Until that instant, Sylvia had forgotten May stood beside her. May nodded at Mack. "Good morning, Deputy Mackey. If you two will excuse me, there's someone I'd like to talk to." She walked toward the door of the church to where Caleb talked to Tabitha. Sylvia would've loved to hear what her friend had to say, but she had a tall, broad-shouldered man staring at her, waiting.

"Good morning, Adam." She let his given name roll off her tongue, seeing his steel gray eyes flash. "How are you?"

"To be truthful, I'm not certain."

Her eyes widened. "Oh?"

His lips drew into a thin line, eyes narrowing as he studied her face. "Do you need more time to make a decision?"

Sylvia felt her body tremble, words stalling as his intense stare sparked a wave of anxious anticipation. She knew what she wanted to say. She just needed the courage to get it out. Looking around, seeing no one within earshot, she opened her mouth.

"As I understand it, I have two choices. Consent to you courting me with the prospect of a marriage without love, or refuse to see you again. Do I have it right?"

He gave a curt nod, his face devoid of expression.

"Good. I'd hate to think I misunderstood my choices. However, I'd like to offer a third possibility."

Crossing his arms, his hard gaze didn't flinch away from hers. "Go ahead."

Feeling an extreme tightness in her chest, she cleared her throat, wanting to sound firm and resolute.

"If I consent to a courtship, you'll allow me to attempt to persuade you to reconsider your stance on love."

A brow lifted. "Reconsider my stance on love?"

"That's correct. I won't marry without love, and you won't marry with it. I'd like the opportunity to change your mind."

He didn't immediately respond to her request, his mind wrestling with the idea any woman could get him to reconsider his position on marriage. Staring into her determined gaze, a flash of unease gripped him. If any woman could make him rethink his opinion on love, it would be Sylvia Lucero, someone he had no desire to lead on or give false hope. Mack would never intentionally hurt her, would feel the pain himself if he did.

"How long a period of time would you request to try and change my mind?"

Her brows furrowed. "How long?"

"If I agree, how much time would you want to change my mind about love? A week, a month, three months? How long, Sylvia?"

She gripped her bonnet as a gust of wind tried to dislodge it from her head. "Well, I, uh...I hadn't thought of a specific amount of time."

A wry grin lifted his lips. "Perhaps you should."

Biting her lip, she nodded. "All right." She thought a moment. "One month. If you feel nothing for me in four weeks, I'll bother you no further, and you'll not call on me again."

Mack swallowed. He hadn't expected her to agree to a time limit or come up with one so quickly. The thought of seeing her every day, learning everything about her and growing close, only to have it all ripped from him scared Mack more than any Confederate bullet ever had.

He wasn't after love, but he did want a solid bond, a deep friendship with a woman he admired and respected. A strong woman he could build a life with, who'd bear his children. Every instinct told him Sylvia was that woman. Could he walk away after a mere four weeks, knowing from the start she'd never receive the love she wanted and deserved?

Rubbing his jaw, Mack ignored the church bell signaling the start of services. She stood before him, her hopeful gaze searching his face, waiting for an answer.

"Four weeks."

She nodded once. "That's right."

"And if I'm unable to offer you a marriage based on love, you'll walk away with no further expectations?" Even though her offer matched his needs, his gut clenched hearing himself speak the words.

"Of course, I would hope we could remain friends." She cringed at the slight tremble in her voice.

"Of course," he repeated, still grappling with an internal struggle that surprised him. Mack knew he should accept the offer without further thought, but something held him back.

"Well, Adam. What do you think?"

He'd given her little time to consider his proposition. Now she was doing the same to him.

The muscles in his jaw flexing, he gave her a curt nod.

"All right. Four weeks."

She seemed pleased at his agreement. Why couldn't he feel the same joy?

# Chapter Eleven

Morgan Miller sat near the back of the church, his attention wavering away from the choir to watch the couple a few pews from the front. Sylvia and Mack walked in a few seconds before the choir started, sitting next to each other, their shoulders touching.

Anger rolled through him at the ridiculous notion a simple deputy could capture the interest of such a lovely creature as Miss Lucero. She was too refined, much too beautiful to tie herself to a man who shared a small house with a fellow deputy, had nothing more than a monthly salary, a horse, and his saddle. As far as Morgan could discover, Mack didn't even own an account at the bank. He'd never be able to support Sylvia in the style she deserved.

Morgan could. His growing ranch provided solid profits, and he had no reason to believe his success wouldn't continue. Especially when he and his family took over the land now owned by the sheepherders, Elija and Ebenezer Smith.

They'd been having problems. Big ones, judging by the way Morgan had been questioned by Deputies Mackey and Covington. Although he had no idea who killed their sheep, he wasn't unhappy about how it affected the Smith brothers. The sooner they left the territory, the sooner the Miller family could expand their holdings.

Beyond his ranch, Morgan and his brother shared an estate their maternal grandmother left them. It didn't make them wealthy, but it did provide each with a sizable sum tucked away in an east coast bank. Enough to provide Sylvia with anything she'd want for a long time.

"Mackey couldn't even provide a house," Morgan mumbled to himself, drawing a glare from the older woman seated next to him. Gladys Poe, if he remembered right. A self-righteous busybody, according to his father and brother. Ignoring her, he continued to watch Sylvia and Mack, the skeletons of a plan forming as Reverend Paige stepped up to the pulpit.

"I've been invited to the Pelletier ranch for Sunday supper. Will you accompany me?" Mack watched Sylvia's reaction, searching for any sign of hesitancy.

"Would my presence be all right with Dax and Rachel?"

"Rachel already told me I could bring someone."

She lifted a brow. "Someone?"

Taking her elbow, Mack guided her away from the open area in front of the church. The service ended fifteen minutes before, allowing them to mingle with their friends for a while before everyone dispersed for their private Sunday plans. Stopping next to the St. James Hotel, Mack faced her.

"Rachel heard from Lena Evans we were courting. Which means her invitation includes you."

Sylvia felt heat rise on her face.

Mack smirked. "Which makes me wonder if you told Lena about me courting you."

"No. I mean, well...May Bacon might have mentioned something at supper with Lena on Friday."

"May?"

Straightening, she squared her shoulders. "May is my closest friend. Of course she knows we've had supper a couple times. Do you have a problem with people knowing?"

Stepping closer, he ran a finger down her cheek, his voice low. "No, I don't. Do you?"

The touch caused a slight shiver to run through her. Swallowing, she shook her head. "No."

Dropping his hand, he took a step away. "Good. It's settled."

"Settled?" she choked out, missing his touch.

"Our agreement. Supper with the Pelletiers will be the start of our official courting period. Four weeks from today, we'll both know what our future will be."

A chill washed through Sylvia, along with a good amount of doubt. Four weeks didn't seem like much time to make such an important decision. And to think it had been her idea. One more example of a hasty decision she should've taken more time to consider. If she had it to do over...

"Are you ready, Sylvia, or do you need to get something from your room?"

Looking down at her reticule, her lips twisted as she thought. "Perhaps a shawl."

He held out his arm. "I'll walk you to the boardinghouse before checking to see if Noah has a wagon I can rent."

"I can ride," she blurted before slipping her arm through his.

Mack chuckled. "Is that so?" He guided her up the steps to the boardwalk, a skeptical look on his face.

Annoyance gripped her at his doubtful expression. "Of course. I grew up on a ranch for heaven's sake."

Approaching the boardinghouse, he stopped. "Are you saying you'd rather ride to the Pelletier's?"

Her excited gaze met his. "Can we?"

The sight of her bright smile and expectant look made Mack feel as if he'd been punched in the stomach. Clearing his throat, he nodded. "If that's what you want. I'll get my horse and another for you. We'll meet back here in a few minutes."

She didn't wait to hear more before dashing inside and up the stairs to her room. Going to the wardrobe, Sylvia pulled out the riding skirt she hadn't worn since boarding the stagecoach to Philadelphia. A few minutes later, she hurried down the steps and burst outside.

Seeing Mack at the livery, holding the reins of two horses, she smiled, not waiting for him to come to her. Crossing the street, she walked past the telegraph office to stand next to him. Running a hand down the neck of the horse she knew he'd saddled for her, Sylvia let out an excited sigh.

"Whose horse is he?" She stroked his neck again.

"Abby Brandt's. His name is Hasty." He ran a hand down the gelding's nose. "Are you ready?"

Taking the reins from his hand, she slipped her boot into the stirrup and swung into the saddle. Settling, she glanced down at Mack. "Well, are you coming?" Reining Hasty around, she clucked, heading toward Redemption's Edge.

Chuckling at her eagerness, he mounted, catching up by the time Sylvia passed the lumber mill. Mack kept glancing toward her, admiring the way she looked atop the horse. Back straight, a loose grip on the reins, her relaxed manner giving the impression of an accomplished horsewoman. Perhaps he'd misjudged her experience.

They'd ridden about ten minutes before he spoke. "Tell me more about your family's ranch."

Her joy at riding after so many months faded a little. She didn't want to tell him the truth, how she'd run away looking for love, when what Mack offered was the same as her father.

Well, not exactly the same. It wouldn't be as if they'd be connecting two wealthy families. She constrained the bitter laugh that bubbled up. If she went along with Mack's description of a marriage, she'd live as a deputy's wife in a frontier town a long way from her family. They'd have children and live a quiet life, her loving him while he'd go through his days content with the companionship she offered— but nothing more.

The thought made her wonder if marriage with a man she didn't love might be easier on her heart than living with someone who could never return her feelings. As hard as she found it, it was a notion worth considering. Sylvia could leave, return home, allowing her father to partner her with one of the young men near Whiplash. There'd be money, social status, and parties. She'd have all her parents shared. It just wouldn't be with a man she loved.

"There isn't much to tell. My father runs cattle with my two older brothers. I come from a small town where marriage prospects are few." The comment was partly the truth, partly a lie. "My older brother intends to marry someone he's loved since they were children."

"What of your other brother?"

She shrugged. "I don't know what his plans are."

"Why did you leave?"

Sylvia glanced at him before returning her attention to the trail ahead. "As I said, there were few prospects for me. At least no one I could love."

Even if he'd expected the answer, it still hit him in the gut. She'd traveled hundreds of miles as a mail order bride to find love. Instead, she'd found a jaded, ex-Union major with no desire to ever fall in love again.

Neither spoke the rest of the ride.

*Denver, Colorado*

Dominic ran his hands along the tall, muscled stallion, picking up one leg after another to check the hooves. He stroked the horse's nose, looking into the animal's stormy eyes.

"I'll take him." Dominic looked around the livery. "Do you have a saddle and tack I can buy?"

The older man pointed behind him. "Inside. There are a few saddles you can choose from. Got saddlebags, too." His rough voice suggested a lifetime of smoking, alcohol, and late nights.

Following him inside, Dominic checked four different saddles, selecting one along with the rest of the tack he'd need, including the saddlebags. Reaching into a pocket, he pulled out enough money to pay the amount the man quoted.

"Where you headed?"

Dominic laid the bills in the man's outstretched hand. "North to the Montana Territory."

"Big Pine?"

Shaking his head, he lifted the saddle and tack, carrying them out to the stallion. "Splendor."

"Heard of it. Never been there. A couple ex-Texas Rangers own the biggest ranch in those parts."

That got Dominic's attention. "You know their name?"

Rubbing his jaw, the man's lips twisted, eyes narrowing before he snapped his fingers. "Pelletier."

He finished cinching the saddle, secured the saddlebags, then slipped on the bridle. Walking the horse through the back gate, he swung on top.

"Thanks for your help."

The older man nodded, lifting a hand in the air. "Yep."

Reining north, Dominic followed a well-used trail. He passed a few other riders heading to Denver, but after a while, no one else appeared. The sheriff told him it would take at least two weeks to reach Splendor, assuming they didn't get early snow. If that happened, it could be three weeks or longer. As an afterthought, the sheriff warned him about the Cheyenne, Sioux, and Crow he might encounter along the way, saying if he did, it might take him a bit longer.

Continuing along the trail, Dominic snorted as he thought about the sheriff's comment. He supposed it was the only way to think about traveling through territories inhabited by various Indian tribes. Along with the thought, he reconsidered his decision to not tell his family where he was headed. If anything happened, no one would learn of it. His would be one more death in a dangerous land where outlaws and Indian encounters were more common than many understood.

By the time the sun crested, beginning its afternoon descent, he'd traveled a good distance. The weather ahead stayed clear, as did the trail, becoming almost lonely in its quiet.

The silence allowed him time to think about Sylvia and what he might find when he reached Splendor. Dominic didn't care to follow any of the scenarios that sprung to mind whenever he thought of his younger sister. All he cared about was finding her alive, happy, and possibly ready to come home.

"All I'm saying is another bull would push the breeding along." Luke Pelletier took another spoonful of potatoes.

Dax Pelletier set down his fork, staring at his brother. "You don't think three bulls is enough for a herd our size? Seems to me they've been doing their job."

Sylvia sat between Rachel and Mack, a smile sliding her lips upward at the conversation. The similarity between the talk around this table and the one at home struck her, making her chest squeeze.

Rachel gave her an apologetic look. "Sorry. Sometimes my husband and Luke get carried away when they talk about the ranch."

"Don't apologize. I've heard this type of conversation my entire life. My father and brothers never worried about what they said at the supper table."

"Do they run cattle?" Rachel asked.

She nodded. "My grandfather started the ranch before my father was born." She looked at Dax and Luke. "The last I recall, my brothers were arguing for buying a fifth bull, but Father wasn't having any of it."

"Five?" Rachel asked the same time Mack did.

Sylvia froze, realizing what she'd admitted.

"They must have a good-sized spread if they already have four bulls and are looking at buying another." This came from Luke, who sat across the table with his wife, Ginny.

She could feel Mack tense next to her, her mind racing at how to respond. Chewing on her lip, she shrugged before lifting her chin. "Several families go together to breed cattle. My brothers are the ones who usually negotiate the deals."

"I heard about families going together to ranch when Luke and I worked as Texas Rangers." Dax stabbed another piece of roast.

Her eyes widened, glad for the opportunity to change the subject. "You were both Rangers?"

Luke nodded. "For a while before coming to Splendor."

"One of my brothers has talked about becoming a Ranger. I'm afraid it will take an act of God to get our father to agree." She moved potatoes around on her plate, staring down at them.

Dax raised a brow. "How old is your brother?"

"Twenty-three."

Luke glanced at Dax, then back at Sylvia. "Old enough to make his own decisions. I don't see why your father would have much say in it."

Sylvia choked out a laugh. "You don't know my father. Anyway, it's doubtful my brother will ever go against him."

The conversation turned away from her family to other topics, Sylvia and her Texas roots forgotten. Instinct told her the subject of the family ranch was far from over between her and Mack.

Taking a few more bites so as not to appear flustered by the twist in the conversation, a twist that was her fault, she set down her fork. Trying to ignore the uneasy sensations rolling through her, she concentrated on what the others were saying, the paintings on the wall, the flowers in a glass vase on the buffet. She attempted to focus on anything but the man beside her.

"You and I need to talk, Sylvia." She felt his breath wash over her cheek as he leaned closer. "There seems to be a lot you haven't told me."

Stiffening, she shifted in her chair to put a few inches between them. "I'm certain there's much you haven't told me as well. Isn't that why people court?"

Drawing away, he snickered. "I suppose you're right."

Letting out a breath, the tension began to seep out of her. Sylvia didn't know why it was so important Mack not learn about her family, their ranch, or wealth. In Whiplash, she didn't know the real reasons eligible young men let their interest in her show.

Well, maybe she did. Her family's status in central Texas drew many potential suitors. Her father sent them all away, suspecting the same as Sylvia. They were looking for a piece of the Lucero money and she was the way to get it.

Mack knew nothing about her background. Although his thoughts on marriage weren't the same as hers, she knew he wasn't after anything except the woman he'd met in Splendor. Not her money or a slice of her family's large ranch. If he proposed, it would be because he wanted her, nothing more.

The clarity of the thought stayed with her as they rode back to Splendor. After they'd taken care of the horses, he walked her to the front door of the boardinghouse, taking her hands in his.

"We have four weeks, Sylvia. The way I see it, that's plenty of time for us to talk. All I ask from you is honesty. If you're going to tell me something, make sure it's the truth." Mack paused, studying her face. "I'll keep nothing from you, and I expect the same in return. Are you agreeable to this?" He lifted a hand, stroking his knuckles down her face, his gray eyes darkening.

Loving the heat his touch caused, her gaze locked with his. "Yes, it's agreeable."

Leaning down, he covered her mouth with his. It wasn't a hard or demanding kiss. Instead, it was an achingly slow kiss, promising more.

Lifting his head, he placed one more kiss on her forehead.

"Good night, Sylvia."

"Good night, Adam."

# Chapter Twelve

Morgan Miller sat at a table in the saloon, sipping his whiskey, waiting to see if Mack came into the Dixie. He'd heard the deputy spent most nights in one of the three saloons, often going upstairs after several drinks and a few rounds of cards. This evening, Morgan had been having supper at the boardinghouse when he'd heard Caleb telling Dutch that Mack would join them at the Dixie later. He had been in the saloon ever since.

He'd stayed after church, hoping to speak with Sylvia, perhaps talk her into having supper with him. Morgan watched as she and Mack talked with friends until the deputy escorted her to the boardinghouse. Thinking this was his chance to see her, he'd waited outside the Dixie, his heart rate picking up when she'd emerged wearing a riding skirt.

Before he had time to call to her, she'd dashed across the street, meeting Mack in front of the livery. They took the trail north, riding in the direction of the Pelletier ranch.

Five days later, he had no better luck. He'd ridden into town late each afternoon, hoping for a chance to talk with her after she left the general store. Each evening, Sylvia met Mack, who took up all her time until escorting her back to the boardinghouse. Twice, he'd followed them, turning away in disgust when Mack took her in his arms, kissing her the way Morgan could only dream about.

He wasn't certain what brought him back to town tonight. On Fridays, he often rode to his father's for supper, sometimes spending the night, more often riding back to his own ranch. As much as he tried, Morgan couldn't stay away.

All he needed was to catch Mack following a saloon girl upstairs once. Without knowing her well, he knew the information would distress Sylvia, perhaps to the point she'd call off the courtship.

"Courtship," he muttered to himself, angered the deputy had beat him to the prize. Picking up the bottle on his table, he poured another drink, tossing it back before refilling the glass a fourth time.

"Are you interested in a game of cards, Miller?"

A man Morgan recognized but couldn't recall his name, stood next to the table with another man. He had no interest in cards, but it would pass the time until Mack arrived.

His gaze moved to Caleb and Dutch, who shared a table on the other side of the saloon. They'd walked in an hour ago and had a couple drinks, acting as if they waited for someone. A knowing smile curved Morgan's lips.

He sat back in his chair, playing cards, his attention straying to the two deputies every few minutes. Restless anticipation passed through him.

He knew it wouldn't be long before Mack joined them, and if his habits stayed the same, within an hour of arriving he'd be following one of the ladies upstairs.

"Thank you so much for inviting us to supper, Lena. The meal was wonderful." Sylvia felt Mack's hands brush against her as he settled the shawl around her shoulders.

Gabe and Lena had also invited his sister, Nora, and her husband, Wyatt Jackson, along with Isabella and her husband, Travis Dixon. The eight of them had a marvelous time, and Sylvia found herself wishing the evening didn't have to end.

Lena smiled. "We'll do this again soon, Sylvia. With all of you living in town, it's easy to get together."

Sylvia had learned a lot tonight, the same as she had at Sunday supper at the Pelletier's. Travis and Wyatt worked at Redemption's Edge, breaking and training wild horses. The men and their wives lived in houses behind the bank, close to the house Mack shared with Caleb, making the trip to the ranch each morning and returning each evening. The arrangement worked for both couples.

The couples loaded into a wagon, the men in back, the three women on the seat, Nora taking the lines. Shouting their goodbyes to Gabe and Lena, it took less than twenty minutes to reach town. Nora stopped the wagon in front of the livery. Travis and Wyatt jumped down, unhitching the horses before securing the wagon for the night.

Taking Sylvia's hand, Mack walked her to the boardinghouse. Instead of going to the front door, he walked around the building to the creek in back. He stopped at the water's edge. Watching it ripple past, Mack turned her to him.

"I'm not ready to let you go quite yet." Leaning down, he pressed a light kiss to her lips before wrapping his hands around her waist, tugging her close.

Sylvia couldn't remember when she'd been so happy. He hadn't pressed her about her family, and she'd allowed him the same respite. Instead, they'd talked of more trivial things, laughing at stories each told, making vague references to a future. After almost a week, neither knew what the future held, but she sensed both wanted it to include the other.

"I think Isabella is anxious to start a family."

Mack squeezed her waist, glancing down at her. "I'm not surprised. Travis lost his wife and daughter during the war. From the way he is with the children at the Pelletier ranch, I'm sure he'd be a good father."

Sylvia tilted her head, considering his words, wondering if Mack thought he'd be a good father.

"Isabella said she either needs to find a job or have children."

Chuckling, he shook his head. "From what I know, she has money from her previous marriage, and Travis wouldn't want her to work. Guess that leaves children."

Her face brightened. "That's almost exactly what Isabella said."

"Did you work in town or stay on the ranch back home?"

Mack's question surprised her. Recovering, she kept her gaze on the moving water. "I helped my parents on the ranch. I can ride as well as my brothers and have almost as much experience as them on cattle drives."

"Do you miss it?"

Her brows rose. "Yes, and no. I do like the work Mr. Petermann gives me at the store. I help with orders, inventory, and he trusts me to work on the books. My father would never let me help with the accounts, although my brothers often assisted him."

"And the ranch work?" Mack watched her face, looking for any sign she regretted the changes in her life.

"I do miss riding every day. It would be nothing for me to saddle my horse right after breakfast and stay out most of the day. I'm trying to save enough money to buy my own horse." Sylvia didn't say her bank account already had enough money for a horse, saddle, and tack. She wanted to do this on her own. Mack didn't need to know. At least not yet.

"I'll buy you a horse, Sylvia."

An almost shocked expression stared back at him. "I couldn't possibly allow you to do that, Adam."

"Why not? It's my money and I can do with it what I want."

"Because it simply wouldn't be right. What if, well...what if after four weeks we end up going our separate ways?" She worried her lower lip, returning her gaze to the water.

"Do you believe that's going to happen?"

Without looking at him, she drew in a breath. "Do you believe you can fall in love with me?"

He hated hearing the tremor in her voice. Clutching her shoulders, he turned her to face him. "I care about you, Sylvia. More than I've cared about anyone in a long time. Can't you accept what I can give you and not focus on what I can't?"

He felt her shoulders slump, releasing his hold. Mack hated disappointing her, but knew they couldn't build a life based on a lie, and it would be a lie if he said he loved her.

Doing her best to push aside her distress, she gave him a tentative smile, hoping he didn't see how much she wanted his love. "I'm trying to accept what you want. It's just..." Her voice trailed off.

Mack felt a sharp pain in his chest at the look on her face. "It hasn't been a week. Let's not speak of this again until three weeks have passed." He lifted her chin with a finger. "All right?"

She nodded, determined to show him no matter how the courtship worked out, he didn't need to worry about her. "You're right. I want to enjoy all the time we have together and not examine each day as if it might be our final one."

Again, his gut clenched. This wasn't a conversation he wanted to have tonight...or ever again. They could have such a wonderful life, if only she'd take what he could give.

They stayed beside the creek several more minutes before Mack escorted her inside the boardinghouse to the base of the stairs. Bending, he placed a kiss on her cheek.

"Are you working at the general store tomorrow?"

"Yes."

"I'll come by to see you. Gabe has me working also. Allie and Cash asked us to have supper with them tomorrow night. Are you all right with us going to their place?"

Her eyes lit up. "Yes. I'd love to see the apartment they have above her store."

Pressing a kiss to her forehead, he stepped away. "I'll let Cash know."

She started up the stairs, then turned back. "Good night, Adam."

A lopsided grin appeared on his face. "Good night, Sylvia." He took a couple steps, then stopped, something nagging at him. Turning around, he called to her. "Sylvia?"

She glanced over her shoulder. "Yes?"

Shoving his hands into his pockets, he struggled with what he wanted to say.

Her heart began to pound when he didn't speak. "What is it?"

"You know what I said about the saloons?"

Throat tightening, she nodded.

"I just want you to know I'm meeting Caleb and Dutch for a drink before heading home. I, well..." His voice faded, seeing the stress on her face. "I won't be seeing any women. Just having a drink with friends."

Walking back down the stairs, she placed a hand on his arm. "I trust you, Adam."

He placed his hand over hers and squeezed, loving his name coming off her lips. "Good." Mack waited until she'd walked to the second floor before leaving for the Dixie.

Striding the short distance to the saloon, he drew in a deep breath of cool night air, glad he'd said something to her. Mack never wanted her to wonder about him or his actions. He'd been on the other end of deceit and knew how it felt. After all this time, it still burned a hole in his gut. The fact Sylvia said she trusted him eased his mind. The problem wasn't so much her trust in him. He didn't know how much he trusted her, especially with his heart.

Pushing open the doors of the Dixie, he spotted Caleb and Dutch at a corner table, playing cards with a couple other men. Heading to the bar, he ordered a drink before joining them.

"You want to play?" Caleb asked.

Pulling out a chair, Mack sat down, taking a sip of his whiskey. "A couple hands, then I'm done. I've got the early shift tomorrow."

After a few more than a couple hands, the other two men stood, excusing themselves. Caleb waited until they'd walked out of earshot before dealing the cards for another round. Picking his up, he looked over the top of the cards at Mack.

"How's the campaign going?"

Mack lifted a brow. "Campaign?"

"To convince Sylvia to marry you without loving each other."

Dutch choked on the whiskey.

Cursing, Mack threw down the cards, resting his arms on the table, an angry glare pinning his friend. "What the hell are you talking about?"

Caleb shrugged. "You heard what I said. It was a pretty clear question."

"Hell," he groaned, scrubbing both hands down his face, looking at Caleb. "How did you hear about it?"

"Does it matter?" He lowered his cards.

Mack had an idea how Caleb heard about his stipulations for marriage, but let it go. He looked at Dutch. "This goes no further."

Dutch held up his hands, leaning back in his chair.

Giving a curt nod, Mack scowled at Caleb. "You, more than anyone, should know why I'm not interested in forming a union based on the elusive notion of love. It means nothing. My experience is you can't build dreams or a future on something that changes faster than the wind."

"Not all women are like your fiancée."

"*Ex*-fiancée," Mack growled.

"If you ask me, you're better off without the faithless shrew. Her marrying your cousin allowed you to meet Sylvia."

The air left Mack's lungs, his anger lessening.

"Do you have any idea how many men will gladly take your place if the courtship doesn't work out?"

Mack shook his head at Caleb. "I hadn't thought about it."

"Maybe you should."

His jaw worked, but Mack didn't respond.

"I've known you for years and have never seen you behave with other women as you do around Sylvia. It may be time for you to consider forgetting what happened before and think about what losing her will cost you."

Mack stared at the ceiling, hands clasped behind his head—the same position he'd been in for hours as Caleb's words forced their way into his head. No matter how he tried, he couldn't shove them aside, nor could he allow himself to agree with his friend.

He already knew the prize he had in Sylvia. Ignoring his suspicions she hadn't been honest with him about her family, she was everything he desired in a woman. He simply didn't understand the problem with his concept of marriage. It wasn't new. Many couples married for reasons other than love.

If they chose to go forward with marriage after the four weeks ended, he'd take care of Sylvia and their children, and she'd never have to wonder about him being faithful. He'd be a devoted husband, showering all his attention on her. What else could a woman want from a union?

Mack had no issue supporting Caleb if he chose to marry for love. Each man had to make his own decision. Why couldn't his friend support him the same way?

Even though it had only been a week, Mack felt certain he could convince Sylvia of the wisdom of his thinking. She may believe love critical, but he knew he could convince her otherwise. Never had a woman been as responsive to his kisses as her. Once they wed, he had no doubt their lovemaking would be nothing short of extraordinary. To his irritation, the thought had his body hardening.

Mack thought of the few times he'd taken her in his arms. Sylvia's touch settled and aroused him at the same time. She'd already become a critical part of his life, someone he needed to see each day. The time he'd spent with Cash in Big Pine had been difficult, reinforcing the void he felt without her.

She'd thought her mentioning the saloon women he'd been with would turn him away. Continuing to stare at the ceiling, he almost chuckled at the thought. Short of lying, he knew nothing she could say would change his mind about their courtship.

The more time he spent with Sylvia, the more time he wanted with the beautiful woman. He hoped to take her riding after church on Sunday. Suzanne already offered to pack food, and Noah confirmed Hasty would be available for Sylvia to ride.

He planned to take her to Rogue Rapids, a swift, churning section of Wildfire Creek bordering the southwestern edge of Redemption's Edge. Mack had been there many times. He'd found it by accident one afternoon while on a solitary ride.

Mack had never invited anyone else to join him or spoken of the spot to Caleb. Nor had he mentioned it to Sylvia. He wanted her first impression of his favorite place to be spontaneous, not based on anything he might have said.

Mack had no doubt she'd love it as much as he did. He winced at the use of a word he wanted to avoid.

"Love," he hissed, whispering it to himself in his darkened room. Mack didn't understand why saying or thinking it resulted in what felt like a physical blow. His stomach clenched and chest squeezed each time the concept came to mind. He knew why, but couldn't get the sharp, painful reaction to stop. The same happened tonight when Caleb insisted on talking about it.

The ache in his chest had become so great, Mack had to fight the urge to stomp out of the Dixie. Only a fool would base his future on such a fleeting emotion. He knew Caleb was no one's fool. Still, Mack had no choice but to believe his friend somewhat delusional. He hoped Caleb never had to face the cold truth about the notion of love.

Closing his eyes, an image of Sylvia wearing a wedding dress crossed his mind. Along with it came an unmistakable sense of urgency.

No matter the obstacles, he would convince her to marry him—without the love she so fervently believed in.

# Chapter Thirteen

*Big Pine, Montana Territory*

Dominic rode down the bustling street, surprised at the size of the territorial capital. He hadn't expected more than one bank, a couple hotels, and a few saloons. Instead, he counted three banks, several hotels of various sizes, restaurants, a large mercantile, saddlery, two liveries, and at least six saloons. He suspected there were more businesses on the back streets, but didn't want to take the time to look.

The sheriff in Moosejaw knew of the Pelletiers, but nothing about a group of mail order brides coming through months before. He suggested Dominic would have better luck getting his questions answered in Big Pine.

He'd allowed himself and his stallion to rest two days in Moosejaw before riding on. Dominic had pushed them both over the last two weeks, sparing little time for rest on his mission to find Sylvia.

The jail was located at the far end of the main street, part of the original buildings when the town was founded. Reining up, he dismounted and stretched his arms over his head before opening the jail's door. Sterling Parker glanced up from the newspaper sprawled across his desk.

"Good morning, Sheriff." He took off his hat, moving toward the desk. "I'm Dominic Lucero. I wonder if I might have a word with you."

Reaching out his hand, Parker shook Dominic's, introducing himself before gesturing to a chair across from him. "Take a seat and tell me what I can do for you."

Dominic's gaze landed on the stove and the pot of coffee sitting on top. "Do you mind if I have a cup?"

"Help yourself." Folding the paper, Parker set it to the side, waiting for Dominic to explain what brought him to Big Pine.

Taking a sip of the tepid brew, he sat down, letting out a deep breath. The stark office reminded him of every other jail he'd seen, including the Texas Rangers' headquarters. "I'm looking for my sister, Sylvia Lucero. She came through here several months ago as a mail order bride. My understanding is she ended up in Splendor."

Parker's gaze narrowed. "If you know all that, I'm not sure why you need my help."

"I have some questions. I'm hoping you can supply answers before I ride out."

The sheriff blew out a breath. "Go ahead."

Finishing the last of his coffee, he set down the cup. "I bought my horse from a man in Denver who mentioned the Pelletiers." Dominic saw recognition in Parker's eyes. "I'm a Texas Ranger. The man said the Pelletiers used to be Rangers. Do you know if that's true?"

"Yep. It's true. Any reason it's important?"

Dominic shrugged. "I thought I'd look them up while I'm in Splendor. I'm curious as to why they left the Rangers to start a ranch all the way up here."

Parker leaned back in the chair, setting his booted feet on the desk, crossing them at the ankles. "They inherited it from another Ranger. I'll let them tell you the rest of it."

"Fair enough."

Parker lifted a brow. "What else do you want to know?"

"Tell me about Splendor. My sister came all the way from Philadelphia to find a husband."

Chuckling, Parker shook his head. "Son, there's no telling why a woman does what she does. I've sure never been able to figure it out." He steepled his fingers under his chin. "I don't know why she'd go all the way across country unless they already had a man picked out for her. That's the way it usually works."

"They sent my sister out with three other brides."

Parker's eyes widened. "Well now, that is interesting. I know they've got a good number of single men in Splendor, but..." He shook his head, chuckling again. "Anyway, there are some good people there. From what I recall, several of Gabe's deputies are single."

"Gabe?"

"Gabe Evans. He's the sheriff in Splendor. A good man, as are all the deputies he hires. Wish I had some of them over here in Big Pine."

Dominic had heard enough. He'd hoped to get a little insight into the small frontier town and be better prepared to see his sister after almost a year. Instead, nothing Parker told him helped. Dominic couldn't imagine Sylvia moving hundreds of miles from home to marry a lawman or small-time rancher.

Then he thought of the reason she'd left. His sister wanted love. He wondered if the man's profession would matter if she found what she craved—love, desire, and passion. Getting to Splendor took on a new urgency. Standing, he settled his hat on his head.

"Thanks for your help, Sheriff. Anything I can relay for you?"

"You can tell Gabe if he's got any deputies ready to move to a bigger town, send them my way."

*Splendor*

Sylvia stood behind the counter in the general store, tapping the top with her fingers. "Friday afternoon," she mumbled to herself, wondering if Mack might stop in before she left for the boardinghouse.

Sunday would be the start of their fourth week—seven days left to change Mack's mind about marriage. So far, she saw no sign the stubborn lawman felt any more for her than he had when the courtship began. Her heart cracked a little more each day, a pain she carried with her from dawn to dusk.

Three wonderful weeks had flown by with them taking long rides, many to visit his favorite spot. Rogue Rapids captured her heart the same as the man who'd shared it with her. They'd spent more time with the Pelletiers, had supper with Beau, Cash, and their wives, and ended most evenings with a long walk.

It broke her heart knowing all those wonderful days and nights would end in a week. As much as she loved Mack, Sylvia knew committing to a marriage without love on both sides would eventually end in bitterness. It would be better to walk away, allowing him to find a woman who shared his views.

As much as it stung her already fractured heart, she'd made the difficult decision to return to Whiplash and whatever her father planned. If she were going to agree to a union, it might as well be to the heir of a ranch near her family. At least she'd be close to her mother and brothers, far away from seeing the man she couldn't have with other women.

The bell above the door drew her attention, ending her depressive thoughts. She startled at the sight of two men walking toward her.

"Mr. Miller. It's been a while since you've be in." She glanced at the other man, someone she'd never met.

"Good afternoon, Miss Lucero." He gestured to the man beside him. "This is my brother, Curtis. He owns a ranch next to mine."

Touching the brim of his hat, Curtis gave her a wary grin. "Ma'am."

"It's nice to meet you, Mr. Miller." She focused on Morgan. "Do you have a list of what you need?"

He leaned a hip against the counter. "Actually, we didn't come in for supplies. I wanted to see if you have a night available for me to escort you to supper."

She opened her mouth to answer when the door burst open, two men walking inside, their rifles pointed at the Miller brothers. Morgan held up his hands, taking a few steps away, while Curtis stood his ground, smirking.

"You Millers have gone too far." Ebenezer Smith's lips slipped into a grim line.

Curtis moved toward them, stopping at the look on Elija's face. "I don't know what you're talking about."

"Six more sheep were slaughtered last night. Someone used a knife on them." Ebenezer took a menacing step forward. "You won't drive us off our land. Not even if you kill every one of our animals."

That drew a laugh from Curtis. "And how will you take care of your family without your herd? You'll starve." He slowly moved his right hand up to rest on the handle of his gun.

"We won't starve because the killing is going to stop." Ebenezer lifted the rifle to his shoulder. "Right now."

The front door slammed open, Mack, Caleb, and Dutch charging inside, guns drawn.

"What the hell is going on here?" Mack shouted, sending a concerned look at Sylvia. "Miss Lucero, you need to head out the back door and go to the boardinghouse."

Her features hardened. "I don't want to leave—"

"*Now*, Sylvia." His booming voice allowed no argument, even as his gaze stayed locked on the Smith brothers. "I'll come get you when this is over."

Morgan glanced over his shoulder. "He's right, Miss Lucero. It's best if you leave."

If Sylvia wasn't mistaken, she thought she heard a low growl from Mack. Nodding, she took one last look at him before leaving out the back.

"Elija, do you want to explain what you and Ebenezer are doing?" Caleb asked, taking a few steps to his side to get a better position. The Smiths hadn't moved, their backs to the deputies.

"Six more sheep were slaughtered. We all know the Millers are responsible. We're not going to wait around for them to kill our entire herd."

"So you plan to kill them right here in Petermann's?" Dutch moved around a barrel full of cornmeal.

"If we have to." Elija settled his rifle against his shoulder.

Mack took slow steps until he stood next to him. "You don't want to do this, Elija. You and Ebenezer are good men. Put down your rifles and let us sort this out."

"We can't do that, Deputy. There's too much at stake."

Mack slid his six-shooter into the holster, placing a hand on Elija's shoulder. "If you shoot them, you'll force us to arrest you. You'll stay in jail until the circuit judge comes. He'll find you guilty and you'll hang. Is that really what you want for your family?"

Elija's hands shook, his jaw tightening. "No."

Mack held out his hand. "Give me the rifle before you do something you'll regret."

A shaky breath blew through his lips as he lowered the rifle, allowing Mack to take it.

"Don't," Caleb growled, aiming his gun at Curtis when he saw the man's grip tighten on the handle of his gun. Curtis dropped his hand to his side.

Dutch moved next to Ebenezer. "Lower your gun. We'll work this out another way." He watched the man's hands tighten on the rifle.

"What they're doing isn't right," Ebenezer choked out.

"No, it's not. But this isn't the solution. Give me the gun, Eb." Dutch held out his hand.

A minute passed, no one moving as Ebenezer struggled with what to do. Finally, he lowered the rifle into Dutch's outstretched hand.

Curtis took a threatening step forward. "I want them arrested."

"Stay back, Miller. We're going to handle this." Mack sent an unyielding glare at Curtis and Morgan. "Everyone is coming to the jail so we can figure out what happened."

Curtis's face reddened. "It's clear what happened. These two walked in and threatened Morgan and me. They should be arrested and put on trial."

Caleb moved next to Curtis. "They're going to jail, all right. But you and Morgan are coming along. Now, let's get going." He indicated for the Millers to walk out first, escorting them to the jail while Mack and Dutch accompanied the Smith brothers.

Gabe sat at his desk, Cash in a chair across from him while Beau stood by the stove, pouring coffee into a cup. The door flew open, Caleb shoving the Miller brothers inside. Before Gabe could question his deputy, Mack and Dutch escorted Ebenezer and Elija into the jail.

Standing, Gabe grabbed the keys to the cells.

"We need to lock all of them up until we get some answers."

Curtis glared at Mack. "We didn't do anything. It was them two who threatened us."

Ignoring him, Mack nodded for Caleb to take the Miller brothers to the back, the Smiths following. When all four were inside the cells, Gabe locked the doors, motioning for his deputies to follow him back to the front.

Ebenezer and Elija sat down on the cots, staying silent. In contrast, Curtis kept yelling, insisting he and Morgan had done nothing wrong, his words punctuated with a continuous string of curses.

Setting the keys on a hook, Gabe lowered himself into his chair. "Who's going to tell me what happened?"

Caleb and Dutch turned toward Mack, who shrugged.

"The Smiths found six more sheep slaughtered. I don't know how they knew Morgan and Curtis were in town, but they found them in the general store, threatening the Millers with rifles."

While Mack spoke, Caleb and Dutch checked the two rifles.

"This one's empty." Caleb set the rifle down.

Dutch shook his head. "Same with this one."

Cursing, Mack scrubbed a hand down his face. "Eb and Elija were threatening the Millers with *empty* rifles?"

Caleb's mouth twisted. "Seems that way."

Crossing his arms, Dutch leaned a hip against Gabe's desk. "What would make them threaten the Millers with unloaded rifles?"

"Maybe they were just trying to get Morgan and Curtis to confess." Beau finished his coffee, setting the cup aside.

"If that's what they were after, those boys were taking a helluva chance. Either of the Millers could've drawn on them."

"I don't think they cared, Cash. Eb and Elija want the killing to stop, even if they put themselves in danger." Mack stared toward the back, gritting his teeth at Curtis's loud voice. "Somebody shut him up."

Chuckling, Beau walked to the back. "Quiet down, Miller, or we're going to keep you longer than you'll want."

"We haven't done anything." Curtis's voice rang with anger.

"So you say. Now, quiet down or you and I are going to have some serious words." Beau returned to the front, his mouth twisted in a grimace.

Gabe leaned back in his chair. "I'm going to let Curtis cool off for a spell before talking to him and the others. Did the Millers ever draw their weapons?"

"No," Dutch answered, Caleb and Mack shaking their heads. "Curtis thought about it, but changed his mind when Caleb stopped him. Morgan never made a move for his gun."

Blowing out a breath, Gabe stood, grabbing his hat. "We've got ourselves a real dilemma, boys. Eb and Elija have been pushed to their limit, and we're all agreed the Millers are somehow involved in the deaths of the sheep. We need proof before the Smiths lose their ranch." His gaze moved between the five deputies in the room. "Hex and Zeke Boudreaux are on patrol." Gabe mentioned his newest deputies, brothers, two of the three men who came from Big Pine and decided to stay in Splendor. "Dutch and Caleb, tomorrow morning I'd like you to ride out with me to the Smith ranch."

Both nodded.

"I want to leave early, before the Millers are released. There's no good reason to keep them here, but I figure we can hold them until noon tomorrow, which should give us time to search the area where the sheep were slaughtered. Mack, I'll need you to stay at the jail tonight. I'm not comfortable leaving either of the new deputies in charge with four men in the cells. Tomorrow, I want you to speak with Miss Lucero, learn what she saw before you, Caleb, and Dutch arrived at the general store. Beau, Cash, I need you and the Boudreaux boys to take care of the town while we're gone tomorrow."

"Yes, sir," Beau and Cash answered together.

Mack let out a breath. He'd hoped to have supper with Sylvia tonight. That wasn't going to happen. "Whatever you need, Colonel."

Gabe raised a brow, ignoring the comment and shaking his head. "I'm having supper at the Eagle's Nest with Lena, Jack, and my father tonight." He mentioned their young son. "Afterward, we'll be heading home. Ride out if anything more happens, Mack. I'll stop at the boardinghouse and have Suzanne send over meals for you and the prisoners."

A few minutes later, Mack sat alone in the jail, listening to Curtis continue his grumbling. Scrubbing a hand down his face, he thought about Sylvia and the last three weeks. They'd spent every evening together during that time, getting to know each other. Even with all the hours, Mack's instincts told him she still held important information from him. He didn't know what or why, but she didn't trust him completely. Then again, he didn't trust her, either. Mack had no intention of trusting a woman again, not after the debacle with his fiancée.

It was Friday evening. Sunday would start their fourth week, their final seven days before a decision would be made. Looking into her eyes each evening, he had no doubt Sylvia loved him. It pained him to know he could never return her feelings.

He'd forced himself to ignore Caleb's words of warning. His friend meant well, observing the same wonderful qualities in Sylvia which drew Mack to her. Everything he ever wanted was embodied in this one woman. Without an ounce of doubt, he knew no other woman could ever fill the place she held in his life.

Still, he refused to fall in love with her. Mack's offer would remain the same. He just hoped it would be enough to keep her.

# Chapter Fourteen

Dominic stopped on the small rise, his gaze fixed on the town a mile away. Larger than he'd anticipated, Splendor bustled with activity on the clear Saturday morning. From his vantage point, he could see a church at one end and what appeared to be a lumber mill at the other. There were tall pines and smaller shrubs on the outer edges of the town boundaries, a creek meandering behind a long line of buildings. The hills surrounding the town hid everything else.

He stroked the roan stallion's neck, the white hairs mixing with the dark coat, giving the horse a gleaming blue color. The hue inspired Dominic to name the magnificent stallion Blue. Chuckling at the simplicity of it, he kicked the horse lightly.

Spending a couple days in Big Pine gave him ample time to learn all he could about Splendor. Almost every conversation included a mention of the Pelletiers, as well as Sheriff Gabe Evans. No one knew anything about a group of mail order brides, a fact which bothered him more than a little. The confidence he'd harbored the entire journey, the firm belief he'd find Sylvia in Splendor, wavered with each conversation.

Riding down the hill, he rubbed his jaw. Perhaps four eligible women passing through the territorial capital didn't interest the vast number of single men in Big Pine. In his experience, any unattached woman traveling through an isolated frontier town drew a good amount of notice, sometimes prompting fights between lonely men looking for companionship.

Nonetheless, Dominic refused to lose the hope of finding Sylvia in Splendor. Keeping his gaze trained on the town, he took in the scenery, including the majestic mountains rising to the west. Even in the early fall, the tops were covered in snow, a sight rarely seen where his family lived.

The Lucero ranch in central Texas was dotted with rolling hills covered with mountain cedar, sycamore, elm, and maple. Some elms had grown to over sixty feet, a few sycamores close to one hundred. The trees in western Montana were different, but no less beautiful.

His gaze had been so focused on the striking scenery, Dominic almost failed to notice he'd reached the southern border of Splendor. He first noted the church steeple before his gaze moved to a large, elegant hotel. *The St. James*, he read, riding down the main street. Reining Blue to a slow walk, he took his time, taking in the other establishments, thinking there was much more to Splendor than he'd originally believed.

He noted the seamstress and millinery shop, bank, law offices, general store, saloons, barbershop, gunsmith, and land office before his gaze landed on what he sought. The jail. Taking in a deep breath, Dominic reined to a stop. Looking around, he stared at the door, not quite ready to walk inside. After a while of sitting motionless, he saw a man with overly long blond hair approach, a badge pinned to his shirt.

"Are you looking for something?" he asked, staring up at him.

Dominic looked down at the man. "Someone. Gabe Evans."

"The sheriff isn't here right now. He and a couple men rode out to a ranch south of here. He might not be back for hours. I'm Cash Coulter, one of his deputies. Can I help you with anything?"

Sliding to the ground, he tossed the reins over a rail, hiding his disappointment. "I was hoping he could help me locate my sister. She came to Splendor several months ago."

Cash studied him a moment before nodding toward the jail door. "Follow me inside and you can tell me about her."

Following him inside, Dominic glanced around the front room. After stopping at several jails on his way to Splendor, he'd come to learn the similarities between them. Four walls, a stove against one, hat hooks on another, a window in the front. A desk and several chairs were scattered about. He knew the large opening in the back wall would lead to cells.

A moment before Dominic pulled his attention from the opening, a man with a star on his shirt walked out, coming to an abrupt stop.

"He's looking for Gabe," Cash said, pouring a cup of coffee. He looked at Dominic, nodding to the other deputy. "This is Beau Davis. I figure between the two of us, we can help you find your sister, Mr…"

"Lucero. Dominic Lucero."

Cash's gaze shot to Beau, the men exchanging a look Dominic didn't miss. Lowering himself into a chair, Beau rested his arms on the desk.

"Would your sister be Miss Sylvia Lucero?"

Dominic took a step closer, eyes flashing, an unsteady grin tipping up the corners of his mouth. "She's here? In Splendor?"

Beau nodded. "If in fact your sister is Sylvia Lucero, then yes, she is. Came into town months ago with three other mail order brides."

Dominic's voice rose with excitement. "That's my sister. Where can I find her?"

Cash sat down, making no move to answer the question, preferring to ask one of his own. "How do we know you're Miss Lucero's brother?"

Nostrils flaring, Dominic's hands fisted at his sides. "What would you accept as proof?"

Beau chuckled. "Do you have anything in your pockets or saddlebags proving who you are?"

Lips slipping into a thin line, he reached into a pocket, his fingers gripping the badge. "Will this help?" He tossed it onto the desk.

Beau glanced at it, his gaze meeting Cash's.

"Well?" Dominic asked.

Picking up the badge, Beau studied it before handing it to Cash. "What do you think?"

Tilting his head, Cash shrugged. "I won't tell you where she is—"

Dominic cut him off. "But—"

Cash held up a hand. "I'll take you to her."

Heading to the door, Dominic grabbed the knob before realizing Cash hadn't moved from his chair. "Well?"

"Don't you want to ask how she's doing or if she's married?"

Dropping his hand, Dominic shifted back toward Cash and Beau, cursing. "Is she?"

"What?" Cash asked.

"Married?" he spat out.

"No."

The tautness in Dominic's shoulders eased as he exhaled a relieved breath.

"She *is* being courted." Cash watched his face tense. "He's a good man."

Dominic glared at him, placing fisted hands on his hips. "That's for me to decide."

Beau threw his head back, barking out a laugh. "I sure would like to witness that conversation with your sister."

Removing his hat, Dominic threaded a hand through his hair, searching for calm. Looking at the ceiling, he sucked in a slow breath. Beau was right. Sylvia wouldn't be dictated to, not after living on her own for so long.

Standing, Cash grabbed his hat, settling it on his head. "Come on. Might as well get this over with before she leaves the general store."

Dominic's brows drew together. "General store?"

Cash pulled the door open. "It's a few doors away."

His mouth twisted in frustration. "How do you know Sylvia will be there?"

Cash looked at Dominic with an amused grin. "It's where she works."

Sylvia dusted the remaining books, turning toward Mack. "You've asked me the same question two times. If I answer, are you going to ask a third time?"

A smile tugged at the corners of Mack's mouth. "Depends on your answer."

Straightening, she crossed her arms. "The Smith brothers walked in with their rifles raised and pointed them at the Millers. Ebenezer said they'd gone too far."

"Gone too far about what?"

"I didn't know at the time, but it became clear the Smiths blame the Millers for the slaughtered sheep. I believe they said six were killed. The Millers denied it."

"Did either Morgan or Curtis draw their guns?"

Sylvia shook her head. "Not that I saw. Morgan moved away from Curtis. I don't recall him saying much of anything. Curtis was the one who did the talking." She took a breath, her lips curling as she thought. "Ebenezer said no one would run them off their land."

"Did Eb or Elija ever say they were going to kill the Millers?"

"Not that I heard. You, Caleb, and Dutch came inside shortly after it all started." Sylvia raised a brow. "How did you know what was happening?"

"Horace Clausen saw Eb and Elija enter the store, rifles in their hands, and ran to the jail. I knew you were here, so..." He shrugged, glancing away.

She stepped closer, resting a hand on his arm. "I wasn't in danger, Mack."

He released a shaky breath. "There was no way to know that, sweetheart." Mack leaned in to kiss her when the bell over the door sounded. Both took a step away, their focus on each other and not on whoever entered the store.

"I didn't know you were here, Mack." Cash walked toward them.

Clearing his throat, he looked behind Cash at a man he didn't recognize. "Gabe wanted me to speak with Miss Lucero about—" Sylvia's shriek stopped whatever else he planned to say.

"Dom!" She brushed past Mack and Caleb, launching herself into her brother's arms. Laughing, she kissed his cheek as he swung her around. Setting her down, he held his sister at arm's length.

"Look at you, working in a store. You're a clerk!" He tipped his head back and laughed. "Father and Mother would never believe it."

Pushing out her lower lip, she frowned. "It's an honest job."

"Of course it is, Syl, and I'm proud of you. Sylvia Maria Pietro Lucero, the only daughter of the biggest landowner in central Texas, working in a store. You have to admit it's rather, well...unexpected."

Sylvia stilled, the hairs on her neck prickling the skin. Slowly, she shifted, her chest squeezing at the stunned look on Mack's face. Within seconds, the shocked expression changed to disbelief, then anger before he walked toward her, stopping a foot away.

Giving Sylvia a cursory look, he stuck out his hand to the stranger.

"I'm Mack Mackey, a deputy here in Splendor."

Accepting the outstretched hand, he grinned. "Dominic Lucero. I'm Sylvia's brother." He looked at her. "I've traveled halfway across the country trying to find you."

Sylvia threaded her fingers together, swallowing the awful feeling building in her stomach. Risking a glance at Mack, she shuddered at the murderous look on his face. Ignoring her, he focused his attention on Dominic.

"I'll leave you two to catch up. I'm certain you have quite a lot to talk about." He spared a cold glare at Sylvia. "Miss Lucero." Without another word, he stalked out.

She felt the color drain from her face, watching him out the front window as he stormed away. Her heart sank. She'd planned to tell him the truth about her family, let Mack know she'd come from money— a great deal of money. Sylvia knew how he felt about any type of deceit and would see her inability to tell the truth about her family as a betrayal of trust. The small amount of hope she still clung to, believing they could somehow build a life together, vanished.

Dominic watched his sister's gaze track Mack as he left the store, her features showing no trace of the joy he'd seen a minute before.

"Are you all right?" He continued to study her face.

She began to shake her head, then forced a smile, ignoring the moisture building in her eyes. "I'm fine, Dom. And so glad you found me." Sylvia glanced at the grandfather clock against the wall. "I don't finish work until five o'clock, then we must have supper together."

Cash stepped next to them. "I need to head back to the jail. Stop by and introduce yourself to Sheriff Evans when you have time."

Dom held out his hand. "Thank you for bringing me to Sylvia."

Cash grasped it. "My pleasure."

Sylvia turned back to her brother. "Do you have a place to stay?"

"Not yet. Do you have a suggestion?"

She bit her lip, brows furrowed for an extended moment. "The St. James Hotel will have a room."

"Where are you living?" He hadn't even considered her living conditions, focusing only on his elation at finding her.

"At the boardinghouse down the street. All of us are living there." She flashed a quick look outside, hoping to see any sign of Mack, knowing she wouldn't.

Dominic lifted a brow. "*All* of you?"

Placing a hand on his arm, she nodded. "There's so much to tell you, Dom. Why don't you get settled at the hotel, refresh yourself, then meet me at the boardinghouse at five thirty. We can eat at the restaurant there."

Dominic stared down at his sister. She still had kindness in her eyes, and he imagined her heart to be as big as always. He saw no sign of the pampered, spoiled young woman who'd taken a stage from Whiplash to settle in a growing town in the frontier of Montana. Instead, he saw an unexpected maturity. He also saw a wave of pain in her expression, something he'd ask about at supper. Leaning down, he kissed her cheek.

"I'll see you at the boardinghouse."

"Yes, at the boardinghouse, Dom."

Her joy at seeing Dominic had faded at the scorn on Mack's face when he stalked from the store. She hadn't missed the look of betrayal in his eyes.

A cold knot of regret coiled in her stomach, making her gasp at the pain. When she'd awoken that morning, she knew there were but a few days left to change Mack's mind about love. She now doubted he'd give her even that much time—and it was no one's fault but her own.

Mack walked to the back of the jail, checking on the Smith brothers still secured in cells. They'd finished the meal Suzanne delivered from the boardinghouse, saying little to anyone other than each other.

He doubted Gabe would hold them much longer. Although they'd threatened their neighbors, the rifles weren't loaded. Neither had meant the Millers actual harm, intending to scare the men enough to stop the slaughter. Mack doubted they'd accomplished their goal.

Morgan and Curtis Miller were released a few minutes after noon, the older brother spitting obscenities at Mack and Beau before the two left town.

Mack now sat alone in the jail after Cash started another turn around town. Besides the troubles between the Smiths and Millers, little had gone on in Splendor over the last few weeks. For him, his own excitement had come from courting Sylvia.

The thought of her caused a dull ache to form in his chest. Lifting a hand, he rubbed the spot close to his heart, then dropped his arm when he recognized the location of the pain. He forced himself to embrace the anger he'd felt at Dominic's words.

She'd lied to him. Her family wasn't of meager means, working a small ranch. According to her brother, the Luceros owned the largest ranch in central Texas. They were wealthy, well-known, and powerful. Sylvia had been raised in a wholly different fashion than she'd led Mack to believe.

Instead of a simple life, working alongside her family, she'd been born into what many would refer to as Texas royalty.

"I hoped I'd find you in here."

Mack shook his head, shoving aside thoughts of Sylvia's lie to focus on Dutch. "Were you looking for me?"

Dutch held up a piece of paper. "I finally received a reply from Pinkerton about your inquiry into Miss Lucero." He sat down, leaning back in the chair. "Quite interesting."

Mack reached out, taking the telegram from Dutch's outstretched hand. Scanning the short message, he choked out a bitter chuckle.

*Sylvia Maria Pietro Lucero. Twenty-one. Only daughter of Antonio Lucero. Lucero Ranch largest in central Texas. Over eighty thousand acres. Two older brothers, Cruz and Dominic. Disappeared months ago. Mr. Lucero has retained our firm to locate his daughter.*

Dutch watched the expression on his fellow deputy's face, cocking his head. "I saw Cash on my way here. He said Dominic Lucero rode in today. I'm sure his arrival surprised her."

Folding the telegram, Mack slipped it into a pocket, letting out a breath. "Yes, it did."

"I suppose you'll be having supper with them tonight."

"It's doubtful."

Dutch's eyes widened, deciding to keep his thoughts to himself. Standing, he headed to the door. "Well then, I'll get supper before coming back to take your place."

Mack nodded, his expression bland. A few spoken words had changed all his plans. Not just for today, but for the next week. A few days remained to fulfill their agreement. He no longer looked forward to his time with Sylvia.

In fact, he didn't anticipate any further time with the woman he evidently hadn't known at all.

# Chapter Fifteen

Sylvia's hands shook, fumbling with the closures on the dress she'd changed into for supper. Mack had already asked her to supper in the boardinghouse restaurant. They were to meet at five thirty, the same time Dominic would arrive downstairs. She couldn't help wondering if Mack would appear or stay away. A slice of pain claimed Sylvia, recognizing she expected the latter. Opening the pendant watch on the dresser, she checked the time. Five thirty.

Placing a shawl over her arm, she walked downstairs, her hand gripping the rail much tighter than needed. Most evenings, Mack waited at the bottom, flashing a warm smile in greeting when he saw her. Staring at the empty space before her, Sylvia's heart tripped. No one waited.

Reaching the bottom, she glanced around, not seeing Mack but spotting her brother standing by the front door. A wave of disappointment so intense she had to steady herself on a nearby table washed through her.

"Are you all right, Sylvia?" Dominic stepped beside her, grasping her arm, his eyes full of concern.

Heat colored her cheeks at the worry on his face. She plastered on a fake smile. "I'm fine, Dom.

A little clumsy is all." Her gaze continued to dart around the dining room, reality smacking her in the face. Mack hadn't come.

Mack stood in the shadows across the street from the boardinghouse. Crossing his arms, he leaned against a post, staring through the window. Sylvia looked so beautiful tonight, tendrils of silky dark hair framing her face. Then again, she looked beautiful every night.

He could see her look around the restaurant before casting a disappointed look at Dominic. Guilt sliced through Mack, knowing she searched for him.

"I'm guessing you had no idea Sylvia came from money."

Mack startled at Cash's voice, caught off-guard by his friend's sudden appearance. He shook his head at allowing himself to become so distracted. Inattention to your surroundings could be dangerous for any lawman.

"She told me her family owned a small spread in Texas. Made it sound like any average cattle ranch, living from one trail drive to another."

Cash leaned down, resting his hands on the top rail of the boardwalk. "Is her being from a wealthy family a problem for you? 'Cause I'm telling you, if I weren't already married to the best woman in Montana, it sure wouldn't be a problem for me."

Mack chuckled at Cash's shameless praise of Allie. The deputy hadn't wasted any time letting the other single men in Splendor know he'd taken an interest in Alison McGrath not long after she'd arrived in town. His face sobered as he thought on Cash's question.

"Sylvia lied to me, Cash. Why didn't she tell me the truth?" He couldn't hide the extreme frustration at her lack of honesty.

"Are you thinking of letting her go because of it?"

He dropped his arms to his sides, straightening before scrubbing a hand down his face. "Thinking about it."

Cash narrowed his gaze on Mack. "You may want to think about it real hard. If you call off the courtship, she will barely catch a breath before others are at her door. Sylvia is a beauty and a real nice lady." He clasped Mack's shoulder. "Don't let your pride lead you toward a big mistake." Taking a step away, Cash looked up and down the street once more. "Guess it's time for me to head home for supper. You might want to think about going to the boardinghouse for the same."

Mack watched him walk away, understanding the meaning of Cash's words. He'd never considered himself a man who allowed pride to interfere with his decisions. The thought caused him to reconsider his decision to let Sylvia go. Maybe she had a good reason for not telling him the truth about her family.

Taking a deep breath, he shoved aside his uncertainties and stepped down from the boardwalk. Keeping his gaze on Sylvia through the dusty restaurant window, he walked inside, making his way to the table.

Removing his hat, he looked at her. "I apologize for being late, Miss Lucero. Is it still all right if I join you?" Any uncertainty he felt disappeared at the relieved expression on her face.

"Of course it's all right. I'm so glad you came."

The joy on her face caused a slight tinge of guilt to flash through him. It was a good decision to reconsider, shove aside his doubts and make an appearance, as she'd expected.

Dominic stood, shaking Mack's hand before indicating a chair next to Sylvia. After they'd both taken seats, her brother leaned forward.

"Sylvia just told me you've been courting her." He lifted a brow, his gaze boring into Mack's.

Clearing his throat, Mack nodded. "For three weeks now." He glanced at Sylvia, unsure what else to say.

"Don't take this wrong, Mack, but Sylvia allowing herself to be courted by a lawman is a surprise. I always thought she'd marry one of the ranchers around Whiplash."

"Dom!" Her face heated in embarrassment. "We're only courting. We've never discussed marriage."

Mack tilted his head, his brows lifting, silently telling her that wasn't exactly true.

She bit her lower lip, forcing her gaze away from Mack to focus on Dominic. "Well, we have mentioned it, but there's been no decision. We're, well...getting to know each other."

Dominic sensed a thread of tension between his sister and Mack, deciding to ignore it for now. "I'm sure you already know Sylvia is a woman with a mind of her own. I believe it's why she left our ranch. To build her own life, not the one our father requires."

Mack's features stilled. "Requires?" He looked at Sylvia.

Shifting in her seat, she opened her mouth to explain, stopping when Tabitha walked up with three plates.

"I saw you join them, Deputy Mackey, and decided to bring you the same as Sylvia and Mr. Lucero. It's Suzanne's venison roast." Tabitha set down the plates.

"The roast is perfect. Thank you."

Tabitha smiled. "Would you like coffee?"

Mack nodded at her, his gaze returning to Sylvia when Tabitha left to fill a cup for him. "You were about to tell me about the life your father would require."

The fork stalled a few inches from her mouth. Lowering it, she licked her lips, wanting to ignore the fact her brother shared their table. She was closer to him than anyone else and knew he'd understand. Still, this was a conversation she and Mack needed to have alone.

Her pleading gaze locked on his. "Would it be all right if we spoke of this later?"

"Of course. As long as we *do* have the discussion, Sylvia." His firm voice told her how serious the conversation was to him.

Dominic glanced between them. Knowing Sylvia, she'd kept the specifics about their family from Mack. He didn't blame her, but he did understand Mack wanting to know as much about her as possible before making a decision about continuing to court her. He'd do the same if he were in the man's position.

"Father brought a woman around for me to meet. Well, her and her family." Dominic flashed Sylvia a smirk, getting the response he hoped for. Her face brightened into a smile.

"As if you'd ever let Father choose someone for you."

"She seemed nice enough, but she wore this hat." Dominic grimaced.

"A hat?" She slid a bite of roast into her mouth.

He nodded, the grimace still on his face. "It was pretty, well...awful."

This brought a deep chuckle from Mack.

Dominic shrugged, swallowing his food with a sip of coffee. "Anyway, it's what made me decide to find you."

Her eyes danced with amusement. "A hat made you decide to leave the ranch?"

"Well, that and the woman wearing it."

Mack and Sylvia both laughed, the mood shifting as Dominic had hoped. They ate for a few minutes in silence before her gaze fastened on her brother.

"How *did* you find me?"

It took him a few minutes to explain his trip to Philadelphia and visiting Pettigrew's, using his badge to get the information about her coming to Splendor.

Sylvia's eyes widened. "You're a Texas Ranger, Dom?"

Pride infused his grin. "I am. They accepted me a week before I left to find you." His gaze narrowed, lips pressed into a thin line. "Father doesn't know." He took a sip of coffee, setting the cup down. "Which reminds me, I need to send a telegram to my captain, letting him know I'm in Splendor."

"How long can you stay?"

Dominic saw the hope in her eyes. "As long as I can, Syl." He glanced at Mack, wondering about the man's intentions toward his sister. Tension still crackled between the two, and Dominic had no plans to leave until he knew Sylvia would be all right.

Mack listened to the exchange, watching their faces. He began to understand how close the two were and the battles each must have fought with their father. Although his reasons were different from theirs, Mack knew about being estranged from your family, being the one to ride away.

"Suzanne said to make sure you all have a piece of her apple pie." Tabitha set a slice in front of each of them. "I had a little earlier, and it's wonderful." She grinned at Sylvia. "More coffee?" When they all nodded, she filled their cups, leaving to seat new arrivals.

"How long have you been in Splendor, Mack?" Dominic put a piece of pie into his mouth, groaning in pleasure.

"A year."

Dominic took another bite. "Do you have other family around here?"

"No."

When Mack didn't say more, Dominic looked at Sylvia, lifting a brow. She hesitated a moment, unsure how much she should say, deciding a little information wouldn't upset Mack.

"He's originally from New York, Dom." Sylvia's sweet smile moved from her brother to Mack, seeing a flash of something on his face before it disappeared.

"A Yankee, huh?"

Mack gave a curt nod, adding nothing more.

The gesture wasn't lost on Dominic. Finishing his pie, he pushed the plate away, drinking the last of his coffee.

"If you don't mind, Syl, I'm going to find a game of cards at the Dixie." Reaching into a pocket, he pulled out money, setting it on the table. "I'd like you to meet me at the St. James for breakfast in the morning, unless you have other plans."

Sylvia glanced at Mack, his expression neutral. Before learning about her family's wealth, he would've mentioned how they always attended church together on Sunday mornings. Tonight, he said nothing, moving his gaze between her and Dominic. She cocked her head at Mack, hoping for some reaction, disappointed when he ignored her silent question.

"We, uh...usually have breakfast early before going to church. Would you like to join us?"

Dominic pushed away from the table but didn't stand. "Us?"

"My friends, May, Tabitha, and Deborah walk to church with me. I've been sitting with Mack the last few weeks."

"I won't be able to make it to church tomorrow. I'll be working at the jail." Mack didn't sound apologetic or notice the brief look of disappointment on Sylvia's face.

She refused to let him know how the distance he'd begun to put between them hurt. Forcing a smile, she turned away from him to face Dominic.

"Would you mind meeting us here tomorrow morning for breakfast?"

Standing, he looked down at her. "Only if you'll allow me to escort you and your friends to church." He flashed her the charming grin she'd seen numerous times when he flirted with young women in Whiplash.

"Wonderful. I'm anxious to introduce you to my friends. All except Tabitha, who you've already met."

"Tabitha?" He didn't remember meeting any of her friends tonight.

"The woman serving us." She nodded toward where Tabitha stood next to another table, talking to three cowboys. They could hear her sparkling laughter across the room.

Dominic's eyes lit at the knowledge. "Well then, I'll definitely be here tomorrow morning." He looked at Mack. "I'm sure we'll be seeing each other again before I leave."

Standing, Mack shook Dominic's hand. "Enjoy your evening. I may join you at the Dixie."

"I'll buy you a drink." He gave Sylvia a playful smile. "See you in the morning."

Waiting until Dominic left, Mack walked behind her chair. "You and I need to talk."

The cool evening breeze washed over Sylvia's cheeks when they left the warm interior of the restaurant and stepped outside. It wouldn't be long before the first snow would fall, blanketing the streets in a thin veil of white.

Anticipation overtook her at the thought it wouldn't be long before the entire town would be covered in snow. Sylvia couldn't wait to celebrate Christmas. Until that afternoon, she believed the holiday would be spent with Mack. Doubt now clouded that certainty.

She'd arrived in Splendor the previous winter, surprised at how simple it had been to adjust to the cold weather and often blustery winds. Deborah had the worst time, while Tabitha, May, and Sylvia loved the beauty of a Montana winter.

Everything was new and exciting, so different from growing up in Texas where each day seemed the same as the last. Being with Mack had given her yet another perspective on the land she had come to love.

He'd introduced her to so much, Rogue Rapids being the most spectacular. She wondered if any other man would've taken such pleasure in sharing his private places.

Sylvia also wondered if any other man would've been as honest about his feelings concerning love and marriage. Mack had shared what his fiancée and family had done, how they'd betrayed him.

It wasn't quite dark as they stepped off the boardwalk, continuing toward the school. A wave of guilt hit her. Mack had been completely honest, holding nothing back, but she hadn't.

Neither spoke as they walked to their favorite spot along the creek near the back of the school. Noah had completed the bench Mack ordered, the two men placing it under a stand of maple trees next to the water.

Most evenings when they walked, Mack would hold her hand or put an arm around her waist. Tonight, he did neither, keeping at least a foot between them from the moment they left the boardinghouse until he gestured to the bench.

"Sit down, Sylvia."

She lifted her chin. "I'd rather stand."

He shrugged, ignoring her defiant pose. "If that's what you want." Mack took a seat on one end of the bench, stretching out his legs and crossing his arms. "Tell me why you lied about your family."

# Chapter Sixteen

*Miller Ranch*

Norman Miller shouted another round of orders to his foreman, Buster, anger pulsing through him. "I want men along the border of our ranch and the Smith ranch at all times. I don't want those sheepherders coming onto our land to protect their herd."

Buster rubbed his stubbled jaw. "We'll need to hire more men, boss."

"Then hire them." Norman scowled at the man who knew him better than anyone.

Curtis had sent a rider to let his father know his sons had been hauled to jail after they'd been threatened by what all considered to be their meek neighbors. Thanks to a visit from the sheriff and two deputies, Norman already knew the details of their arrest.

Ebenezer and Elija were known for turning away at any perceived wrong. They weren't men who stood up to others, believing words worked better than bullets. When faced with ruination, even men such as the Smiths could be pushed to violence.

"What do you want to do about the rest?" Buster crossed his arms, ready for another explosion.

Running a hand through his hair, he murmured a string of curses. "Hell if I know. I can't stop the sheriff and his men from questioning my ranch hands. The man is thorough. I'd do the same in Gabe's position."

"Yep, you would, but that doesn't solve our problem."

Norman shot a dark look at Buster. "Continue doing what we discussed and hire more men. And send someone to fetch my sons. I want to talk to them tonight."

"It's already pretty late, boss."

"I don't care if it's midnight. Send them to me tonight."

After Buster left, he walked to the window, watching the foreman take his usual long strides toward the corral. In spite of the looming darkness, a few men continued to work with the horses. Stopping next to one of them, they talked a moment before the cowhand grabbed the reins to his horse, mounted, and rode off.

Scrubbing both hands down his face, he lowered himself into the desk chair, settling his arms on top. This entire situation had gotten well out of hand. Norman knew what the outcome would be if the attacks on the Smiths continued. The two brothers didn't have the money to sustain persistent slaughter of their herd.

The thought should've brought him a measure of satisfaction. With the Smiths gone, their land would go up for auction. No matter the way it came about, Norman meant to be the first in line.

*Splendor*

Sylvia didn't sit next to Mack, preferring to stand, giving herself whatever advantage possible. There was no one to blame except herself for the tension between them.

Before Dominic arrived in town, she and Mack had been getting along well. Very well, if she ignored the fact he still stood firm on his stance about love. Except for that one important part, she'd never expected to have this kind of bond with any man. She didn't want to lose it.

Blowing out a slow breath, Sylvia accepted it might already be too late to reverse the damage caused by her lack of honesty. It might be different if Mack hadn't been adamant about his thoughts on lying and betrayal from the beginning. They were words he linked together when he spoke just one of them.

She understood why he tolerated nothing less than complete honesty. He hadn't taken the betrayal of his fiancée and cousin well. He'd also never confronted either them or his family, who'd stayed silent while the couple ripped out Mack's heart. Yes, Sylvia could definitely understand his stance on being truthful.

Shoving aside the remorse, she controlled her features, holding his gaze. "First, I'm sorry I didn't tell you the complete truth about my family."

He didn't move, continuing to stare at her.

"My grandfather arrived in the country from Spain as a young man. With determination and hard work, he built the Lucero ranch, starting with a few acres, building it to thousands before his death. When my father took over, he continued what grandfather started, quadrupling the size by the time my oldest brother, Cruz, turned eighteen. He's twenty-four now."

Stopping a moment to judge the effect her words had on Mack, she squared her shoulders, letting out a breath when his expression didn't change. It continued to be as devoid of emotion as he had been when she started.

"You have to understand something about my family. According to my mother, my grandfather and grandmother married for love. My father and mother married for love." Pain flashed across her face before she could conceal it. "At some point, Father changed. Family became less important than the size of our ranch and building more wealth. He enjoyed the attention paid to him by others, even those envious of what he'd accomplished. That's when he decided it would be best for him to choose who his children married. Cruz was lucky. The girl he'd fallen in love with years ago comes from a wealthy family. They are also *ranching elite*, as Father would say. Dom told me tonight they plan to marry before Christmas."

Taking a few slow breaths, she considered her next words. "You heard what Dom said at supper. Father has been trying to pick his wife from the time he turned twenty. He's twenty-three now." A grim smile tilted the corners of her mouth. "Dom's a champion at avoiding Father's schemes. Before I made the decision to leave, my parents invited numerous eligible bachelors to their annual Christmas party."

For an instant, she thought Mack's back stiffened, then assumed she'd imagined it when he continued to watch her.

"Not one caught my interest, but Father didn't care. He wanted a match of land and wealth, not love, and I was the inducement." She choked out a pained laugh. "Well, the land, power, and money were the incentive. I was the sacrifice. I left soon afterward, taking a stagecoach out of Whiplash, then a train to Philadelphia and then Pettigrew's Mail Order Bride Company." She shrugged. "You know the rest."

Sylvia felt a measure of pride at the steadiness in her voice. She had no intention of showing any weakness in front of Mack. He needed the truth, which she'd given him. He didn't need to know how much it would hurt if he chose to call off their courtship. She'd put herself in this position and would accept whatever he decided.

Mack continued to study her another minute before patting the bench. "Sit down, Sylvia."

He'd watched the play of emotions cross her face as she explained her family and her reason for leaving. Determination, obstinance, frustration, and hope.

She hesitated a moment before relenting to take a spot at the other end of the bench. Most evenings, they'd sit close, his hand entwined with hers. Before they'd leave, he would kiss her...long and deep until she felt breathless and a little unsteady when he'd help her stand. It would be his excuse to take her in his arms once more to kiss her again. Sylvia expected none of that tonight.

So when he moved to her, settled an arm over her shoulders, and drew her to him, she shuddered. When he lifted her chin, lowering his mouth to hers, she moaned. This wasn't the gentle kiss of other evenings. His mouth covered hers with an intensity implying he'd never get enough, deepening it until she clutched at his shoulders, heat pulsing through her.

He felt her tremble at the same time he let out his own low groan. Tightening his hold, he splayed his hands across her back, holding her as close as possible without hauling her onto his lap.

That came a moment later. He never broke the kiss as he settled her across his thighs, feeling her arms wrap around his neck. Her lips were warm and soft, molding to his as if they were made only for him. Her mouth was searching, persuasive in a way he didn't expect from an inexperienced lover. The thought stopped him, his smile curving against her lips. She'd learned a lot about kissing over the last three weeks, and each lesson had been a pleasure for him to give.

Feeling his body harden beneath her, he kissed her one more time before pulling back, resting his forehead against hers.

"There are still things I need to say," Mack whispered, not moving her off his lap. Rubbing soothing hands over her back, he tucked Sylvia's head against his chest, resting his chin on top.

She sucked in an unsteady breath to calm her racing heart and prepare herself for whatever he meant to say. No matter his decision, she'd never regret a single minute they'd spent together.

Sylvia cleared her throat. "All right." She swallowed, clutching her hands to her chest.

"Thank you for telling me the entire story of why you came to Splendor. I understand why you left and your need to make your own choice about marriage. I still don't understand why you were so clear about your family having a small spread. Are you embarrassed about their success?"

She shook her head against his chest. "No. I'm proud of what they've achieved."

"They why not tell me the truth? Why not trust me with the truth?"

*And there it is*, Sylvia thought. He believed she hadn't trusted him enough to be honest.

"It wasn't a matter of not trusting you. Well...not really." She opened her hands to rest her palms on his chest. "The men Father brought around weren't interested in me. At least that wasn't their motivation for a match. They were after the money and land, the power that came with the Lucero connection. I was the path to secure a union."

Understanding rushed through Mack. "A marriage without love."

He felt her nod against his chest before she breathed out a weak, "Yes."

Continuing to rub circles over her back, he closed his eyes. She'd come to Splendor to find love. Instead, she'd fallen for a cynical lawman—a man who had no use for love or a marriage based on anything more than mutual commitment and respect.

Worse, he had no wealth to offer, not even a house. Nothing a woman from her background would want if she shared her life with a man who could never return her love. And if Mack hadn't known before tonight, he now understood with complete certainty—the women in his arms loved him. The thought delighted and sickened him at the same time.

Mack's honor would never allow him to marry a woman who'd traveled hundreds of miles to find love, only to shackle herself to a man who'd never be able to offer it.

Sylvia was too fine a woman, too much of a prize to lock herself into a union based on anything except love. His desires held no weight when compared to what she'd be sacrificing if he continued the courtship.

Lowering his hands to her waist, he set her aside, putting a slight amount of space between them. He forced himself to look at her. What he saw made him feel as if he'd been punched in the chest. Her eyes were glassy, lips swollen, a satisfied but somewhat dazed expression on her face.

Shoving aside the doubt clawing at his brain, he cleared his throat, taking one of her hands in his. "You know I care about you, Sylvia."

Something in his voice warned her she wasn't going to like what came next. "Yes."

"And I'd never do anything to hurt you."

She nodded, allowing herself to look at him for the first time since he removed her from his lap. "Yes..."

Restless, he stood, moving to look down at her. "You need to know I do understand why you didn't tell me about your family's wealth. There are men out there who would take you as their wife for what your family offers." He paced a few feet away, sucking in a deep breath, returning to sit next to her. "I'm not that kind of man."

Sylvia glanced at him, sorrow already showing in her eyes. "I know."

"I'm also not the kind of man who would keep you from your dream of marrying for love. I now understand why it's so important to you." Turning his head, he watched the creek several feet away, needing to get the rest out before his courage failed. "It wouldn't be fair of me to continue to court you knowing I'll never be able to fulfill your dream."

Her gaze moved away from him, her body stilling, expression tight and strained.

Mack reached over to take her hand in his. "I'll never allow myself to love again. You deserve so much more. You deserve it all, including love."

She didn't look at him, didn't respond. A moment passed before she pulled her hand from his.

Mack never expected the slice of pain ripping through him, pulsing and throbbing, as if he'd been cut in two. He stopped himself from pushing his palm against his chest to relieve the intense ache. He'd gone too far to falter now.

"Sylvia, look at me."

Her jaw tightened, eyes blinking to stop the tears she would not allow to fall. "I understand, Mack." She hated the way her voice cracked. "Truly, I do."

He gave her a few minutes before standing, reaching out his hand. "I'll walk you back to the boardinghouse."

Sylvia didn't move, shaking her head. "I'd like to stay here a little longer." When he dropped his hand, moving to sit back down, she shook her head. "Alone, if you don't mind."

"I can't leave you out here alone."

Without sparing him a glance, she nodded once. "Yes, you can. The boardinghouse isn't far. I can certainly make it there alone. Good night, Mack." Sylvia did her best to sound calm, accepting, even if everything inside her screamed with pain.

"But—"

"I'm staying here alone for a while. I'd appreciate it if you wouldn't argue this any further."

He wanted to take her in his arms, tell her he'd find some way to love her, give her what she wanted. Instead, he took a step away.

"Then I'll say good night."

She didn't look up or acknowledge what amounted to an unqualified goodbye. Clenching both hands in her lap, Sylvia continued to stare at the moving water, wishing it would wash away the sound of his footsteps as he left her.

Sylvia didn't know how long she sat there, gathering what was left of her pride. She'd never felt such intense pain, making it hard to breathe or think. He'd never love her.

Hope had been the refuge she'd flee to when life overwhelmed her. The last three weeks with Mack were the best in her life, making her hope grow out of all reason. All this time, she'd been duping herself, believing Mack cared more about her than he did.

Twisting her cotton dress with her hands, Sylvia let out a broken breath. She'd been a fool. Unfortunately, the realization didn't do anything to soften the pain lodged deep in her chest.

After a good, long time, Sylvia decided she had enough of thinking about something she couldn't change. He'd made his decision, not wanting to include her in his future.

She'd lost the man she loved. The logical part of her insisted she'd get over him...in time. The part around her heart knew it wouldn't be easy and might get worse before getting better.

Standing, she steadied herself before walking toward the boardinghouse. While still under the canopy of branches, Sylvia swiped at the moisture on her face, satisfied no one would notice the silent tears—the reason she'd stayed so long on the bench.

Straightening her back, she lifted her chin, reminding herself she was Sylvia Maria Pietro Lucero, the daughter of the largest landowner in central Texas. Sucking in a breath, she stepped to the front door, forcing herself to walk inside, the same way she intended to force herself to forget Adam Mackey.

# Chapter Seventeen

Mack stood in the shadows across the street, leaning against the door of the telegraph office. That was as far away as he intended to go until Sylvia was safe inside the boardinghouse.

He hadn't anticipated the kick to his stomach when he watched her emerge from the cover of the trees. His chest squeezed when she'd brought her hand to her face, wiping away what he believed to be tears. It was the last bit of vulnerability he saw.

It had never been his intention to hurt Sylvia. Not ever. The hurt came anyway, regardless of any intentions he held. Regret, more potent than what he'd felt at the news about his cousin and fiancée, sliced through him, confusion clouding his mind.

He still couldn't force himself to leave his post, even after watching Sylvia step inside the boardinghouse and close the door. Observing her through the glass, he saw her stop to speak to Cash and Allie on one of their rare nights out. Their pleasure at seeing Sylvia didn't change as they spoke, telling Mack she hadn't spoken of his decision to discontinue their courtship.

Cursing himself, he stepped away from his spot, realizing what he'd forgotten to say before leaving Sylvia alone. In her mind, and probably everyone else's, she'd been rejected, seen as not good enough for him.

Spitting another series of curses, he tried to think of a way to fix his mistake. He cared not at all what people thought about him. What they thought about Sylvia meant everything. Mack knew the pain of being the one spurned. For her, it would be twice as bad. She loved him, and he'd rejected her love.

"Damn it all..."

Feeling a hand on his shoulder, he whipped around, ready to draw his gun before recognizing Caleb.

His friend held up his hands. "Hey. I just wanted to see if you're all right."

Settling fisted hands on his hips, Mack shook his head. "Hell no, I'm not all right."

Caleb studied his face, not liking what he saw. Then his gaze moved across the street, seeing Sylvia, Cash, and Allie inside the boardinghouse. "Did you just leave Sylvia across the street?"

Mack winced. "In a way." Letting out a breath, his solemn gaze met his friend's. "I, uh, well...I called off the courtship tonight."

Caleb's jaw dropped. Stepping away, he crossed his arms, his voice hard and unflinching. "You truly are an idiot."

Mack's eyes widened. "What the—"

"She's a woman any man would give his right arm to have. Beautiful, smart, funny, and from what I've heard, an excellent cook."

Mack lifted a brow, surprised and unamused at Caleb's ire.

His friend's displeasure continued, unrelenting. "As if you need reminding, she's in love with you. What the hell were you thinking?"

Opening his mouth to argue, Mack closed it. Caleb spoke the truth. Everything he'd said Mack had told himself over and over since he'd walked away from Sylvia.

"I was thinking it best to allow her to find a man who could love her the way she deserves. Sylvia doesn't need to be saddled with a cynical deputy with nothing to offer. A man who can't love her."

Caleb didn't respond, the expression on his face saying it all. Shaking his head, he settled a hand on Mack's shoulder. "You are going to regret letting her go." Without another word, he shook his head once more, then turned and left.

Mack watched him walk away, afraid his friend was right.

Awakening in slow stages, Sylvia stretched her arms, a tired grin spreading across her face. An instant later, the pain of last night returned. She could no longer look forward to suppers or long walks with Mack. Nor would she experience passionate kisses each evening, sending her to bed hot and needy. It was over.

Staring at the ceiling, she allowed herself a few minutes to adjust to the loss. At least she had Dominic.

She shot up. "Dom," she gasped. Jumping out of bed, she rushed her ablutions and dressed. He'd be waiting for her downstairs. Hurrying out the door, she took the steps quickly, slowing as she reached the bottom. Her brother stood at the entrance of the restaurant, a smirk on his face.

"Late as usual, Syl."

Stopping next to him, she took the arm he offered. "How late am I?"

Pulling out his pocket watch, he counted out loud. "One, two, three...it seems you're at least ten minutes late."

"No..." A small grin lifted her lips.

"I'm afraid so. How can you hold a job with such tardiness?"

"My smile?"

Dominic threw back his head and laughed, drawing Suzanne's attention.

"I see Sylvia decided to join you, Mr. Lucero." Suzanne studied Sylvia's face, a frown forming. "Are you all right?"

Sylvia's stomach clenched. "I, uh...I'm fine. At least I will be after one of your breakfasts." She tried to sound amused, knowing she failed.

"You look a little pale. Are you certain you're all right?"

"I'm absolutely fine, Suzanne."

Raising a brow, Sylvia's friend shrugged, showing them to a table. "Will Mack be joining you this morning?"

Pain flashed across her face before Sylvia shoved the hurt aside. "Not this morning. May I have coffee with eggs and toast?"

Nodding, Suzanne looked at Dominic. "I'll have the same, plus ham or bacon, whichever you have."

"How about I bring both?"

He flashed her a charming smile. "Perfect, Mrs. Barnett." She chuckled, walking away. He waited until Suzanne was out of earshot, turning a somber expression to Sylvia. "Now, tell me what's bothering you. And don't consider lying to me."

She'd thought of just that. Her bravado shifting, Sylvia leaned forward. "Mack decided to call off our courtship."

It wounded Dominic, hearing the pain in her voice. Then anger set in at the man who'd dared hurt his sister. "The rogue."

"Mack was always a gentleman, Dom." She wouldn't mention the scorching kisses.

He snorted. "Did he give you a reason?"

She lifted a shoulder, the color draining from her face. "He doesn't love me."

He murmured a curse, then glanced around, relieved no one seemed to hear him. "The man's a fool, Sylvia," he ground out, her answer doing nothing to quell his anger. "Do you love him?"

She glanced away, unable to hide the truth from a brother who knew her so well. Reaching over, Dominic covered her hand with his.

"I'm so sorry, Syl."

Staring down at their joined hands, she bit her lip, voice strained. "It's odd, isn't it? I traveled all this way to avoid a marriage to join lands, only to fall in love with a man who only desires a union based on respect and companionship. Mack doesn't believe in love at all." She looked up, swallowing the ball of regret. "He'll never love me."

He squeezed her hand, his compassionate eyes meeting the distress in hers. "Mack isn't worth your sorrow, Syl. If he can't see the wonderful treasure you are, he's not worthy of you."

She worked to hold onto the tiny sliver of composure, her lower lip trembling.

"I'm serious, love. Give yourself some time and you'll see I'm right." He leaned closer. "It won't be long before he realizes his mistake and begs you to give him another chance."

The thought stalled her sorrow. "No. I'll not let my heart be ensnared by him again. It's over, Dom. It's best I look to the future and not the past."

Studying the way her features began to move from grief to determination, his lips twisted into a reassuring grin. "That's the sister I remember. Strong and independent. They've served you well in the past and they will again." Seeing Suzanne approach with their meals, he lifted his hand, resting it on his thigh.

As Suzanne placed the plates before them and moved off, Sylvia clung to his words, more determined than ever to push Mack out of her heart.

Sylvia tilted her chin up as she and Dominic walked down the church's center aisle to a row near the front. She'd have preferred to sit at the back where her presence might be ignored by the small group of women who thrived on gossip. It wouldn't take long before news of Mack's decision swept through town. Nevertheless, Sylvia refused to be intimidated by the harpies or think less of herself because of his rejection.

Spotting May and Tabitha in the second row, she leaned up to speak in Dominic's ear. "There." She indicated the seat with a nod of her head. "Next to my friends."

Sitting down, she allowed herself a quick look around, recognizing the Pelletiers, Gabe and Lena, Gabe's father, and several others. All offered her smiles and nods of recognition. They obviously hadn't heard about Mack's decision. Some of her tension lessened and she let out a relieved breath.

Sylvia had taken a seat next to May, noticing her friend glance around the church as the choir finished a hymn. It wasn't hard to guess she searched for Caleb. Although he'd made no hint of an intention to court May, he'd walked her to the boardinghouse a couple times and joined her and Sylvia for breakfast several times. She found herself praying if Caleb ever did voice his intentions to May, their courtship would end better for her than it had for Mack and herself.

Watching out the window of the jail, Mack's throat tightened at the sight of Sylvia and Dominic leaving the boardinghouse for church. As much as he believed the decision he made served them both better than a misdirected marriage, he couldn't stop the claws of regret.

A sharp pain in the area of his heart startled him. He'd felt it once before when his aunt sent news of Mack's fiancée's marriage to his cousin.

Although he didn't recall the ache being as intense as this morning.

Ignoring it, he paced away to sit at Gabe's desk. Opening a drawer, Mack grabbed the newest wanted posters, doing his best to concentrate on the images and descriptions. No matter how long he stared at each sheet, Mack couldn't remember any of what he'd read.

Blowing out a frustrated breath, he dropped the posters back into the drawer. Caleb had taken the first rounds of town, leaving Mack to man the jail. Gabe had sent the Smith brothers home after giving them a stern warning to never again threaten anyone unless they meant to make good on their threats.

Gabe had been more than a little frustrated at his inability to discover anything to identify who'd slaughtered the sheep. Miller maintained his and his sons' innocence. He hadn't denied the benefits to his family if the sheepherders left the area, reminding Gabe he wasn't the only rancher who coveted their land.

Even Dax and Luke Pelletier had met with Ebenezer and Elija, talking of their interest if the Smiths ever decided to sell. Unlike Miller, Gabe knew his friends had offered their help if the sheepherders ever needed it.

With the Smiths gone, no one remained at the jail for Mack to guard. Unable to staunch his restlessness, he grabbed his hat, deciding to take a turn around town. He knew a special stagecoach run would be arriving late in the morning. Sunday arrivals were rare, unless important supplies or people were aboard.

Mack had no idea which to expect. He hoped if the stage brought passengers, Sylvia's father wouldn't be among them. She didn't need the humiliation he felt certain the man would rain down on her once he found Mack had called off the courtship.

The sick feeling returned, turning his stomach inside out. Another wave of guilt had him turning in the direction of the church. He needed to see Sylvia, explain how he preferred she tell people she'd called off the courtship and not Mack. He didn't expect an argument or hesitation. It would be to her benefit, and Mack felt certain Sylvia would jump at the chance to cast him as the scoundrel.

Crossing the street, he passed the Dixie, newspaper office, and St. James, arriving at the church as the first of the parishioners walked outside. He couldn't account for the tightening in his chest as he waited. All he had to do was explain his reasoning, obtain her agreement, and leave. How hard could that be?

"No. I'll *not* lie about how our friendship ended." Sylvia didn't look at him, her attention on anyone but him.

Mack winced at her choice of words. He expected her to say courtship or relationship. Instead, she'd emphasized how his rejection ended not only spending each evening with her, but any chance of continuing their friendship. The truth stung.

"You wouldn't be lying. Not exactly." Mack glanced behind him, seeing Dominic speaking with the Pelletiers, even though his gaze stayed fixed on him and Sylvia.

Her gaze lifted to his for an instant, brow lifted. "Not exactly?"

Rubbing the back of his neck, Mack's jaw clenched. "It seemed an inevitable end. You knew from the start my feelings on love and I knew you felt the opposite. Neither of us planned to change our minds. If we'd continued another week, it would have ended the same." He saw the flash of pain in her eyes, wincing at hurting her again. "Can't you allow me to take the fault?"

Hands tightening on her reticule, she glanced away, blinking to staunch the moisture in her eyes. She would not allow him to see her reaction. Squaring her shoulders, she glared at him.

"If you knew how this would end, why didn't you do it right away? Why keep seeing me, making me believe there might be hope for us?"

Her questions seared through him, the ache bringing another round of guilt. She deserved his complete honesty. "Because I couldn't let you go."

Sylvia took a small step away, stunned. He hadn't been able to let her go, but after he knew of her love, he'd sent her away, unable to handle feelings he couldn't return.

Taking off his hat, Mack threaded a hand through his hair. "I did you a disservice not calling it off sooner. For that, I am truly sorry."

She stiffened, seeing Dominic striding toward them. "Regardless, you called off the courtship and that's what people will learn. I'm a strong woman, Mack. Believe me, I can handle their derision at being rejected. Now, if you'll excuse me."

Brushing past him, she stopped Dominic's forward progress, her brother wearing a murderous expression. Slipping her hand through his arm, she swallowed the bile Mack's request caused. Nothing he said made anything better.

Morgan Miller stood next to his horse, arms crossed, watching the exchange between Sylvia and Mack. Even if the break happened only a few hours earlier, word traveled fast in a town the size of Splendor.

Sylvia whispered the information to May and Tabitha after church. Her words hadn't gone unheard by Gladys Poe, the town's worst gossip. Within minutes, everyone still standing outside the church knew Mack's decision, sparking anger at him and sympathy for Sylvia.

Morgan felt neither. A sense of triumph washed through him. He'd been waiting, knowing the deputy would make a mistake, although he'd never considered the mistake would be so massive.

Tossing the reins over a hitching post, he followed Sylvia and her brother the few feet to the St. James. He continued behind them as they entered the dining room, making a slight cough, catching Sylvia's attention.

"Mr. Miller. I didn't see you at church."

Removing his hat, he offered a sly grin. "I sat at the back." He looked at the man next to her, already knowing their relationship.

"Mr. Miller, this is my brother, Dominic Lucero. Dom, this is Morgan Miller. He owns a ranch south of town."

The men shook hands, studying each other the way men do. "Won't you join us, Mr. Miller?" Dominic asked, noticing Sylvia's eyes widen a little.

"It would be my pleasure. I'd appreciate it if you'd call me Morgan." He turned toward Sylvia. "Both of you."

Sylvia felt a slight lightening in her chest. "All right."

"And you'll call me Dom."

"May I show you a table?" Thomas stepped beside them.

"Yes, please. For three." Sylvia slipped her arm through Dominic's, a little bit of her misery retreating. Reaching their table, Morgan pulled out a chair for her.

"Sylvia?"

"Thank you, Morgan."

Thomas waited until all three sat down, taking their orders before disappearing into the kitchen. They fell into an easy conversation about Morgan's ranch, Dominic's arrival in town, and his new job as a Texas Ranger.

Their discussion slowed as they ate the meals Thomas set before them. After a while, Morgan looked at her.

"Excuse me if I'm intruding on something I shouldn't, Sylvia. I heard you are no longer seeing the deputy."

Dominic whipped his head toward his sister, seeing her stiffen. He opened his mouth to speak, closing it when Sylvia answered.

"That is true."

Morgan waited a few moments, setting down his fork. "If it's not too soon, I'd be honored to accompany you to supper."

Sylvia wasn't surprised by the invitation, other than the speed with which the man had moved after hearing about her and Mack.

"I'd love to have supper with you, Morgan."

Relief flashed in his eyes. "Wonderful. Would Wednesday evening suit you?"

She glanced at Dominic. At his nod, the corners of her mouth slipped into a grin. "Yes, that would be fine."

Morgan couldn't hide an upsurge of satisfaction. "I'll look forward to it."

# Chapter Eighteen

Sylvia had awoken Wednesday morning with more confidence than she'd felt when climbing from bed Sunday. She'd worked Monday and Tuesday, relieved Mack hadn't made an appearance. The less she saw him, the easier it would be to shove the handsome deputy from her mind, forgetting him as one did yesterday's trash.

Hearing the bell over the door, she stopped dusting the shelves to see who'd entered. She straightened, a smile on her face when she saw May walk inside.

"Aren't you working today?"

May rushed up to her, eyes bright with excitement. "Did you hear who came in on the stage Sunday?"

Sylvia's forehead bunched. She shook her head. "No. Is it someone important?"

"Well, I'm not sure. It was an older woman. Very beautiful and obviously from wealth. She's staying at the St. James."

Brows lifting, Sylvia looked out the front window. "Is she tall with dark hair streaked with silver?"

May nodded. "She's quite elegant, don't you think?"

Pursing her lips, Sylvia thought of the woman she'd seen walking on the boardwalk the night before. She'd wondered about her, but didn't know who to ask.

"I thought she looked elegant and sophisticated. Do you know why she's in Splendor?"

"No one at the St. James seems to know anything about her, other than she's from Boston. Oh, and Thomas says she's a widow. She keeps to herself, taking walks, asking few questions."

"Do you know her name?" Sylvia asked.

"Mrs. Billings." May opened her pendant watch, checking the time. "I'd best get back to the hotel. The cook needs my help with supper." She started to leave, then turned back. "Are you still having supper with Morgan Miller tonight?"

"I am." A curious mixture of excitement and resignation tugged at her, but she shook off both. She'd approach supper with cool detachment, not allowing herself to let down her defenses for an instant. This evening was her way of getting over Mack, nothing more. It didn't have anything to do with the successful rancher.

Sylvia found Morgan compelling and attractive, although she felt none of the desire she had for Mack. Sadness streamed through her, knowing the odds she'd ever be fortunate enough to meet another man as captivating as Mack weren't good. Still, she had to try. She believed Dominic when he'd told her it would be the best way to mend a broken heart.

"I thought you had a supper engagement this evening, Sylvia." Stan Petermann stood a few feet away, a tender look on his face. In a few short months, he'd become somewhat of a surrogate father, and she knew he saw her as a substitute daughter. It was one reason she hoped to still build a life in Splendor—the friends she'd made since arriving.

"Mr. Miller is to meet me at the boardinghouse at six."

Stan looked at the time. "Then you should be leaving to get ready."

"Are you sure?" She couldn't hide the delight in her voice.

Chuckling, he pointed to the door. "Go on with you, and have a wonderful evening."

Grabbing her shawl and reticule, she made for the door. "Thank you, Mr. Petermann."

Mack walked past Ruby's Palace, the tinny piano music spilling onto the street, luring him inside. Stopping for a moment, he stared at the door, knowing Malvina would welcome him with open arms. The comfort she would offer held no appeal. He wanted only one woman but no longer had the right to call on her.

Jaw clenching, he moved on, passing the clinic, schoolteacher's house, and the house he shared with Caleb before reaching the end of the street. Ahead and to his right stood Noah's blacksmith shop, livery, and saddlery.

He took a few steps toward the blacksmith shop, halting when he recognized a rider rein to a stop. Mack moved into the shadows of an unoccupied house.

Sliding to the ground, Morgan Miller led his horse toward Noah, who stood just inside the door.

"I'd like to board my horse for the evening."

Noah grabbed the reins. "Are you spending the night in town?"

"I'm escorting a young woman to supper and expect to be up late. I'll pick him up early tomorrow morning."

Nodding, Noah shook Morgan's outstretched hand. "You won't have to worry about him."

"Thanks. I'll see you in the morning."

Mack's hands clenched at his sides, nostrils flaring. He knew of only one woman who'd captured Morgan's attention. Sylvia.

Unexplained anger sliced through him. He had no interest in seeing any other woman, yet she'd accepted a supper invitation within days of Mack ending their courtship.

Emerging from the shadows, he followed Morgan around the outside of the telegraph office, watching as he entered the Wild Rose. He hesitated a couple minutes before continuing inside, walking straight to the bar, nodding at Al, the longtime bartender.

"Mack. What can I get you?"

"Whiskey, Al."

Pouring it, he set it in front of Mack. "Not having supper with pretty Miss Lucero tonight?"

Snorting, he picked up the glass, tossing back the amber liquid, letting it burn a path down his throat. "I thought you'd have heard by now. I'm no longer courting her."

Al's brow raised. "Too bad. She's a mighty fine lady."

Mack mumbled a curse. He'd heard the same several times until he felt ready to punch something...or someone. Instead, he lifted his empty glass, waiting as Al filled it. "Yes, she is."

"Heard about the trouble with the Smiths and Millers last week." Al shook his head. "I've met Eb and Elija at church. Seem like good people."

"And the Millers?"

"Morgan is good enough. Curtis is a little rougher, but not a bad sort. Their father, Norman, is a hard man, always expected a lot of both boys."

Mack shrugged. "A lot of ranchers are hard on their sons."

Al rested his arms on the bar, leaning forward, lowering his voice. "I mean *real* hard. Not spankings, but whippings and beatings. I've heard both boys have scars to prove it. With their ma gone, no one was around to stand between Norman and the boys. I've heard Buster, their foreman, often tried to intervene. Don't know how successful he was at stopping Norman." Straightening, he grabbed the whiskey bottle, filling Mack's glass once more. "It's all rumor, though. I've never heard either Curtis or Morgan mention it." Al moved off to help a group of cowboys who took places at the bar.

Picking up the glass, Mack took a small sip, deciding it best to nurse this one. Shifting, he saw Morgan at a table near the piano, playing a game of cards as if he had no other place to be. Mack wondered if he'd misheard the man's conversation with Noah. Lifting the glass for another sip, he stopped when Morgan tossed down his cards and stood.

He walked around the table, approaching Mack, stopping a couple feet away. Tilting his head, Mack lifted a brow.

"I understand you no longer have an interest in Miss Lucero. Is that so?"

Throat tightening, Mack forced a curt nod.

"In that case, I'm letting you know my intention to take up where you left off. Do you have a problem with that?"

Mack hated it, but he refused to let Morgan see it. Features impassive, he shrugged. "Sylvia's free to have supper with whomever she wants."

Staring at Mack another moment, one side of his mouth tilted upward. "Good."

He watched Morgan leave the saloon and head straight to the boardinghouse. Mack's anger boiled inside him, wishing he'd gone with his initial urge to land a blow to the man's jaw.

"Sonofabitch." The mumbled oath preceded Mack slamming his glass on the bar, getting Al's attention. "Give me the damn bottle."

Sylvia studied the short, handwritten menu Thomas handed her. Glancing at Morgan, she saw him doing the same. As always, the table at the Eagle's Nest looked beautiful, the lanterns around the room set at the right level of light, the aromas from the kitchen playing on her senses.

Everything was wonderful, except the wrong man sat next to her.

"Do you know what you want?" Morgan asked, his warm gaze searching hers.

She felt a tinge of guilt, wishing the man who rode all the way to town was someone else. "The rabbit fricassee. And you?"

Morgan grinned. "A steak and sourdough cornbread. I've heard it's real good here."

"I've had it, and yes, it is good." Setting down the menu, Sylvia picked up her wine glass, taking a sip. She had the oddest urge to pick up the bottle in the middle of the table and drink it down without regard for the consequences tomorrow.

Thomas took their orders and poured more wine into their glasses before leaving them alone. Morgan rested back in his chair, his glass held between strong, tanned fingers.

"Do you enjoy working at the general store?"

Her shoulders relaxed, a smile touching her lips at his easy question. "Very much. Mr. Petermann lets me do much of the bookwork, ordering, and organizing the products when they arrive. The pay is fair, and he allows me time off when needed. I can't imagine another job I'd like more."

He seemed to consider her answer, his gaze narrowing. "Does that mean you plan to stay in Splendor?"

"For now. I'd like to be here through a full winter. I'll make a decision in the spring, after I've been in Splendor a year. It wouldn't be fair to Lena and the others who paid for our travel to leave before then."

Morgan nodded. He'd heard of the local women who'd brought the four mail order brides to Splendor. None had married, although he'd heard

Caleb might have an interest in May Bacon. As a bachelor with little time to search for a bride, Morgan welcomed the arrival of the young women. His gaze moved to the entry, eyes widening a little.

"It appears your brother will be having supper here as well."

Sylvia shifted in her chair, looking over her shoulder to see Dominic walk into the restaurant. Her mouth dropped open, noticing the woman on his arm—Tabitha. Setting her napkin on the table, Sylvia stood, a sparkling smile greeting the two when they stopped by the table. Morgan rose to stand next to her.

"Good evening, Syl." Dominic kissed her cheek, turning toward Morgan and extending his hand. "Hello, Morgan. This is Tabitha Beekman."

Accepting the outstretched hand, he nodded at both. "Good evening, Dominic, Miss Beekman." He'd seen her working in the boardinghouse several times. "Would you care to join us?"

Sylvia sent her brother a pleading glance, hoping he'd accept.

Dominic understood the look in her eyes. "If we wouldn't be intruding…"

"Not at all." Morgan stepped aside to let them pass by toward the two empty chairs. While Dominic pulled out Tabitha's chair, Morgan motioned for Thomas.

Retaking her seat, Sylvia felt a surge of relief. Within minutes of arriving at the restaurant with Morgan, she knew it had been a mistake. Accepting a supper invitation so soon hadn't helped put Mack behind her.

Instead, the memories of being at the Eagle's Nest with him overwhelmed her. Inexperienced at being courted, except by one man, she didn't know how miserable spending time with someone else would be. Maybe it would be different in a few weeks or months. Tonight, she found comfort in having her brother so close.

A commotion at the entrance had everyone in the restaurant turning. Curtis Miller looked around the room, his gaze landing on Morgan. Ignoring the stunned look on the faces of the other diners, Curtis's face reddened, the cords in his neck rigid. Except for his brother, he didn't spare anyone else at the table a glance.

"You need to come with me."

Morgan jumped to his feet. "What is it?"

"We've been attacked. At least one of Pa's cattle was slaughtered and several more missing. He wants everyone at his ranch." Their father's property bordered the entire length of the Smith's, the other two Miller ranches to the west of his.

"Do you think it was the Smiths?"

Curtis rested fisted hands on his hips. "Not sure. Pa sent Buster over to their place. They'd been attacked, too. Eight more from their herd had been slaughtered."

Morgan rubbed the back of his neck. "Could be they're retaliating by taking our cattle."

"Maybe. But this whole thing strikes me as strange." Curtis let out a frustrated breath. "Buster is over at the jail now. We're going to need help hunting down whoever is doing this."

Morgan turned to look down at Sylvia. "My apologies, but I must leave." He glanced at Dominic. "Would you mind seeing your sister home?"

Standing, Dominic shook his head. "Not at all. Do what you need to do."

"Let's go, Morgan," Curtis growled behind him. "We can ride back with the sheriff and deputies." He left without a backward glance, uncaring of the spectacle he made by stomping out of the dining room.

Morgan shot another apologetic look at Sylvia before following his brother.

"What was all that about?" Tabitha's brows pulled together in a frown.

Sylvia saw the same confusion on Dominic's face. From conversations with Mack, she explained what she knew about the slaughtered sheep, as well as what happened between the Smiths and Millers at the general store. "Many thought the Millers were behind the killings."

Dominic rubbed his jaw. "It seems they're being attacked as well. Is there another landowner who'd benefit from ruining both?"

Sylvia shook her head. "I don't know much about the other ranchers in the area. From what I've seen, most get along quite well with each other."

Dominic's face sobered. He'd seen range wars and hoped this didn't escalate into a conflict where men, as well as animals, died. "Well, someone's behind this. They'd better find out who it is before there are any more killings."

Caleb stormed into the Wild Rose, his gaze swinging around the room.

"He's over there." Al pointed to a table in the corner.

"Ah, hell." Caleb couldn't hide his disgust at finding Mack passed out, his head resting on the table, his hat on a nearby chair. Striding to him, he cursed again at what he saw. "How long has he been this way?"

Al scratched the stubble on his chin. "At least an hour. He finished an entire bottle of whiskey after a short conversation with Morgan Miller."

"Damn," Caleb mumbled. He'd heard Miller had asked Sylvia to supper. He now regretted not telling Mack about it before he heard it from Morgan. "Do you have any coffee?"

"Not a drop."

Letting out a breath, he grabbed Mack's collar, yanking him up in the chair. "I need to get him to the jail. Most of us are riding out and need him there."

Al chuckled. "He won't be any use to you. Even coffee isn't going to help much." Reaching behind him, he grabbed a pitcher of water, walking around the bar to the table. "Give this a try."

Grabbing the pitcher from Al's hand, he poured the contents over Mack's head, stepping back when his friend jumped up, roaring a string of curses. Staggering, he scrubbed both hands down his face, rubbing red-rimmed eyes before looking around, his hard gaze landing on his friend.

"What the hell, Caleb?"

Snorting, he looked at Al. "It worked."

Crossing his arms, Al nodded. "That it did."

Mack started to lower himself back into the chair before Caleb's hand shot out, gripping his arm to stall his movement.

"We need to get to the jail."

Mack glared at him, reaching out to steady himself against the table. "What the hell for?"

"Someone went after Norman Miller's cattle. Killed one and stole several more. The Smiths also lost more sheep tonight. Gabe wants everyone at the jail."

Shaking his head, Mack nodded. Grabbing his hat, he plunged it onto his soaked hair, grimacing. "This is going to hurt tomorrow," he mumbled, following Caleb outside.

# Chapter Nineteen

Sylvia stared at the jail from the window of her bedroom. Dominic had walked her and Tabitha back to the boardinghouse after supper, deciding to check with Gabe to see if there was anything he could do to help.

He returned a few minutes later, knocking on Sylvia's door. Gabe and most of his men had already ridden off, leaving one of the new deputies and a very drunk Mack at the jail.

Sylvia crossed her arms, a foot tapping on the floor. "Drunk?"

A broad grin spread across Dominic's face. "Very."

"What is so funny?"

Chuckling, he sat down on the one chair in her room. "Seems he learned Miller was taking you to supper."

Her mouth twisted, brows furrowing. "Why would that bother him? He's the one who called off the courtship."

"Yep, he is." Dominic continued to grin.

She glared at him. "Well?"

Holding out his hands, palms up, he shrugged. "Well what?"

"Why would it bother him, Dom? I don't understand."

"I don't have an answer for you, Syl. That's something you're going to have to ask Mack." It wasn't the complete truth. Dominic had a pretty good idea why the deputy buried himself in a bottle tonight, but he had no intention of sharing his thoughts with his sister.

She lifted a brow. "Was he drunk downstairs in the saloon or upstairs?"

Dominic frowned before understanding her meaning. "Downstairs, Syl. All alone at a table with the empty bottle of whiskey. I wouldn't want to be him tomorrow."

Plopping onto the bed, Sylvia let the misery she felt show on her face. "He can be such an idiot."

"Yes, he can," Dominic agreed, believing his meaning was a little different than his sister's. Sitting back, he stretched out his legs, resting his hands in his lap, waiting for Sylvia to say more.

"It's so hard, Dom." She stared out the window, not meeting his gaze.

"What's hard, love?"

She blew out an agonized breath. "I thought having supper with Morgan would help me forget Mack. Instead, I miss him even more."

Pushing out of the chair, Dominic sat on the bed next to her, settling an arm over her shoulders. "You're a strong woman, Syl. You traveled across the country, came to a town no one has ever heard of, and made a life for yourself. You enjoy your work and have made many friends. You *will* get over Mack, love. It may take time, but soon, you'll wake one morning and realize he no longer owns your heart. That is when you'll be ready to venture out again. Don't rush it. Let it come in its own time."

Leaning into his shoulder, Sylvia sighed. "How do you know all this?"

He let out an amused chuckle. "I was naïve enough to consider myself in love once."

Pulling back, she stared at him. "You were in love? When and with whom?"

A wry grin crossed his face. "I was seventeen. She was fifteen and new to Whiplash. Her father bought the mercantile and her mother opened the millinery."

Her eyes widened. "I know who you mean, but I can't remember her name."

"Mattie. Well, her real name was Matilda, but she preferred Mattie."

She leaned back against his chest. "What happened?"

His voice turned cold. "Her father learned of my interest and sent her away to school back east. She never returned before her parents sold their businesses and moved away."

A few minutes passed before Sylvia spoke again. "Have you never cared about a woman since?"

He rested his chin on the top of her head. "What for when there are so many wonderful women out there for me to meet? Why settle for one when I can have—ow, Syl. What was that for?"

She laughed, having stopped him with a jab to his chest. "I don't want to hear about all your conquests. I heard enough about them back home."

Pulling away, he looked down into her eyes, lifting a brow. "People spoke of the women I knew?"

"Don't seem so surprised, Dom. You're a Lucero. We were always one of the main topics of gossip in Whiplash. But I believe you were the number one source of good stories. Such as what happened with Mary—"

He covered her mouth with his hand. "Enough, Syl. I do not want to hear what my sister knows of my liaisons."

Her mouth tilted into an impish grin. "They *were* quite educational, Dom."

Groaning, he removed his arm from her shoulders and stood. "On that, I believe I'll head to the hotel." Leaning down, he kissed her forehead. "Meet me in the St. James dining room for breakfast tomorrow."

Her face brightened. "I'd love to." When he moved to the door, she called his name. "Dom. I'm so glad you're here."

A grin lifted the corners of his mouth. "Me, too, Syl."

"What do you want us to do now, boss?" One of the Miller ranch hands stood in the shadows of the barn, his worried gaze darting toward the house every few seconds.

"Nothing for now. We need to wait for things to cool off, then start up again. No use taking risks at this point." The tall, lanky man scratched his chin, seemingly unconcerned by the number of lawmen roaming the ranch and Gabe's many questions.

"They know something's not right. Sooner or later, they're going to figure this out." The ranch hand turned and spat, wiping a sleeve across his mouth. "I say we stop now. It's going to take a lot more than a few dead sheep and missing cattle to accomplish what he wants."

"As long as he's willing to pay us and offer up the land he promised, I plan to keep following his orders. What you do is your decision."

The ranch hand glared at the man who'd hired him a few years before. He owed him for taking a chance on someone with no experience, except a year fighting for the losing Southern cause. Being a Confederate soldier gave him purpose, a direction in life. Afterward, he'd wandered across several states, never knowing where he'd find his next meal. One hot, dusty afternoon, he'd landed at the Miller ranch, parched and almost starved. Death would've claimed him if the grizzled foreman hadn't taken pity on him.

"I'm with you on this, boss. I know what Miller did to you and sure as hell know it wasn't right."

"He'll get what's coming to him. All men like Miller eventually do." He said the words with great conviction. The truth was Buster Maddox no longer believed justice would prevail or a man's word was his bond. It certainly hadn't been with Norman Miller.

Hex Boudreaux jostled Mack's shoulder, shaking his head when he heard the muffled groan. Shaking him again, he jumped back when Mack roared to life and reached for his gun, finding only empty air. Confusion clouded his face as he turned his attention to one of the newest deputies.

"You took it off last night." Hex nodded to the hook on the wall. "I'm thinking it was a mighty fine decision." The young man grinned, moving toward the door. "Thought I'd make the rounds. There's coffee ready. You may want several cups before venturing out."

Mack sat back in the chair, grimacing at the light streaming through the grimy window. Rubbing his eyes, he cursed himself for being such a fool. He'd known the folly of his ways with each swallow of whiskey. Still, he'd continued, unable to push aside the image of Sylvia with Morgan. *His* Sylvia.

The smell of coffee forced him to stand. Hex was right. It would take several cups to counteract the damage he'd done the night before.

He'd just taken a sip when the door banged open. Dutch strolled inside, followed by Hex's younger brother, Zeke. Both men stopped and stared at Mack as if he were some type of apparition.

"Glad to see you're alive." Dutch removed his hat, tossing it on the desk.

Mack grunted, taking another sip.

"We were taking bets on if you'd make it or not." Zeke grabbed a cup, filling it with coffee. "Caleb said he'd never seen you so, well..."

Mack lifted a brow. "Drunk?"

Zeke grinned. "I believe *soused* is the word he used."

Dutch opened a drawer in Gabe's desk, tossing a packet of headache compound toward Mack. "You're going to need this. Maybe a couple of them."

He had barely lifted the packet when Gabe, Caleb, and Cash walked in, staring at him with the same expression as Dutch and Zeke. Mack lifted a hand.

"Don't say it," he warned. "In fact, don't talk at all."

Gabe chuckled, making him feel worse. In all the years he'd known Gabe, Mack had never seen the man drunk or out of control. Then again, he'd probably never done something as foolish as shove the woman he loved from his life.

Mack stilled, the cup partway to his mouth. *Love?* He shook his head, refusing to believe that was what had lured him to drink an entire bottle of whiskey. And he sure as hell hoped the ridiculous notion of loving Sylvia had only been a remnant of his currently pickled brain.

"Did you find out who killed the animals?"

Gabe glanced at Mack, shaking his head. "No. I have an idea of what's going on, but no proof."

Caleb crossed his arms, leaning against a wall. "Tell us what you're thinking."

Lowering himself into his chair, Gabe rested his arms on the desk. "Whoever is doing this is close by. I can't see the ranchers who live near Norman participating in the killings or thefts. The closest ones are the Murtons, and I'll bet my badge neither Ty nor Gil would ever agree to these intimidation tactics. The families south and west of the Smiths are also sheepherders and friends of Eb and Elija. They wouldn't do anything to hurt them."

"Where does that leave us?" Dutch asked.

Caleb rubbed his jaw. "Someone who works for Miller?"

Gabe nodded. "That's what I think."

"But you've no proof." Mack finished his third cup of coffee.

"None. I'm going on instinct."

Zeke leaned a hip against the edge of Gabe's desk. "I can understand someone working for Miller killing the sheep, but why kill and steal cattle? It doesn't make sense to me."

Pinching the bridge of his nose, Gabe nodded. "That's the one part I can't figure out. Maybe it was done to throw us off, make us think the Smiths retaliated." He let out a heavy breath. "It's speculation, nothing more."

Cash had been silent, listening to everyone before commenting. "Since we've nothing else, it's as good a guess as any. Do you have any idea who?"

Gabe grimaced, shaking his head. "None."

The room quieted as each of them considered Gabe's theory.

"I don't think it's either of his sons." The men shifted their gazes to Cash. "Curtis is hotheaded, but not the type to run the Smiths off, no matter how much he hates having the sheepherders in their part of the territory."

"What about Morgan?" Mack asked, wishing he'd kept his mouth shut when Caleb lifted a brow at him.

Cash's mouth twisted. "He's less probable than Curtis. Morgan attended college to be a doctor. As I recall hearing, Norman came down with a severe fever during his son's second year of school. He wasn't expected to live, so Morgan agreed to come home. He never returned to school after his father recovered. Morgan's more of a healer than a killer."

Zeke straightened from his spot against the desk, glancing around the room. "What about the foreman, Buster Maddox?"

Dutch frowned. "I understand he's been with Miller for years. What do you think, Gabe?"

"I don't see Buster doing anything without Norman's order. There's just one way to find out."

Cash nodded. "We need to post ourselves near the Miller ranch and watch. I don't see any other way to figure out who's doing this."

"I'll go." Mack had no reason to stay in town.

"As will I." Caleb walked to the stove, pouring a cup of coffee, wincing at the taste of the tepid brew.

"Everyone will take turns until we figure out what's happening. Two deputies, two nights. Dutch and Caleb will ride out first. Cash and Beau next, Hex and Zeke after them."

Mack's brows furrowed. "What about me, Gabe?"

"I'll need you to stay in town with me. Can't leave the townsfolk unprotected."

Irritation pinched Mack's features. "They won't be unprotected. Even with two deputies watching the Miller ranch, there'll still be five of us in town."

Gabe ignored the protest, looking at Dutch and Caleb. "You two get ready to head out. The rest of you get back to your duties." He waited until everyone had left before turning a hard gaze on the only man who remained.

"Dammit, Gabe. I need to get away from here."

"What you need is to get your head straight."

An incredulous expression glared back at Gabe. "Get my head on straight? What the hell are you talking about?"

Standing, Gabe walked around his desk. "You're no good to me until you figure out what you want."

Mack shook his head, brows drawing together. "What are you talking about?"

Gabe crossed his arms. "Why'd you bury yourself in a bottle last night?"

Jaw tightening, Mack glared back. "That's my business."

"You've made it my business by almost killing yourself with whiskey. I don't know what's going on in your head, but whatever it is, straighten it out. You're no good to anyone right now, not even yourself." Picking up his hat, Gabe walked to the door. "Go home, Mack, and get some sleep. Maybe that will help you sort it out."

Mack paced the small area in the front room of the house he and Caleb shared. He couldn't sleep, his head throbbed, and his stomach roiled at even the thought of food.

Gabe's words locked in his head, forcing him to do some hard thinking. Unfortunately, he wasn't in any condition to consider anything other than simple subjects, and anything involving Sylvia wasn't simple.

Whether Mack wanted to admit it or not, she was the reason he'd drowned himself in whiskey. Being honest, his decision to end their courtship was the reason, mocking him every minute from the time he woke until he dropped off to sleep. He should've known it wouldn't take long for a new suitor to appear, attempting to take what Mack still considered his.

His reasons seemed so clear a few days ago. He couldn't offer Sylvia what she wanted, what she deserved. The proper decision was to walk away, let her find a man who could fulfill all her dreams, including marrying for love. A few days ago, Mack knew without a doubt he wasn't that man. Then he'd learned of Morgan's invitation to supper.

He'd wanted to bury his fist in the man's face, watch in satisfaction as he crumbled to the floor. Instead, he'd secured a bottle of whiskey, sulked off to a table, and tried to forget his greatest mistake by numbing his brain and body.

Mack should've known it wouldn't work. When his head cleared, he'd still have to deal with the same laughable decision. He just wished he could find any amount of humor in his actions.

Unrelenting pounding on the front door stopped the pacing. Mack turned, wanting to ignore whoever stood outside. He'd decided whoever knocked had given up when the pounding started again. Letting out a breath, Mack relented, stepping to the door.

Opening it, he'd been ready to deliver a terse greeting when his eyes widened. An instant later, a fist connected with his jaw.

# Chapter Twenty

Before he opened the door, Mack didn't believe he could feel any worse. Lying on the floor, rubbing his jaw, he rethought the assumption.

"What the hell?" Mack mumbled, his gaze fuzzy even as he perceived the shadow looming above him.

"Do I have your attention?" Dominic reached out a hand, yanking Mack upright.

Continuing to rub his jaw, he blinked to clear his vision. It took him a few moments to recognize Sylvia's brother standing before him. Gritting his teeth, Mack accepted his day was going to get worse before getting any better.

"Do you want a whiskey?" he ground out, relieved his jaw still worked.

Dominic snorted. "Haven't you had enough for a dozen men?"

He cringed, wondering if everyone in town knew about the previous night. Letting out a frustrated breath, Mack moved to the sofa and sat down. Ignoring Dominic's question, he ran a hand through his hair.

Crossing his arms, Dominic looked around the small house, noticing two doors he suspected led to bedrooms. He'd already heard Mack shared the place with Caleb. Sylvia deserved better, but she loved the man and that was all her brother needed to know.

"I want you to stay clear of Sylvia." Dominic lowered himself into a chair, leaning forward, his features hard as granite. "She deserves better than the way you treated her."

Mack agreed. "It wasn't my intention to hurt her."

"Yet you did. I'm guessing you knew you would walk away the entire time you courted her."

Mack grimaced, unable to argue the point. He'd learned what she wanted not long after they'd started courting, but continued seeing her, knowing he'd never be able to provide the love she desired.

"This is a small town. With her working at the general store, it'll be impossible for me to stay away from her."

"It won't be for long."

Mack's gaze shot to his. "What do you mean?"

"I intend to take her back to Texas."

Lips pressing together, he swallowed the bile Dominic's words caused. "Is that what she wants?"

"What the hell do you care what she wants?"

Muttering a curse, Mack shook his head. "I just want her to be happy."

"Right now she's nowhere close to that, and won't be as long as she stays in Splendor. I plan to take her with me to Austin. It's growing, with a lot of single men looking for wives. I'm betting it won't take long for her to forget about you."

Dominic's words ran together in Mack's mind, his attention focused on the possibility Sylvia might leave Splendor. A ball of ice began to form in his gut, growing with each passing minute. He'd never considered Sylvia leaving, couldn't imagine going through each day without a glimpse of the beautiful woman he cared so much about.

"She loves Splendor."

Dominic shrugged. "She can fall in love with Austin—and a different man." Standing, he moved to the door. "I expect you to stay far away from Sylvia until I can get her out of town."

"Most days I take my meals at the boardinghouse."

"There's the Eagle's Nest and McCall's. Eat at one of those places until she's gone." Dominic set his hand on the doorknob before turning back to glare at Mack. "If you do anything to hurt her again, I'll find you, and I guarantee you won't like the outcome."

Stepping out into a beautiful fall afternoon, Dominic smiled with a sense of satisfaction. All he had to do now was wait, hoping his visit would generate the desired result.

If not, then Adam Mackey truly wasn't the man Sylvia needed.

*Miller Ranch*

Dutch crouched behind a stand of thick bushes and low-hanging elms, his field glasses focused on the main house and barn. From their current position, he stared into the sun's glare. "We're going to have to move closer once the sun sets."

"I'm thinking over by the stables." It would be too risky to get close to the buildings on this side of the house during daylight.

"Agreed." Dutch handed the glasses to Caleb, keeping watch for anyone approaching from behind.

"If whoever is doing this comes from here, they won't ride out until dark."

They were fortunate Norman's house had been located near the property line with the Smiths. The position would be easier to spot anyone riding in the direction of the sheepherders.

Caleb lowered the glasses, looking at Dutch. "I'm guessing Miller believed he'd be the one buying the land west of him or he wouldn't have built so close to the boundary. It must have come as quite a shock when the Smiths bought it out from under him."

"Harold Clausen said it was a sale between two parties who knew each other." Dutch removed his hat, running a hand through his dark red, unruly hair. "The banker knows a lot about everyone in Splendor. As I recall, either Eb or Elija is married to the previous owner's daughter."

"How do you hear all this stuff, Dutch?"

He shrugged. "I meet Clausen for breakfast every few weeks. It's a habit I gained while working for Pinkerton. Allan liked us to stay close to town leaders." Dutch chuckled. "It's amazing what you learn over eggs and coffee."

Caleb snorted. "Maybe we should've asked Clausen who he thinks is killing the Smith's animals."

"If we don't figure it out, I'll be sure to ask him the next time we have breakfast."

Dutch's droll response had Caleb chuckling. Lifting the glasses, he aimed them toward the barn. "Looks like the men are coming in for the night." Caleb passed the glasses back, scooting back several feet to stand and stretch. "I'm hungry. Do you want some hardtack and jerky?"

Dutch nodded, not lowering the glasses. "It looks like Buster's walking into the main house. I'm not sure I agree with Gabe about the foreman."

"I think Norman is ordering Buster and a few men to drive out the Smiths." Caleb took a bite of hardtack, handing a biscuit and a piece of jerky to Dutch.

They stood in the shadow of the trees, eating while keeping watch on Miller's ranch. It wasn't long before the sun settled behind the western mountains, the sky darkening with a slim sliver of moon to light the land.

After a while, they left their horses behind, bending low as they ran across the long expanse of open space to huddle beside the stables. From their position, they'd be able to spot anyone riding south toward the Smith property. Unfortunately, it would take them several minutes to return to their horses and follow.

"Over there." Caleb's voice had dropped to a low hiss. "There are two men entering the barn."

They watched for several minutes, disappointed when they left the barn for the bunkhouse. When an hour passed with no other activity, Dutch slid to the ground.

"This could be a long night. Get some sleep, Caleb. I'll take first watch."

Sliding down beside Dutch, he lowered his hat, closing his eyes. Within a few minutes, Caleb fell into an uneasy sleep.

Mack rubbed the sleep from his eyes, squinting at the sunlight shining through a slit in the curtains. Three days had passed since Dominic visited. Three days of Mack fighting with himself over what to do about Sylvia.

As hard as it had been, he'd heeded Dominic's request and stayed away from the general store and boardinghouse. Twice he'd spotted her through the windows of each, a lump forming in his throat before he moved on.

He felt a little ridiculous this morning watching her cross the street to the general store. In the evening, he'd watch Dominic escort her home. Mack couldn't help thinking he should be the one by her side, not her brother.

Stepping away from the jail's window, Mack tried to make sense of his unrelenting desire for Sylvia. He never imagined it would be so hard to walk away, settle her into a distant slot in his memory. Knowing of Morgan's interest in her, and recalling Dominic's warning, the loss seemed so much more tangible.

"Are you just going to watch her?" Caleb chewed a piece of jerky, a smug grin tipping the corners of his mouth.

It had been four days since Gabe's men started watching the Miller property. None of the deputies had seen anything suspicious. It was as if the rancher knew they were being observed, which Gabe believed he did.

Hex and Zeke had replaced Cash and Beau that morning. In two days, Caleb and Dutch would switch with them, starting the cycle again. All the men knew it could go on for weeks until whoever was behind the actions believed it safe enough to ride out again.

Mack hesitated a moment before answering. "I haven't decided." Caleb's jaw dropped enough for him to notice. "Don't look so surprised. You're the one who told me I was a fool to let her go."

"I've never known you to take my criticisms seriously in the past."

Crossing his arms, Mack snorted. "I don't recall you ever commenting about my decisions in the past."

Caleb lifted a brow. "True, but I never felt the need to point out your flaws before now." He bit off another piece of jerky, chewing slowly.

"Dominic plans to take her back to Texas. To Austin."

Caleb pointed the dried meat at Mack. "Now there's a place I'd like to see. Maybe I'll ride along with them."

Picking up his hat, Mack settled it on his head. "She's not leaving." He didn't wait to hear more from Caleb, heading outside to take long, determined strides to the general store.

Stepping to the front window, he looked through the glass, gratified to see Sylvia alone. He didn't wait before pushing the door open to walk inside.

He saw the moment she noticed him. She straightened, eyes wide, inhaling a sharp breath. Recovering quickly, Sylvia lifted her chin.

"Deputy Mackey." Her voice quivered a little. Otherwise, she showed no sign of how she felt at being so close to him. "What can I get for you?"

Mack furrowed his brows, realizing he hadn't thought beyond seeing her again. Not from across a street or through a window, but standing a few feet away. He didn't know how long he stared before Sylvia cleared her throat.

"Can I help you find anything, Deputy?" Her voice was clipped, impatient, as if she wanted to be anywhere except standing in front of him.

"No. Yes..." Mack glanced away. He had no idea what to say, and for an instant, didn't know why he'd even come. "I, um...wanted to see how you were doing."

Sylvia crossed her arms, her mouth twisting. She looked at him as if seeing him for the first time, not liking what she saw. "How I'm doing?"

Disgust rose within him. Not at her, but at himself and the way they'd parted. Blowing out a frustrated breath, he met her skeptical gaze.

"I've missed seeing you, Sylvia."

Her closed features softened. Not much, but enough for Mack to notice. "You've missed me?"

"Does that surprise you?"

She took a slight step away, wishing someone would enter the store, ending this conversation. Sylvia didn't want him so close, asking questions, telling her things she didn't want to hear.

"Well, yes, it does."

He noticed her move away in slow increments until at least a yard separated them. Unwilling to allow it, Mack moved closer, noting her swift intake of breath.

"It shouldn't, Sylvia."

Shoving aside a combination of surprise and hurt, she turned, walking to stand behind the counter. A relieved breath crossed her lips. Setting both hands on the counter's edge, she narrowed her gaze.

"I never expected to see you again, except in passing. You made it quite clear you no longer wished my company."

He shook his head, voice calm. "You're twisting my words."

Her back stiffened. "Not at all." Pressing her lips firmly together, she seemed to weigh her next words. "I've had time to think about what you said, and you were right to end it."

Mack stilled. "I was?"

Her fingers dug into the counter. "As much as I wanted you to care enough to marry me, you were right not wanting to shackle yourself to someone you didn't..." She swallowed, "couldn't love. We both deserve better."

His chest tightened, squeezed to a degree the breath stuck in his lungs. "I would never have felt shackled to you, Sylvia. Not trapped or chained or imprisoned. Not in any way."

Her brows drew together. "I don't understand what you're trying to say."

Mack blew out a humorless laugh. "I'm not certain, either, other than I can't sleep or eat. Nothing feels right."

She quirked a brow. "And you're drinking more."

A tight smile cracked his otherwise somber expression. "You heard about that, did you?"

"I'm afraid most everyone in town did." She felt her pulse increase under his intense stare. "So, what is it you want from me, Mack?"

His expression didn't change. "I don't want you to leave Splendor."

"Leave?" The word had barely left her mouth when the door of the general store burst open.

"Mack, you need to get your horse and be ready to ride." Caleb glanced between his friend and Sylvia, giving her a contrite grin. "Something is going on at the Miller place and Gabe wants us to ride out. I need to find Dutch."

Mack turned back to face Sylvia. "I have to go."

"I know."

"We aren't done with this conversation." He started to move toward the door.

"Maybe we should be."

Turning abruptly, he stalked around the counter to within a few inches of Sylvia. Before she knew what he intended, Mack leaned down, brushing his mouth across hers.

"As I said, we aren't done with this conversation."

# Chapter Twenty-One

"Tell me what happened?" Mack finished saddling his bay gelding, Apollo, and swung into the saddle.

"Eb sent his son to town. He says there's shooting going on at Norman Miller's ranch. Hex and Zeke are there, but are pinned down by gunfire." Caleb shot him a look. "At least they were when Eb's son rode out."

Dutch rode up next to them. "Gabe and Cash will ride with us. Beau will stay here with Eb's son."

An instant later, Gabe rode up on Blackheart, the stallion dancing around while his owner surveyed the men before him.

"I don't know what we'll find, so be ready for anything. Let's move." Gabe led the way, riding down the length of the main street, reining his horse southwest toward Norman's ranch.

On a normal ride, it would take them almost an hour to reach the Miller ranch house. Mack expected them to cut the time in half, Gabe's pace not slowing over the curving trail. He knew the sheriff's thoughts were on his two newest and youngest deputies.

As the miles passed, Mack couldn't keep his thoughts from straying to Sylvia. A smile tugged at the corners of his mouth, remembering her shocked expression at the quick, unexpected kiss. He'd meant his last words to her. Their conversation wasn't finished. Mack didn't know what else he intended to say to Sylvia, other than he had no intention of letting her leave town. Not even if it meant fighting Dominic to stop her.

He did have one hesitation. How would he respond when she asked if he loved her? Without doubt, Sylvia would want to know if he'd changed his mind. So far, Mack had no good answer. At least not one she'd like.

Living without her wasn't an option, but did he love her? Mack honestly didn't know. By the time they spoke again, he had to have an answer, something guaranteed to keep her in Splendor.

"Hold up!" Gabe raised his hand. Halting near him, his men looked around, wondering at the reason for the sudden stop. "Riders coming." He nodded to the trail ahead.

They didn't have to wait long before Hex and Zeke rode up, Zeke's pants covered in blood, his face pale.

Hex's gaze landed on Gabe. "We need to get him to the doctor."

Gabe turned, motioning for Dutch. "Get Zeke to the clinic." Shifting back to Hex, his voice rose. "Tell us what happened."

Hex's worry was etched on his face, watching Dutch take the reins of Zeke's horse. "Shouldn't I go with him?"

"Dutch will make sure he's taken care of. I need you to explain what happened at Norman's ranch."

Sucking in a breath, Hex nodded. "Eb and Elija Smith were with their herd. They'd driven them right to the edge of their property, right up against the Miller place."

"Did Norman and his men fire on them?" Gabe asked.

Hex rubbed a hand across his forehead. "No. The shooting started inside the house. It all happened real fast, Gabe. A few men came running outside, guns drawn, firing into the house. That's when Zeke and I moved out of our hiding place, yelling for them to stop."

He paused a moment, trying to remember the details of a skirmish taking no more than five minutes. "One of the men outside turned and shot Zeke. When he fell, I fired at another one, hitting him in the shoulder or chest. I'm not sure which. I dragged Zeke behind the shrubs, then continued to fire."

"What did Elija and Eb do while this was going on?" Gabe asked.

Hex blinked, trying to remember the details of the gunfight. "I saw them raise their guns, but don't recall if they fired or not. All I could think of was getting Zeke out of there."

Cash moved to him. "Did any of them ride off?"

"Two."

"Did you recognize either of them?"

Hex shook his head. "One was tall, real skinny. The other shorter and round."

Gabe looked at the others. "Could've been Buster."

"Sorry, boss. I was worried about Zeke and didn't get a good look before they rode off."

"Which way did they ride, Hex?" Mack asked.

"North."

*Splendor*

Sylvia finished placing the new merchandise on shelves, logging each item into the journal. Stan Petermann had left for Big Pine the night before, leaving her in charge of the store for two days. Three if he couldn't find what he sought.

She'd looked forward to his absence, mentioning it to Dominic at supper the night before and breakfast that morning. Unsurprising, he'd supported her excitement, something Sylvia felt certain her father would never have done.

Setting the last item on a shelf, she stood. Tilting her head to one side, then the other, a frown tugged down the corners of her mouth. Bending, she moved the article an inch to the right, the frown turning into a smile at the symmetry created by the simple change.

Rearranging the merchandise gave her time to think about Mack's visit and the confusion it caused. Sylvia didn't know why he'd sought her out, showing up days after not seeing him, doing all she could to avoid him. His visit had unsettled her, making her want things he refused to offer.

Seeing his handsome face and beloved features reignited the deep pain she'd fought to ignore since the night by the creek. Why did he have to return now when she'd begun to move ahead with her life? It wasn't fair of him to tease her with his presence and a vague promise of...

"Of what?" Sylvia whispered, feeling foolish for talking to herself.

It had been difficult, accepting how long it would take to cut her love for Mack from her heart. Supper with Morgan had done nothing to soothe the ache or emptiness. All she'd thought of was Mack, his twinkling eyes and confident smile when he pestered her, seeking a reaction, which she invariably provided.

They'd shared nothing more intimate than passionate kisses and trembling touches, yet their connection had seemed so deep and utterly consuming. Sylvia had never thought she'd feel so much for another person, falling to an unexpected degree for the charming lawman. To her chagrin, she now understood the price of loving a man incapable of matching her desire.

Tucking a loose strand of hair behind her ear with a shaky hand, she shoved thoughts of Mack from her mind. She couldn't wallow in regret, nor do anything about the intense ache still present in her heart.

Hearing the bell over the door, she turned, not recognizing the two men walking inside.

"May I help you?" She moved toward them, hesitating when the taller of the two narrowed his gaze, a feral look in his eyes. He and his companion were covered in trail dust, not unusual in a town where a majority of the men worked on ranches. Still, the expression on their faces unsettled her.

"You must be Miss Lucero."

Taking a step back, she nodded. "Yes, I am. Have we met?"

He shook his head, taking several menacing steps forward. "No, but I've heard a good deal about you. I thought it was time we met. I'm Buster and that is Smalls."

Smalls, shorter with a wide girth, turned, locking the door.

"Why did you lock the door?" She kept her voice firm, almost indignant, although her chest pounded frantically. Sylvia took a few more steps away, meaning to get behind the counter—and grab the shotgun Stan kept on a shelf.

She'd learned to shoot soon after learning to ride, becoming accomplished at both. Few in Splendor would expect either from a young woman who spent her time moving between the boardinghouse and general store.

"Stay where you are." Her movements stalled at Buster's stern command. Shifting his hand to his gun, he lifted it from the holster. "We're going to go through the back and leave, real quiet like."

Shaking her head, she darted away, falling on her face with a thud when he caught the hem of her dress in his strong grip. Pushing up, anger seized her. She kicked at his legs, arms flailing at his chest and face when he bent closer. Opening her mouth to scream, he silenced the attempt with a grimy hand.

Pointing the gun at her head, Buster's hot, acrid breath washed across her face. "This is your only warning. Do that again and no one will ever find your body. Now, get up." Removing his hand from her mouth, he grabbed Sylvia's arm, yanking her to stand. "Move." He shoved her toward the back, glancing behind him to see Smalls looking out the front window once more before joining them.

Buster nodded to the back door. "Open it, Smalls."

Turning the knob, he pushed the door open enough to peek outside. "It's clear."

Yanking Sylvia to him, Buster leaned to within inches of her face. "Our horses are out back. Don't scream or try to get away. If you behave, you might live long enough to see your brother again. Do you understand?"

Her mouth opened on a gasp before she nodded. Buster knew of Dominic, already understanding Sylvia would do whatever he asked to protect her brother.

"Good. Are you ready, Smalls?"

The shorter man gave an abrupt nod, stepping aside.

"Let's go." Buster shoved her ahead of him. "Walk as you normally do over there." He pointed the gun in the direction of the horses, then moved it behind her. When she hesitated, he dug the gun into her back. "Keep going."

Reaching the horses, Buster mounted while Smalls kept his gun aimed at Sylvia. Shoving it into the holster, he gripped her waist, lifting to place her in front of Buster. Mounting his own horse, Smalls nodded. Without another word, they kicked their horses, taking the back street to the south and out of town.

Mack rode right behind Gabe, their pace as rapid as when they'd left Splendor earlier. Cash had ridden ahead to Norman's ranch to check for casualties and talk to those involved in the shooting.

Nothing about the incident between who they believed to be Norman and his ranch hands made sense.

Gabe wouldn't have answers until Cash returned to town. In the meantime, they had to make sure whoever rode off wasn't headed to Splendor to continue with their mindless rampage.

Mack didn't understand the fear gripping him. Even though the gunmen traveled north, it didn't mean they meant to ride into Splendor. Nor did it mean Sylvia was in any danger.

Few people knew her, and almost no one had any idea of her family's wealth. Besides, she worked in the general store. Whoever the men were, they wouldn't stop in the mercantile during an attempt to escape. The thought would've been humorous if unreasonable fear didn't still burn in his chest.

Entering Splendor, Mack didn't stop at the jail, riding the additional feet to dismount before the general store. Tossing the reins over a rail, he turned the doorknob, knocking when it didn't open. Pulling out his pocket watch, he checked the time, finding it too early for her to close the store.

"Good afternoon, Deputy."

Mack spun around to see Dominic approaching, stepping onto the boardwalk to stand by him. Without returning the greeting, he turned the handle again. "It's locked."

"She must have closed early." Dominic cupped his hands, attempting to peer through the grubby window. "I don't see her. Why don't you try the boardinghouse while I check the back door?"

Nodding, Mack hurried across the street and shoved open the door, spotting Suzanne entering the kitchen. "Have you seen Sylvia?"

"Not since this morning. Isn't it too early for her to be closing the store?"

"It is. Would you mind checking her room?"

Suzanne didn't argue, noting the anxious look in his eyes and hard set of his jaw. Rushing upstairs, she returned a minute later, shaking her head.

Wasting no more time, he headed back to the general store, coming to a halt at seeing Dominic standing in the open doorway. The hope on her brother's face faded at Mack's expression.

"She's not at the boardinghouse, is she?"

Mack shook his head. Fisting his hands, he settled them on his hips, looking up and down the street. "Where the hell is she?"

"Perhaps she fell ill and went to the clinic." Dominic's voice held little conviction.

"I saw her earlier and she seemed fine."

Dominic's brows rose. "When?"

"A few hours ago, before Gabe led a group of us to Norman Miller's ranch."

The words had just left Mack's mouth when he saw Cash appear on horseback, a wagon close behind him. They turned to the right at the south end of town, taking the back street.

"They must be going to the clinic." Mack rushed off, Dominic following him between the general store and barber shop. They emerged onto the back street as the wagon came to a halt outside the clinic.

"Who do you have?" Dominic asked Cash.

Dismounting, Cash moved to help the wagon driver lift one of the injured men. "Norman Miller and one of his hands. They were hit during a shootout at the ranch this morning."

Dominic and Mack lifted the second man, following Cash to the clinic steps.

A man sitting beside the driver had already gone inside, coming out with Doctor Clay McCord. Clay stood on the landing, motioning for them to take the injured men inside. Once done, Cash, Mack, and Dominic met outside the clinic, waiting when they saw Gabe stalking toward them.

"What did you learn?" Gabe asked Cash.

Removing his hat, Cash scrubbed a hand down his face, a tired breath escaping his lips. "Norman and Buster argued about something. Several other men were in the study with them. A couple supported Miller, a couple siding with Buster." Cash's forehead bunched as he focused on the little he'd been able to uncover. "At some point, Miller pulled a gun on Buster, who pulled his own. Both started shooting."

"Did you learn anything about what started the argument?"

Cash nodded at Gabe. "The two men who brought the wagon to town said it began when Norman questioned Buster about what has been happening at the Smith ranch." Sucking in a breath, Cash's gaze narrowed on Gabe. "If the men are correct, Buster and a couple others are the ones responsible for killing Eb and Elija's sheep. Buster and another ranch hand are the men Hex saw ride off."

Gabe rubbed the back of his neck. "I'll be damned."

"Yeah," Mack agreed.

"Until Norman's able to talk, we aren't going to know exactly what happened," Cash added, looking up to see Dutch join them.

Dutch looked between Mack and Dominic, his features grave.

Mack's stomach clenched. "What is it, Dutch?"

"Al, from the Wild Rose, was leaving Sarah Murton's house." He nodded to her small house next door to the clinic.

Cash's brows rose. "The schoolteacher?"

Dutch cleared his throat, nodding. "The same. Seems they have a, well...some kind of arrangement."

Cash let out a mild oath, remembering how Beau had courted Sarah for a time before Caro returned to Splendor.

Dutch lowered his voice, sending an apologetic look at Mack. "Anyway, when Al left Miss Murton's place about an hour ago, he saw two men ride out of town. He's certain Sylvia Lucero rode in front of one of them."

# Chapter Twenty-Two

*Big Pine*

Buster kept the small derringer pressed into Sylvia's back, guiding her toward one of the cheaper hotels in the territorial capital. The late hour and almost complete darkness helped shield their faces as they walked inside. A lone man stood behind the counter, stifling a yawn as the three approached.

"We need a room."

The clerk's brow rose, his gaze moving over the two men and one tired, but defiant looking woman. "All three of you?" The older man didn't attempt to hide the disgust in his voice.

Buster leaned across the counter, his gaze hard. "Do you have a problem with that?"

The man's voice faltered. "Uh...no, sir."

He straightened. "Good."

"It's too late for baths." The clerk turned the register toward them. "Please sign here." He quoted a price, pulling the journal back to him after Buster signed. Taking the money, he handed him a key. "It's the last room upstairs on the right, Mr. Jones."

Buster increased the pressure on Sylvia's arm, hiding the derringer at his side as they made their way upstairs. Handing the key to Smalls, Buster waited as the man unlocked the door and shoved it open.

The small room included a bed, scarred dresser, and oil lamp. "You get the bed, girl." Buster shoved her toward it. Her face twisted into a hateful expression, receiving a harsh chuckle in response.

Smalls stared around the almost barren space. "Where are we going to sleep, Buster?"

Snorting, he pointed to the floor. "The only place we can."

"I need food." Smalls started for the door. "I won't be gone long."

Buster walked to the window, looking out on the street. Other than the occasional sound of tinny piano music, the town had quieted.

"What do you plan to do with me?"

Turning from the window, Buster studied her. She'd been quiet since leaving Splendor, didn't try to run, and made no fuss in front of the hotel clerk.

"Having you with us is how we'll be able to get out of the territory. I'm certain your brother will send a posse."

Sylvia's voice held firm. "And you believe he'll do nothing if you have me?"

"Exactly."

A chuckle broke the air, a slight grin on her face. "You don't know much about my brother."

Buster moved toward the bed. "Your brother isn't going to endanger you. He'll do whatever he has to in order to get you back safely."

"Oh, he'll make certain I'm safe. But Dominic won't let you get away with taking me. He'll seek justice, and nothing will stop him from obtaining it."

"You have a great deal of faith in him."

A wave of satisfaction washed through her. "Because I know Dominic." Sylvia didn't add her firm conviction Mack would ride with her brother. No matter what had transpired between them, he'd be as adamant as Dominic about getting her back.

*Splendor*

When Norman regained consciousness, he'd confirmed his ranch hand's story regarding the confrontation. Buster and a few others had been responsible for slaughtering the sheep and stealing the cattle. A sadness had overtaken the rancher as he described the shooting. Norman admitted he knew the reason for Buster's actions, although he refused to share the cause with anyone.

Gabe argued for Dominic to wait until morning when they'd have a better chance of picking up Buster's tracks. He'd refused. It came as no surprise

Mack agreed with him or that Caleb insisted on riding with them. Instead of continuing to argue, Gabe sent a telegram to Sheriff Parker Sterling.

They'd left late that night, taking the shortest route to Big Pine. As a group, Gabe and the deputies were certain Buster would head straight for the large town before riding through Bloody Basin, Red Dog, and Moosejaw.

Norman believed Buster's destination to be the Dakota Territory. The man who'd been his foreman for over ten years had an uncle in Yankton, the territorial capital—someone who'd hide him, even from the law. Norman felt certain Buster would let Sylvia go when he and Smalls crossed into the Dakotas.

"We won't let them get that far," Dominic had told Gabe before he, Mack, and Caleb rode out.

They'd reached Big Pine a couple hours before dawn, meeting the sheriff in the jail. They'd barely made it inside when Sterling pinned them with a hard stare.

"I don't want any vigilante antics in my town. We do this my way. If you don't agree, I'll lock all three of you in cells right now."

Dominic moved closer to Sterling. "Does that mean you know where they are?"

He shot a look at his deputies, his mouth drawn into a grim line. "We're real certain they're at a hotel at the east end of town. I'd already spread word, letting the town know to look for two men and a woman riding in late. The clerk hailed one of my deputies not long after they registered using the name Jones."

"Which hotel?"

Sterling crossed his arms. "Well, that's just it, Mack. I'm not letting you know until we're ready to move. I don't want you three doing anything requiring me to arrest you for murder."

Mack swore under his breath, lowering himself into a chair. "What's your plan, Sheriff?"

"It's real simple. My deputies and me go into the hotel. I already know the room they're in and the clerk confirmed all three are in there. They aren't going to have any idea we've discovered them this soon, so it's doubtful one of them is standing guard."

Dominic's jaw tightened. "Buster will grab Sylvia as soon as he figures out what's happening. One of your men could shoot her by accident."

Sterling's gaze wandered over the three men, his features softening. "We aren't going to let that happen. We'll get her out before those two sonsofbitches know what's happened."

Mack hoped to God Sterling was right.

Thirty minutes later, the sheriff and his men were in place, guns drawn, counting the seconds until Sterling gave the signal. Mack and Dominic had been allowed to take positions below the window of the second floor while Caleb guarded the front entrance.

"When we get Sylvia back, you sure as hell better marry her or I'll shoot you myself." Dominic rolled the cylinder of his six-shooter, checking it for the third time. He didn't look at Mack, figuring his message had been clear enough for even a dunderhead such as him to understand.

Mack didn't attempt to lie. "I plan to. If she'll still have me."

Dominic had to concede the point. "Yeah, you surely did stir up a passel of trouble with my sister. It may take her a while to come around. The fact is she might even go to supper with Morgan a few more times just to make you sweat."

"The hell she will," Mack spat out with more force than intended.

Before Dominic could reply, a blast of gunfire rippled through the air. Not long after, a window shattered on the second floor, followed by a body falling to the ground, landing at Mack's feet. Staring at the crumpled form, he pointed his gun at Buster's still body. Hearing a groan, Mack bent down.

"Move, you sonofabitch. Give me an excuse to put a bullet in your head."

Dominic stepped next to Mack. "Like hell. If anyone's going to shoot him, it'll be me."

"No one's shooting anybody. Stand back you two and help an old man out." Sterling walked up, an arm settled over Sylvia's shoulders.

"Syl..." Dominic's voice faded as he moved to her, wrapping her in a tight hug. "My God. I was so worried."

Closing her eyes, she held on, thankful once again her brother had come to Splendor. Opening her eyes, she glanced around him. Mack stood a few feet away.

"Mack." His name came out as a breathless whisper. Dropping her arms from around Dominic, she moved toward him, taking only two steps before he whisked her into a fierce embrace. Burying his face in her hair, he took an unsteady breath.

He didn't know what to say, his throat thick. Instead, he held her to his chest, unwilling to let go.

Pulling back, Sylvia looked up to see his face lined with worry. "I'm all right, Mack."

He brushed hair away from her face, cupping her cheeks with both hands. Leaning down, he brushed his lips over hers, needing the contact to reassure himself Sylvia was safe. Dominic's low cough had them stepping apart.

"Did they hurt you, Syl?"

She shook her head, not ready to release her hold around Mack's waist. Letting out a breath, she turned to her brother.

"Frightened me, but nothing more." Sylvia's attention moved to see two of Sterling's deputies lift Buster, carrying him onto the boardwalk. Looking up, she noticed a sign over one door, indicating they were taking him to the town's infirmary.

The outlaw cried out in pain, one of his legs bent at on odd angle and a deep gash on his face dripping blood. His breath came out in an unsteady wheeze, indicating broken ribs.

"What of Mr. Smalls?" Sylvia asked Sterling, who stood a few feet away.

"Dead."

She shivered, but didn't display any remorse at her kidnapper's death. "What will happen to him?" Her gaze settled on Buster.

"If he lives, he'll go to trial. I don't know all the charges right now, but I'm guessing there will be several for the judge to consider."

"They spoke of killing sheep and stealing cattle from Mr. Miller." She looked at Mack. "Are those the sheep belonging to the Smiths?"

He nodded, controlling the urge to pull her back into his arms. "Yes. They shot Norman and another ranch hand. They also killed another man, but I don't have all the details." Mack glanced behind Sylvia to see Dominic shaking his head, indicating he didn't want Sylvia to hear any more. "But you're safe, and that's what matters." He trailed a finger down her cheek. "Sylvia, I—"

"We should get some sleep before heading back to Splendor." Dominic didn't look at all apologetic for interrupting.

"You'll be more comfortable at one of the hotels farther up the street." The sheriff glanced around. "I'm going to stay until the undertaker gets the body moved and the doctor has had a chance to look at Maddox."

Sylvia's brows scrunched together. "Maddox? Is that Buster's last name?"

"According to the telegram Gabe sent earlier today, it is." Massaging the back of his neck, Sterling blew out a breath. "Glad this ended without you getting hurt, Miss Lucero. It could've been much worse."

Two days later, Sylvia still thought of the sheriff's words, shivering at the truth of them. He'd been right. She'd been fortunate to be rescued before experiencing any real harm.

Buster wouldn't be returning to Splendor. Instead, he'd face trial in Big Pine. The only explanation for his crimes had been his angry tirade against Norman Miller. Buster insisted the rancher had swindled him out of the land Morgan now owned. They'd had a deal and Norman had betrayed him. Miller hadn't come forth to explain his side of Buster's accusation, leaving the town with more questions than answers.

Since returning to Splendor the day before, Dominic had pushed her to head home to Whiplash, or ride to Austin with him. He spoke of the opportunities in the town where the Texas Rangers had their headquarters.

Sylvia might not have listened as intently to his arguments if Mack had made even one attempt to see her. He'd stayed away, not appearing at the store or boardinghouse restaurant. After the kidnapping, she supposed he'd come to the same conclusion as her brother—she'd be safer back in Texas.

Even Stan Petermann had reservations about letting her resume all the duties at the general store. He welcomed her that morning, but stayed close, not leaving to make his normal trip to the bank or walking across the street for food. Instead, he'd sent her out to bring back meatloaf from Suzanne's. It seemed everything Sylvia had gained during her brief time in Splendor slipped away and she could do nothing to stop the downward spiral.

"Good afternoon, Sylvia."

She jolted at the greeting, having been too lost in her thoughts to hear the bell above the door. "Good afternoon, Mrs. Evans. How are you doing?"

"I believe the correct question is how are *you* doing?" Lena ran her hand down a new bolt of fabric, her gaze flickering up to meet Sylvia's.

"Much better now that I'm home." Her heart sank. She'd miss Splendor, but as Dominic reminded her, it wasn't her home.

"Gabe told me one of the men who took you died, and the other is fighting for his life back in Big Pine. If the man lives, Gabe says he'll be facing trial there."

Sylvia had heard the same from her brother. Either way, she'd be expected to testify, which meant leaving Splendor wouldn't be an option until after the trial.

"I won't keep you, Sylvia. I just wanted to see how you were doing after your harrowing experience. You are quite a brave woman."

Sylvia snorted at the comment. "Hardly. I did what Buster and Smalls told me, hoping someone would find where'd they'd hidden me away."

"And someone did. Well, I'd better move on. I still have supper to start for Gabe and Jack."

"How is your son?"

Lena smiled. "Jack is doing quite well. He's eight now and is certain there's nothing more he can learn."

Sylvia remembered she'd thought the same at his age.

"You and your brother should come to supper before he returns to Texas." Lena gave her a knowing grin. "You could also ask Mack to join us."

Sylvia bit her lip rather than share with Lena how she'd not seen Mack since their return to Splendor. "Thank you for the invitation. I'll mention it to Dom."

"This Saturday would be perfect. Do you know if you're free?"

Looking away, she stifled a laugh, knowing nothing would show on her social calendar. "That should be fine."

"Wonderful. Have a good evening and we'll see you on Saturday."

Lena slipped outside as Sylvia walked to the back, meaning to grab her coat and reticule. "I'm leaving now, Mr. Petermann."

Stan stepped out of the small nook he used as an office. "I'll see you in the morning."

The corners of her mouth turned upward. "Yes, you will. Have a good evening."

"You as well." He disappeared back into the cubicle.

Slipping into her coat, Sylvia didn't see anyone standing by the door until almost running into him. "Oh, I..." Her eyes moved upward, words stalling.

"Good evening, Sylvia."

# Chapter Twenty-Three

Mack's eyes crinkled at the corners at the surprise on Sylvia's face. He fingered the brim of his hat, his gaze moving over her, not sure what to say. He'd been trying to decide how to convince her to stay in Splendor since seeing Dominic in the gunsmith shop that morning. Her brother had been firm in his belief she return to Texas, a location he considered much safer and better suited for a woman seeking marriage.

Mack's mood had dampened on the last. In truth, it had diminished with each word Dominic spoke regarding Sylvia's future. After almost losing her to Buster's ill intent, he had no intention of letting her slip away from him a second time.

"Are you finished for the day?"

She licked dry lips, her heart beginning to beat at an erratic rate as she met his gaze. "Yes, I am."

"Would you be available to join me for supper?" He gripped the brim of his hat more firmly.

Her first reaction had been to agree. The part of her insisting she protect her heart from the man who'd already broken it held back.

"I'm not certain it would be a good idea. I mean, you made it quite clear you no longer have any interest in me, and I find it hard to believe you've changed your mind." She tried to step past him, but Mack moved to block her way.

"My decision to call off our courtship may have been premature."

Brow lifting, her lips pressed into a tight smile. "Premature?"

A muscle twitched in his jaw. "That's what I said."

Shaking her head, Sylvia glanced toward the door, wishing he would step aside and let her leave. "I don't know what you want of me. My feelings on love were clear from the start, as were yours. Unless you've changed your thoughts on marriage, I see no point in starting again."

Frowning, Mack shifted his stance, unsure of what more to say. He didn't want to lie, yet refused to lose her without understanding the extent of his feelings for the beautiful woman he couldn't rid from his thoughts.

"I *do* care for you, Sylvia. I care a great deal."

"Caring for me isn't enough."

"I realize it isn't." He looked away, letting out a frustrated breath. Mack couldn't recall a time he'd been so confused, so unsure of how to proceed. All he did know was he couldn't let her go. "I need you, Sylvia."

Her brows wrinkled. "*Need* me?"

Threading fingers through his hair, he gritted his teeth. "Yes, need you. I don't want you to leave Splendor...leave me."

Closing the distance between them, she placed a hand on his arm. "You're the one who left me the night you called off our courtship."

"Ah, Miss Lucero. I was afraid I'd missed you."

Both turned to see Morgan had entered the store.

She quirked a brow at him. "Missed me, Mr. Miller?"

Morgan turned his back to Mack. "I'm in town to see to my father. Since I have to stay the night, I wondered if you'd have supper with me."

Her lips parted, her eyes widened. "Well, I..." She glanced at Mack.

"She's already agreed to join me for supper, Morgan." Shifting to move around him, Mack took a spot at Sylvia's side, looking down at her. "Haven't you, sweetheart?" He winced, seeing her eyes flash.

"Is that correct, Miss Lucero?" Morgan took a step closer to her.

Lifting her chin, she focused her response on Mack. "Actually, I've already agreed to have supper with my brother. If you gentlemen will excuse me, I must be leaving." Opening the door, Sylvia stepped outside, leaving the men to stare after her.

Mack stared at the cooling steak on his plate, unable to summon any level of appetite. He'd chosen to eat at McCall's. Other than the boardinghouse and Eagle's Nest, Betts McCall and her husband ran the only other restaurant in town. He'd brought Sylvia here several times. The food was good and plentiful, and as he stared down at it, he felt a twinge of guilt at leaving it uneaten.

"Is the steak not to your liking, Mack?" Betts stood next to him, her brows knit in confusion.

"I'm sure it's fine. I suppose I'm not as hungry as I'd thought."

Looking around the room, satisfied everyone had been taken care of, she pulled out a chair. Betts sat next to him, patting his arm. "How is that beautiful lady of yours? I haven't seen either of you in quite a while."

"She really isn't *my* lady, Betts."

"Nonsense. It's your fault if you don't see her that way." She chuckled at the blank look on his face. "Come now, Mack. You aren't a stupid man. Surely you know Sylvia's in love with you."

Swallowing, he nodded.

Her gaze narrowed. "It seems that's not the problem then, is it?"

"No, Betts, it isn't."

Sitting back, she considered his words, her eyes widening. "You're the problem, aren't you?"

Mack had no idea why he'd allowed himself to be drawn into a conversation he hadn't expected to have with anyone. He wasn't one to speak of his feelings, admit his mistakes.

"She'll only marry for love."

"And you don't love her." It wasn't a question.

"No, I don't."

Waving to the couple who placed money on the table before leaving, she turned back to him. "Are you sure about that?"

Crossing his arms, he frowned. "I'd know if I did."

At this, Betts threw back her head and laughed.

Narrowing his gaze, he stared at her. "What's so funny?"

"You, Mack. I've never seen a man so smitten with a woman as you are with Sylvia. You may be lying to yourself, young man, but how you feel is clear on your face every time you look at her." Leaning forward, her face sobered. "You know how Cash looks at Allie, Gabe looks at Lena, and Beau looks at Caro?"

He gave a slow nod, unsure where she was going.

"That's how you look at Sylvia." She placed her hands on the table, pushing to stand. "I suggest you take a good, hard look at yourself, Mack. Don't lose what she's offering because you're afraid to grasp it with both hands. Whether you're ready to admit it or not, that girl is your future, and you're hers."

Dominic studied Sylvia's face. Her features were pinched, eyes grim, white lines rimming her mouth. His stomach clenched at the unhappiness she'd been unable to hide from him.

"Tell me what bothers you, Syl."

She knew he wouldn't want to hear about Mack's visit...or Morgan's. He'd made his feelings about the youngest Miller brother clear.

She shook her head. "It's nothing."

Chuckling, he reached over, covering her hand with his. "You may be able to get away with hiding your thoughts from others, but not with me, love. Tell me what it is. Maybe I can come up with a solution."

Shoulders slumping, she sighed. "There's only one person who can provide a solution, Dom."

"Damn that man," he mumbled under his breath.

Eyes wide, she stared at him. "What do you mean?"

"It's Mack, isn't it?"

Pursing her lips, she nodded. "He asked me to supper tonight, but I just don't see the point, Dom.

He's made his feelings about love quite clear, and he knows mine. Why won't he let it be?"

"You mean let *you* be?"

She let out a slow breath. "Yes." Glancing around the room, she saw May walk out of the kitchen with two plates. "May's coming this way."

"We aren't done with this, Syl." Dominic flashed a smile at May, a woman he found to be quite pretty and kind. Unfortunately, his attention had been captured by another of the brides, someone he had no intention of pursuing. His life was in Austin as a Texas Ranger, not in a small town in the remote territory of Montana.

"Here you are. Sorry for the delay." May set the chicken fricassee in front of Sylvia and a thick slice of roast before Dominic. "Would you like anything else?"

He shook his head. "This is fine, May. Thank you." Picking up his knife and fork, he started to cut the roast, stopping when he noticed Sylvia staring at her plate. "Is something wrong?" When she didn't respond, he leaned closer. "Syl?"

Startled, she looked up. "Oh, sorry."

"Is something wrong with your meal?"

"I'm sure it's fine. It's just, well..." She continued to stare at her plate.

"Lost your appetite?"

Sylvia glanced up at the familiar voice. "Mack. What are you doing here?"

"I've come for you." He held out his hand, sending a warning look at Dominic. "We need to talk, Sylvia. I'll not take no for an answer."

When Dominic opened his mouth to respond, she jumped up. "Do you mind, Dom?"

Standing, he glared at Mack. "What are you about, Mackey?"

Mack met his hard stare. "This is between Sylvia and me, Dom. You'll just have to be patient while we talk."

"If you hurt her again—"

Sylvia moved between them, putting a hand on her brother's chest. "It's all right, Dom. I want to hear what Mack has to say."

His features softened. "If you're sure, Syl."

"I am."

Taking Sylvia's hand, Mack turned, almost pulling her behind him in his haste to find privacy.

"Mack?" He turned at Lena's voice. She stood next to an open door. The one leading to the hotel office. "In here."

Jaw clenching, he nodded, changing directions to enter the office. "Thank you, Lena."

Sylvia's eyes grew wide as Mack pulled her past Lena. Once inside, he closed the door, turning to face her.

"Marry me, Sylvia."

Her mouth gaped open. "Wh...what?"

"Marry me. I don't want to live without you. I *can't* live without you. Knowing how you grew up, it won't be easy being married to a deputy with little money and no prospects for much more. But I swear I'll make you happy."

Staring at him, her mind raced. "You don't love me. I've already told you I won't marry…" Her voice trailed off when he placed a finger over her lips.

"That isn't exactly true." Swallowing any doubt he may have felt before, his features warmed. "I spoke with a very wise woman tonight. She helped me see the error in my thinking."

"The error," she breathed out, trying to understand his meaning.

He took her hands in his. "Yes." Chuckling, he squeezed her hands. "I do love you, Sylvia. Much more than I thought possible." Leaning down, he brushed a kiss across her lips. "Marry me." He kissed her again, earning a sigh. "Stay in Splendor and build a life with me."

Seeing the tears in her eyes, he stilled, thinking he'd made one more mistake when it came to Sylvia. Perhaps she no longer loved him, didn't want him, or had developed feelings for Morgan. The last caused a sharp pain to grip his chest. He couldn't bear the thought he might have already lost her.

A moment later, a beguiling smile broke across her face.

"I love you, Mack. I'll always love you."

"Is that a yes?"

She blinked back the tears. "Definitely a yes."

# Epilogue

*Two weeks later...*

Reverend Edward Paige looked across the crowd gathered in the church before smiling at the couple before him. "Ladies and gentlemen, may I present Mr. and Mrs. Adam Mackey."

Scooping Sylvia into his arms, he kissed her, ignoring the gasps, cheers, and clapping from their friends. Without hesitation, he walked down the aisle to the back of the church, feeling slaps on his back. Stepping outside, he set her down, taking Sylvia in his arms to capture her mouth in a searing kiss.

Laughing, she pulled back, not removing her arms from around his neck. "Adam, what do you think you're doing?"

"I'm kissing my wife. I love you, Mrs. Sylvia Mackey."

"I love you, too, Adam. So, so much."

"Congratulations, Mack. Although I still don't think you're good enough for my sister." Dominic held out his hand, shaking Mack's. An almost melancholy grin tipped the corners of his mouth when his gaze met his sister's. An instant later, he wrapped his arms around her, swinging her around.

"I love you, Syl. This man better make you happy or you know I'll have to kill him."

Slapping his chest, she laughed. "I love you, too, Dom, and I'm so glad you stayed for the wedding."

"There wasn't any chance I would've left before Mack made it legal." He shot an appraising look at him.

May pushed through the people crowding around the new couple, reaching Sylvia to give her friend a warm hug. "I'm so happy for you."

May felt Caleb brush her shoulder. He shook Mack's hand, then nodded to the building next door. "Suzanne says it's time for all of us to move into the new community building. The food is ready and the band will start soon."

Taking Sylvia's hand, Mack walked to the new building next to the church. Their wedding reception would be the first big event since its completion a few weeks before. The instant they walked through the door, the band began to play a lively tune.

The building filled within minutes, their friends eating, drinking, and dancing. Sylvia's heart expanded, looking at all the people she'd met since arriving in Splendor. Her gaze moved across the crowd, stopping on a woman she'd seen in town several times but had never met.

If she recalled correctly, someone mentioned the woman arrived on a special stage, one she'd hired to bring her to Splendor. Poised and impeccably dressed, her cool gaze moved across the room, as if searching for someone. Sylvia noticed the instant her attention landed on Doctor Charles Worthington.

"May, have you learned any more about the woman over there, the one in the green gown?" Sylvia nodded across the room.

"Not more than what I mentioned before. Her name is Clare Billings. She's a widow from Boston and is still staying at the St. James. The woman has become quite the mystery at the hotel. Perhaps now is a good time to introduce ourselves."

Before Sylvia could respond, the woman turned away. Head held high, back straight, she moved to the door. Taking one quick glance over her shoulder in the doctor's direction, she stepped outside.

"It appears we've missed our chance. Still, it's time you visited with your guests."

When May took Sylvia's hand to pull her toward Tabitha and Deborah, Caleb moved next to Mack, handing him a cup of punch. Reaching into his pocket, Caleb removed a small flask, pouring a slight amount of whiskey into the otherwise bland drink.

"She's beautiful, Mack." He held up his cup, touching the side of Mack's. "Sylvia is going to make you a helluva wife."

From across the room, Mack watched his wife move from one group to another, smiling, laughing, and accepting numerous hugs. She'd settled into life in Splendor with little effort, even helping move items into the house Mack rented next to where he used to live with Caleb. This evening, he'd carry her into their house for the first time and make love to her as he'd desired for weeks.

Mack sipped the punch, glancing at Caleb. "What about you and Miss Bacon?"

Caleb swung his gaze to him. "May? What about her?"

Chuckling, Mack lifted a brow, his gaze moving across the room to where Sylvia and May stood. "Have you decided if you're going to court her? Formally court her, Caleb, not just the occasional breakfast or supper with Sylvia and me."

Slipping the flask from his pocket, he took a long drink before putting it away. "Just because you've tied yourself to one woman doesn't mean I'm ready to do the same."

Mack's gaze narrowed on his friend, studying his face. "If I'm not mistaken, you aren't much of a rogue. I know you take the occasional trip to Big Pine and once in a great while choose a woman at the Dixie. You certainly don't have the reputation I developed before Sylvia."

Blowing out a breath, Caleb gave Mack a lopsided grimace. "I like May a great deal. She makes me laugh, takes my mind off the past and all we did during the war."

"We did what was required as officers for the Union Army."

Caleb's face sobered. "You're right. I don't regret my actions. But there are times they haunt me."

"Are you referring to your nightmares?"

Caleb shrugged. "That, and Regina's death."

Clasping a hand on his shoulder, Mack lowered his voice. "It's been over four years since your fiancée was murdered. You need to let it go, Caleb. Open up to loving someone else."

Caleb thought of the months after Regina's death at the hands of marauders. A gang who'd been after him, not the sweet woman he would've married if her life hadn't been cut short. He'd been adrift ever since, uncertain of anything except the constant grief. Drinking and spending his nights with saloon whores masked the pain, never eliminating it.

He thought of May, believing she might be his path to redemption and peace. Different in appearance and much shorter than Regina, Caleb found himself thinking of her more each day.

"I've been thinking the same, Mack."

Giving him a wry grin, he tilted his glass toward May. "There's no better time than right now to ask her. I'll walk over with you and retrieve my bride."

A sudden terror tore at Caleb's chest. "Now?"

"Why not? It's not going to get any easier, and you certainly don't want to go through what I did with Morgan Miller...or Dutch, Hex, or—"

Caleb held up his hand. "I understand what you're saying." Sucking in a breath, he finished the punch and set the cup down. "All right."

He took determined strides across the room, stopping within inches of a startled May.

"Oh, Deputy Covington." May flushed, eyes widening.

Swallowing any doubt, he met her confused gaze. "Miss Bacon. I wonder if I could speak with you. In private."

She shot a look at Sylvia, who seemed as surprised as May. "If you'll excuse me."

Sylvia slipped her arm through Mack's, leaning into him. "Of course."

Offering his arm, Caleb led her to a quiet corner, nodding at a chair. When she settled into it, he took a seat next to her. They sat in silence for a few moments, May watching the way he seemed to battle with something. Unspoken emotions crossed his face, making her stomach clench.

Letting out a ragged breath, he stood. "I'd like to know if you would be open to me courting you."

Lips parting, she stilled, unsure she'd heard him right. "You want to court me?"

His brows furrowed. "Does that come as such a surprise?"

Clasping her hands in her lap, she considered the question. "Not really. I do like you very much, Caleb."

He liked the way she used his first name. Sitting back down, he pulled one hand from her lap, holding it. "You don't have to decide right now. It's a big decision, May. Consider it for as long as you need."

Staring into his deep blue eyes, May knew she'd be putting off the inevitable. "I don't need time to consider it. Yes, I'd very much like you to court me."

Eyes sparkling, Caleb squeezed her hand, a relieved smile lifting the corners of his mouth. "That's wonderful." Standing, he helped her up.

Biting her lip, she glanced across the room before gazing up at him. "This may sound silly, but do you mind if I let Sylvia and Lena know you've asked to court me?"

His gaze softened on her. It seemed natural, wanting to let her closest friend and the woman who'd brought her to Splendor know of his intentions.

"Of course not." Placing a hand at the small of her back, he guided May across the room where Sylvia and Mack spoke with Gabe and Lena. Stopping beside them, Caleb settled her in front of him.

Clearing her throat, May looked between the two ladies, ignoring Mack and Gabe. "Caleb has asked permission to court me. I've agreed."

Gabe sent Caleb a questioning glance, saying nothing. Mack simply grinned.

Lena smiled at Caleb. "That's wonderful."

"Yes, it is," Sylvia added.

Lena looked at Gabe, then back at the other two couples. "Would it be too presumptuous of me to invite the four of you to our house for supper on Saturday evening?"

Before anyone could answer, the front door opened on a bang. A woman of indistinguishable age, bright red hair, and heavy makeup walked inside, holding the hand of a small boy. She'd succeeded in getting everyone's attention.

"I'm looking for Caleb Covington. Is he here?"

Brows scrunched in confusion, he stepped forward. "I'm Caleb Covington."

She tightened her grip on the boy's hand and marched forward. She allowed herself a few moments to look Caleb up and down.

"We've traveled a great distance to find you."

Staring at her, he shrugged.

"You were a Texas Ranger, correct?"

He glanced at Mack, then back at the woman. "For a time."

"In Austin?"

"Yes."

"You knew Sadie Moss?"

His eyes clouded in confusion. "Sadie?"

"She was a saloon girl in Austin. Do you remember her?"

Pushing down the dread at her question, Caleb glanced at May before taking a closer look at the boy. His stomach clenched at the blond hair and deep blue eyes gazing back at him. A miniature version of him.

"Yes. I remember her." His voice was low, cautious, and filled with alarm.

Tugging the boy in front of her, the woman settled her hands on his shoulders. "Mr. Covington, this is your son...Isaac."

Thank you for taking the time to read Rogue Rapids. If you enjoyed it, please consider telling your friends or posting a short review. Word of mouth is an author's best friend and much appreciated.

Watch for book twelve in the Redemption Mountain series, Angel Peak.

Please join my reader's group to be notified of my New Releases at:
https://www.shirleendavies.com/contact-me.html

I care about quality, so if you find something in error, please contact me via email at
shirleen@shirleendavies.com

# About the Author

**Shirleen Davies** writes romance—historical and contemporary western romance with a touch of suspense. She is the best-selling author of the MacLarens of Fire Mountain Series, the MacLarens of Boundary Mountain Series, and the Redemption Mountain Series. Shirleen grew up in Southern California, attended Oregon State University, and has degrees from San Diego State University and the University of Maryland. Her passion is writing emotionally charged stories of flawed people who find redemption through love and acceptance. She lives with her husband in a beautiful town in northern Arizona. Between them, they have five adult sons who are their greatest achievements.

I love to hear from my readers!

Send me an email: shirleen@shirleendavies.com
Visit my Website: www.shirleendavies.com
Sign up to be notified of New Releases:
www.shirleendavies.com
Check out all of my Books:
www.shirleendavies.com/books.html
Comment on my Blog:
www.shirleendavies.com/blog.html
Follow me on Amazon:
http://www.amazon.com/author/shirleendavies

Follow my on BookBub:
https://www.bookbub.com/authors/shirleen-davies

Other ways to connect with me:

Facebook Author Page:
http://www.facebook.com/shirleendaviesauthor
Twitter: www.twitter.com/shirleendavies
Pinterest: http://pinterest.com/shirleendavies
Instagram:
https://www.instagram.com/shirleendavies_author/
Google Plus:
https://plus.google.com/+ShirleenDaviesAuthor

# Books by Shirleen Davies

## *Historical Western Romance Series*
## MacLarens of Fire Mountain

Tougher than the Rest, Book One
Faster than the Rest, Book Two
Harder than the Rest, Book Three
Stronger than the Rest, Book Four
Deadlier than the Rest, Book Five
Wilder than the Rest, Book Six

## Redemption Mountain

Redemption's Edge, Book One
Wildfire Creek, Book Two
Sunrise Ridge, Book Three
Dixie Moon, Book Four
Survivor Pass, Book Five
Promise Trail, Book Six
Deep River, Book Seven
Courage Canyon, Book Eight
Forsaken Falls, Book Nine
Solitude Gorge, Book Ten
Rogue Rapids, Book Eleven, Coming next in the
series!

# MacLarens of Boundary Mountain

Colin's Quest, Book One,
Brodie's Gamble, Book Two
Quinn's Honor, Book Three
Sam's Legacy, Book Four
Heather's Choice, Book Five
Nate's Destiny, Book Six
Blaine's Wager, Book Seven
Fletcher's Pride, Book Eight, Coming next in the series!

# *Contemporary Romance Series*

## MacLarens of Fire Mountain

Second Summer, Book One
Hard Landing, Book Two
One More Day, Book Three
All Your Nights, Book Four
Always Love You, Book Five
Hearts Don't Lie, Book Six
No Getting Over You, Book Seven
'Til the Sun Comes Up, Book Eight
Foolish Heart, Book Nine
Forever Love, Book Ten, Coming next in the series!

### Peregrine Bay

Reclaiming Love, Book One, A Novella
Our Kind of Love, Book Two

# Burnt River

Shane's Burden, Book One by Peggy Henderson
Thorn's Journey, Book Two by Shirleen Davies
Aqua's Achilles, Book Three by Kate Cambridge
Ashley's Hope, Book Four by Amelia Adams
Harpur's Secret, Book Five by Kay P. Dawson
Mason's Rescue, Book Six by Peggy L. Henderson
Del's Choice, Book Seven by Shirleen Davies
Ivy's Search, Book Eight by Kate Cambridge
Phoebe's Fate, Book Nine by Amelia Adams
Brody's Shelter, Book Ten by Kay P. Dawson
Boone's Surrender, Book Eleven by Shirleen Davies
Watch for more books in the series!

**The best way to stay in touch is to subscribe to my newsletter.** Go to www.shirleendavies.com and subscribe in the box at the top of the right column that asks for your email. You'll be notified of new books before they are released, have chances to win great prizes, and receive other subscriber-only specials.

Avalanche Ranch Press, LLC
PO Box 12618
Prescott, AZ 86304

Rogue Rapids is a work of fiction. Names,
characters, places, and incidents are either
products of the author's imagination or used
fictitiously. Any resemblance to actual events,
locales, or persons, living or dead, is wholly
coincidental.

Made in the USA
Coppell, TX
30 April 2020

23272914R00184